Cold hands

OLIVER SMUHAR

Published by Mountain Blue Publishing 2022
Copyright © 2022 Oliver Smuhar
www.oliversmuhar.com

Disclaimer
Every effort has been made to ensure that this book is free from error or omissions. Information provided is of general nature only and should not be considered legal or financial advice. The intent is to offer a variety of information to the reader. However, the author, publisher, editor or their agents or representatives shall not accept responsibility for any loss or inconvenience caused to a person or organisation relying on this information.

Cover Design: Oliver Smuhar and Robert Smuhar
Illustrations: Oliver Smuhar
Typesetting: Book Covers Australia.com

ISBN:
978-0-6483320-6-0 (pbk)
978-0-6483320-7-7 (e-bk)

Tyler & Amberley's ~~Bucket~~ List

Cold Hands acknowledges the Traditional Custodians of country throughout Australia and recognises their continuing connection to land, waters and culture. We pay our respects to their Elders past, present and emerging. Furthermore, Cold Hands would like to recognise the Gundungurra, Darug, Darkinjung and the Eora Traditional Owners of the land.

Dear Reader,

First of all, I would like to thank you for your purchase. I have done everything in my power to create an accurate depiction of mental illnesses and their impacts on young adults and adolescents in Australia. It gives me great pleasure to present my most personal treasure, **Cold Hands.**

The first version of Cold Hands was written in 2018, a few weeks after I graduated high school. It was a time of reflection and learning as I transitioned from a student into an adult. Throughout my life, I have suffered from mental health issues, including depression and anxiety. Even now, with the book's release, I still get flustered and nervous while driving, feel almost empty when I see my friend's post photos on social media, and many negative thoughts continue to circle my mind.

I would like to mention that the book's plot is based on the events I encountered in high school. Although the story is fictional, many elements that you will experience are indeed true. I plan to use these experiences to help young people and raise awareness on mental health. And yes, this notion has become more significant with the increase of daily calls to Lifeline Australia during the 2021 Australian Lockdown.

The world is a very complicated place, but just remember you are not alone. We are all in this together. If you see someone who is a little lonely, sad or maybe socially awkward, go say hello. Because one simple conversation can save someone's life. **Trust me, it saved mine!**

If you would like to support my message, please rate and/or review this book online, follow me on social media or tell a friend about Cold Hands. I wish you a fantastic time reading. And don't forget to look out for your friends, family and loved ones!

Sincerely,

Oliver Smuhar

In memory of all the lives lost to suicide in 2019-21.
Always in our hearts and memories.

The Moment x

1. The New Girl 1

2. Enlightened 8

3. The People I Tolerate 14

4. Home 23

5. What Makes You Happy? 31

6. Watching Ants 36

7. To Think and To Know 43

8. The Travelling Package 51

9. Doctors and Parents 56

10. Friends 64

11. Thursday 70

12. The Changing Forest 78

13. Work 87

14. Day Two 94

15. Orange Juice 99

16. May 106

17. Sunsets and Break-ins 114

18. The Party 123

19. Life 131

20. Visiting Hours 137

21. Morphine 149

22. Empty 159

23. Birthday Gifts 167

24. Good Company 175

25. Graduation 180

26. Helping Others   187

27. Finished   192

28. Handprints   197

29. Summertimes   203

30. Nothing   211

31. The New Boy   221

32. Day One   227

33. The People I Fear   235

34. Reminders   241

35. Cold Hands   247

36. The Moment   259

Please Read   270

The Videos and Lectures in Cold Hands   273

Sharron's Letter   274

Tyler's Letter   275

The Quotes in Cold Hands   278

The Art in Cold Hands   279

THE MOMENT

Time moves fast,
getting old?

The past,
the future.

Cold hands,
uncovering rich lands,
in the sight of youth,
through dreams, it depends,
on what is truth.

The smell of the ocean?
Taste of devotion?

Present life,
possibly in knots?
But focus on now.

To have cold hands,
be *nowhere*.

Now here, not for plans,
feeling almost dreamlike.

— Unknown

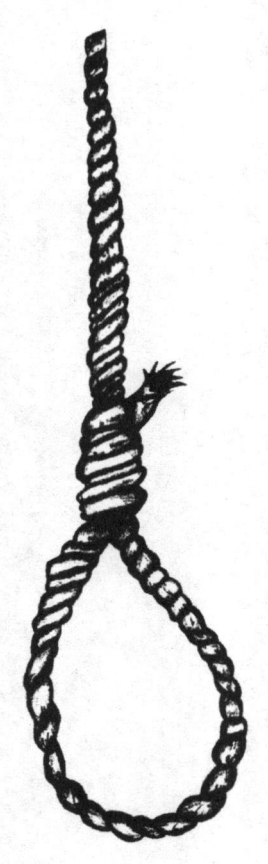

The New Girl

Have you heard that life is best described as 'playful?' It's a type of melody, not a mindless pathway weaved within a so-called journey. For me, I had lost sight of where to go; it felt pointless moving forward. No matter how much I tried, I never found the time to dance upon my path. The music was always faded, and in all honesty, my sad excuse of a life was sick of being playful.

What was the point?

I was always tired, hurt, cold. A sudden itch tickled my skin as a ghastly rope bound my neck with a tight grip. My Adam's apple felt clamped, and like I said, *I was cold.*

The bags beneath my eyes were already pulling me down, and the second-hand rope reeked of mothballs. It took me an hour to figure out how to tie the damn thing onto an old ventilation system. With how neat the noose was, you'd think I was an expert.

Gosh, why didn't I just overdose on pills?

I was empty, like the sound of silence, and I didn't know why. In all the papers and photographs I scavenged through, I never found the answer. I stared at them, scattered across the dark floor; even my birth certificate was sad, its words of ink a poison, burning my chest as it heaved in pain.

I had thought about this over and over again in bed, yet it was a lot sourer up close. The bitter stench of the garage was building, replacing that mothball scent as my swollen eyes drowned in tears.

I'm not crying!

No, I was just confused. The room was pitch black, and the only light was outside the steel roll-a-door. So, once I stepped off the table, it would be done, and I would die.

Will it be worth it? I wasn't sure. No one would care, or notice, or even talk about it.

I heaved on the icky rope, tightening it as I rubbed my moistened cheeks. This wasn't playful! All I felt, besides the subtle air from my nose, was heartache.

My shoes were seconds away from slipping as I admired the garage's walls. Tools and half-painted corners, chipped and dry, strained my eyes. These were the last things I was ever going to see.

I took a wholesome breath and stepped off.

My neck caught my weight as the rope hardened. *It burned!*

When I started crying in pity, I realised how stupid I was. I wanted to do it! I wanted to so badly, but being there, seconds away from death, my gut, my body, my whole life jolted in disgust.

My throat, clenched from the rope's pressure, began to heave as I tried to push out air from my lungs. I yanked against the pain, my hands ripping at the rope's clasp. Squirming above the floor, I was like a dangling chandelier. *Now wouldn't that be playful?*

Soon, my eyes became sleepy, my throat succumbed to the rope's pressure, my hands retreated to my side, and the swinging went silent. The taste of death reassured me, and with my last breath, the world turned black.

...

I gasped at a silent heartbeat. I heard the rope snap and gravity pushed me down, leaving the garage spinning as my head crashed into a blur of concrete and paper.

As I coughed, I was all burnt and red and disappointed. But I deserved it. *Why did I do that? What was I thinking? People would care if I died, wouldn't they?*

I cried until my head stopped feeling dizzy, and laid there, admiring the broken rope. Part of it was still around my neck, giving me an irritating rash.

Someone's voice echoed behind the door as I picked up my shaken body. When I leaned my weight onto my legs, I could barely remember where I had left my things. I searched, half-dazed, finding a blazer and tie over a chair that matched the table. Instead of putting them on, my arm swung hard, knocking my head to the side. It was a hard punch, bringing back the dizziness.

I'm an idiot, and I deserve the pain!

Patting down my white shirt, I wiped away the salty stains under my eyes and threw everything on, leaving as if nothing had happened. I checked my phone to see a notification from Cameron.

Chill this afternoon?

Laughing to myself, I adjusted my tie, feeling the broken rope and seeing it in the reflection of my phone. I ripped at the noose, the straws shredding from my grip and falling onto the papers.

As I forced the steel door open, blue lights blinded my view. It was a cloudy day; there was not a single sliver of sunlight. Throwing my bag over my shoulder, I crawled out of the garage unit and stopped.

Two tradesmen in orange were carrying a wooden post to a construction site next door. I waited, dodging their view until they were out of sight. When I chained the garage door shut, the grey world waited ahead.

I checked the time. *Oh, crud!*

School was in twenty. There was no way I was going to make it. *Not to mention the train trip.*

Wandering through the streets, I passed thrift shops, bakeries and cafes, and finally found a bin for the half-rope scrunched in my hand. It seemed crossing roads was more dangerous once I was doped up on dying. *Gosh, it's not my fault they can't drive.*

I followed a half-arse trail bloated with overgrown grass until the cloudiness gave way to the sun. Its light was a blessing for a short time, but it vanished when I boarded the train.

My head was throbbing as my exhausted body managed to find the school's driveway.

That was quick! I guess going through the park made life a little easier, yet by the time I reached the school's entrance, the bell was going ballistic.

Passing a demountable, I was injected into an orchestra of teenagers, big and small. It was chaos as I pushed through crowds of children who were too confident to be twelve or thirteen. Fortunately, I soon found my year at the back of the eating area where the fake grass sprouted.

The dreary sky made everything so lifeless as students in the same uniform as mine gossiped about their holidays. For some reason, I was annoyed by nothing, so I sat on a wooden seat, its slats as sharp as a hundred swords, and watched the ants beneath my feet.

As I was alone, my ears caught the New Year's gossip.

Everyone was so bland these days and nothing was different for them. It was always the same depressing stuff, like *oh, I worked and made a bit of cash* or some other crap about going to Europe or missing a party.

Taking my bag off, I held its top strap between my legs and began to listen to a silly conversation that echoed into my left ear. Ryan, who was pasty white with stained teeth, had gunk in the corner of his eyes. He chuckled to himself, an innocent kid who hadn't even had his first kiss yet. With him were Josh and Alley.

Josh was shorter than most boys my age and had a half-grown beard that was brown and a ring around his index finger. Alley, on the other hand, was nice to look at, smiling like a bunny with frizzy brown hair and smooth olive skin. She rolled her brown eyes as Ryan bragged about passing his driving test.

And that's when Alley said something interesting.

"Did you hear about the new girl?" she asked.

Ryan paused, eager to hear the news.

"A new girl? What'd she look like?" said Josh.

"I don't know," Alley shrugged. "I haven't seen her yet. Apparently she's starting today. Weird, huh?"

"Weird?" Ryan's brows dropped. "Why? We had like five new people last year. What's the difference now?"

"Just to start at a new school now. At the start of the year, with only three terms left. It's a bit odd, that's all."

"Maybe her parents got a new job. I'm sure there's a reason," said Josh.

Getting curious, I began to pay more attention as the rumour continued.

I turned my ears away from Ryan, Josh and Alley as they ventured into why they were nervous for the extension maths tests. The boys in front of me—you know, the ones who *gym*—they were onto something.

"D'you hear about the new girl, Jake?" Toby asked, playing with his obnoxious stubble. He was a stubby guy with broad shoulders and an angry face.

Jacob's hazel eyes lit up. He was taller than Toby but twice as skinny. For some reason, he always looked like he was tensing his tanned arms as he fixed his perfectly combed-to-the-side hairdo.

"Nah. Dibs if she's hot," said Jacob. "Just putting it out there. How do you know about her?"

"Mrs Mulhall introduced her to Bronte's group," Toby explained. "I saw her with them when I was looking for you this mornin'. She seems quiet."

A taller guy joined them. He had an orange beard with frail soft hair and black bags under his eyes that were almost as bad as mine.

"Sup, Crouchy? Did you hear about the new girl?" Jacob asked.

Crouchy laughed, hugging his binder. "Kind of. Riley and I saw her with Miss this morning. Is she in our year?"

"Yeah. Is she hot?" Jacob muttered like a thirsty hound.

"I don't know," Crouchy shrugged. "I don't really judge girls straight up. I guess. I didn't get a good look. We'll go talk to her at lunch."

With a grin, Toby nudged Jacob. "Let's just hope she's not like Anna. Didn't she move because of you?"

"No! There was a misunderstanding, that's all. She and I were *confusing*, and … I don't really want to talk about it, okay! *Stop laughing.* It's not funny. Guys, come on."

I chuckled to myself, remembering a past I had forgotten.

All of the girls were waiting in their white blouses and navy blazers. I forgot how small they were. But there was no new girl. Toby said she was with Bronte's group, and I was looking right at them. No new face. Nothing.

The girls laughed at each other.

"How was Foster, Bronte?" asked Katie. She had pitch-black hair and small teeth that were almost too perfect. Her starlight-blue eyes focused on Bronte, a tanned girl who looked like she was from the beach, not the mountains.

Bronte fixed her honey-coloured hair and smiled. "Oh my gosh, the water there is so pretty. It was heaps good; bit boring though. We were there for way too long. What'd you guys do?"

Katie started going on about how she went to the snow, and *would you believe it?* Izzy was there too. And Maddy went to her father's house in Queensland, while Alex went here, and Chloe went there, and so on.

But as I was watching them, barely listening to their giggles, one of them noticed me. She was shy, standing in the corner, confused and quiet, not saying a word but smiling when she needed to. Her whole body was weak as she huddled amid the popular girls. She had tied her light-brown hair into a high ponytail that was deliberately lazy, but not *too* lazy. Her lips were perfectly plump, and she had the most beautiful eyes. She had blue eyes, the darkest blue eyes I had ever seen.

Noticing my gaze, she stared at me like there was nothing between us. Her mouth hinted at a little grin, while her eyes judged me from top to bottom, then drifted, focusing on my neck.

I huddled, facing the ground, and covered my rope burn.

That was the new girl! She did exist. Be she wasn't quiet, like what Toby said. She was ... *sad.*

I avoided her grin, keeping my head down.

Suddenly, Xander yelped. He had curly brown hair and thick eyebrows that could cut down a tree. No one did anything as he recovered from Jake's casual punch-to-the-shoulder. It wasn't because he was Aboriginal Australian or because he was pretty mediocre at football—he was just that kid who always gets punched.

Laughing away the pain, Xander caught a basketball. The noise was so loud, my heart ended up racing. Everyone was here, but no one seemed to be worried.

I sighed, sitting alone like usual. There was no point speaking to anyone; I was just a burden. I felt my neck again and it burned. *I wish that rope hadn't snapped. Why did it have to snap?*

As I watched the ground, the ants moved back and forth like the world was on fire. This wasn't playful. *It was just empty.*

Enlightened

I noticed that everyone in white was huddling towards Mrs Mulhall's voice. I lined up and walked into my homeroom from last year, awaiting further instructions.

Like all homerooms, mine came with a new teacher. Mr Taccori, the *big* man himself, stomped through, inspecting our uniforms. Some say he looks like Danny DeVito but with less hair; others say he looks like a bean sprout with two legs. *I* would have said he was a mix.

He waddled down the line and stopped, grinning at me. "Mr McBaker. Good to see you're still around. No trade yet? Hope you had a good holiday."

I nodded with a sarcastic sniff, and he got the idea, continuing down the line.

The vice principal's sharp voice echoed through the speakers. She was facing the students, asking all of us to sit down. She talked about how it was a new year of learning, then lingered on the damn driveway and how it was fixed after being broken for like sixteen years. She went on and on until old mate took over.

The principal addressed the crowd as if he was somehow above us. He said the same stuff but with more angst, and finally, all the year groups got split up. Everyone stood and went wherever they were meant to be, and I followed suit.

I carried myself to the Presentation Space. We were herded like cattle, still talking about the past, until we reached a glass room. I squeezed inside, finding a seat where I knew I wouldn't be bothered.

When I got comfy on the carpet, something caught my eye. The blinding noise became distant as the new girl asked Mrs Mulhall something. She was centre stage, and with me as her audience, I willingly watched her out of curiosity. *She was different.* The way she walked—or strutted, I should say—the way she carried her small bag, and the way she seated herself, it was like watching ballet. A performance she had done a thousand times.

The noises came back, and as she disappeared into the furthest group to my left, I began to hear another conversation.

"Do you know her name?" asked Johnny.

His friend, Nic, laughed. "Haven't heard it yet. I'm sure Miss will tell us; she always does in these year meetings. *Is that what this is?* I hope it is, unless it's English."

"Nic, are you high?

"A little. Wait! Shh, don't tell anyone. Nah, you wouldn't … I'm so hungry."

That idiot. It wasn't the first time he had done it, but why bother? He wasn't going to get a kick out of it.

Well, Johnny sure did, laughing and taking a squat beside me. He said his greetings and waited like everyone else who was clear-minded on the floor.

I yawned, itching my eye as Mrs Mulhall announced the beginning of a new year.

"Hey, guys! Welcome back. We've made it, *finally!* This is the end, but I'll get into all of that at the year assembly. Did we all enjoy the holidays? … Good, good. We have lots to talk about today …"

I'll be honest, I blanked out a little. She's a kind lady, Mrs Mulhall, but she went on about the same stuff they tell you every year. But I didn't ignore her, *no.* She talked about our Year Twelve jackets and what was to come with examinations and *blah, blah, blah.*

Near the end, before the bell blessed us, Mrs Mulhall got excited.

"What else? Oh, we have a new student. Just one this year. Amberley—sorry to do this, but can you stand up please?"

Like the stalking heard of tigers my year was so fond of being, we all targeted the new girl as if she was candy for our carnivorous minds. With her hand wrapped around her opposite arm, Amberley achieved a brief moment of fame as the world felt extra grey. Seconds felt like minutes, and I'm sure for her, this lasted hours, but Mrs Mulhall saved the day and introduced her to everyone.

I, like the rest of my year, found a sudden boredom as Mrs Mulhall returned to talk about learning and expectations.

Why was the new girl so sad? Was it just how I saw things, or could everyone see it behind her grin?

When the bell went, the dark-blue corridors made time trip over itself as the first two periods of math were over in seconds. Recess was served with a platter of chairs. I chose a seat that was bound to be lonely, being in the middle of nowhere; even the paths at school forgot to visit its timber cushions. It was behind the basketball courts and wasn't too close or too far from my classes.

The seat had a backrest, and its sturdy slats were long enough for me to be spread out. Halfway along the slats, a concrete vase cut the chair in half, separating the two sides with a giant stringy shrub protruding against the left of my new spot. I could only have half this seat, but half would do.

Sitting on the right side, next to an unpolished concrete urn, I searched past the shoulder-high shrub. It was too thick to notice anything beyond its ferns, however, gaps of light did glimmer through its stern exterior.

Placing my bag upon the concrete, I unpacked my sandwich. Knowing how crappy it would taste, I unwrapped it, resting my slouched body against the seat.

A small amount of wind picked up, but it wasn't enough to make me shiver. As it blew through the basketball court and down the hill I sat upon, the new girl wandered in the distance. She looked lost.

As she wandered, Amberley covered herself with her binder. Her walk was cautious. All gentle-like, she travelled from group to group, passing them as if the social interactions weren't exhausting.

I nibbled on my sandwich, sighing at how slow today was. The ants beneath my seat scattered like a disaster had struck. When the wind calmed, the new girl was gone.

As I rested my eyes on the floor, the world moved without me. And by the time fifty ants found their home, the bell screamed, and off I went.

People are a lot like ants. At the sound of the bell, we all scattered in search of our next class. I flailed around with my laptop in its case, strolling along a path where everyone else walked the opposite way, their faces all blurred, their leather shoes all shiny.

Climbing some stairs, I grinned at Xander's wave and entered another classroom that felt too warm for this school. The room featured a clean whiteboard, a little man who was too eager to teach and a croaky wooden frame around a windowless aperture—I had found Society and Culture.

Tossing my things onto a vacant table, I sat, stretching my arms.

Xander joined me, chewing gum as if it were the last thing he would ever do. "Tye! How were the holidays, bro?"

I ignored him, nodding with a subtle grin.

He continued, "It's one of those days. I understand, you be you. But if you wanna talk to someone, you let me know. All right?"

Smiling, I gave him a thumbs up and we waited until Mr Taccori instructed us on our major works.

"Now, I hope you've all started something in the past six weeks, or that'll just have been a waste of time. You should have at least started your PIP research or even made a questionnaire. But I'm guessing none of you have done that?"

He had guessed right. Neither I nor anyone else wanted to waste their precious time on something that was rather *unimportant*. Well, not important *now* given that it wasn't due 'til August.

Sir walked around the room, attempting to intimidate us with his ridged stare. He stopped, glancing at my frown.

"Tyler, have you done anything on your personal interest project? Hmm? Surveys, interviews, literature reviews? Anything that might enlighten me?"

He wanted to make himself alpha, but before I had time to lie, someone saved me.

"Excuse me," a voice whispered from the doorway.

Sir pulled a one-eighty, seeing Amberley near the entrance. She asked if this was Main Six and if we were learning Society and Culture. Everyone around became curious. It was like a magical eclipse that burnt my eyes the longer I looked. And as Amberley and Sir discussed the future, she avoided his gaze to stare at me. When it happened, I hesitated and looked at my lap.

Mr Taccori got all happy and asked us whether we knew Amberley. After the new girl joined the others, just a table away from mine, for a hundred and forty minutes, we both sat as if something bad had happened.

And after all that time, even after the bell went, I couldn't fathom why she looked so empty. She'd smile, but behind it all, it meant nothing. It was a facade, an act as clear as day, but it felt like I was the only one who noticed.

Her joyless gaze made my heart burn—she wasn't depressed, no, she was sadder than that.

By the end of last period, I saw her once more. I finally replied to Cameron:

Meet me at Salvos.

I didn't know if he'd read it, but I knew he'd be there anyway.

Amberley walked out of the archway, passing me as if I were

nothing. I rested once more by the steps and analysed everything she did. Not one, but both of her parents picked her up and carried on like she was going to die.

And that's when it happened.

Right there and then, she smiled at me in the sunlight of the afternoon. The clouds seemed distant, and without a wave or even a *hello*, our eyes met, and she revealed a smile worth watching a thousand times.

She planted herself into her parent's car, and when they drove away, I realised how late I was. The back number plate glistened in front of me, and I smiled back, standing up to rub my neck. It still stung! Beneath the neck hairs, it was warm, and I was cold.

Why was that girl so peculiar just then? I couldn't say, and after I had made a few guesses, I found Cameron in a familiar spot.

The People I Tolerate

I like watching ants. Whether they're scattered across a sidewalk, a pile of dirt or a patch of grass, they carry on as if there's nothing wrong with the world. It keeps me calm, staring down at them. Today, the concrete had a grey tinge to it—an almost blue look. It got me thinking about what the ants were doing—what I was doing this morning …

No, no, I'd rather not think about that. And besides, the street was so loud.

I tried blocking out all the honking and yelling. It was like peak hour in the city, but there was no city in sight. I leant back and sighed.

Where is he?

I'd been here for a few minutes, right in the middle of Springwood, a few feet from the shops and the council. With my back against the Salvo's wall, the honking stopped, and this douche decided to park his car right in front of me. You could hear it happening as more ants crawled past like moving polka dots. It was all fuzzy, a murmur in my ears.

And yet, I was so focused, I didn't realise the same murmur was repeating my name.

"Tyler!"

"Huh?" I muttered, blinking past the pathway and finding an old friend. "Sorry. I was just watching the uh—ants … Wait! Why are you …? You don't have your licence."

Cameron laughed, locking the door to his '93 Toyota Hilux.

"Don't be a baby, it's fine. An' besides, I'm leaving Jess here. Sorry it took so long. Actually, have you seen the rope I kept in the back?" He tapped the ute's grey tray and leant forward to investigate.

"What rope?" I coughed, tiptoeing to his side.

"Don't worry. I just needed something to tie my shit down. I'm gettin' the delivery this weekend. I'm sure Haley has it. Come on!"

I followed him behind the shop where the employees' carpark was, and right at the back near an iron door, there were two blue donation bins.

Cameron swung his keys around and kneeled, unlocking one of the tin boxes. He was skinny for his size, a little shorter than me with gaps between his teeth. His brows were heavy, and his freckles were abundant; he grinned like a shark. He always smelt like orange peels—I never knew why. But he was broad and could knock down anyone if he got angry.

Scratching his frail dark brown hair, he slammed his palm against the bin. A metallic echo erupted as he scoffed. Eventually, he threw the door open and took out a brown paper bag. It was rolled up tight, restrained with an elastic band.

Tossing the bag to me, he locked his crimes for another day.

I handed him the bag as we retraced our steps. "Feels bigger than normal. Did you get promoted?"

"Nah, man. New Kev's just got me doin' more stuff." Cameron's brows dropped and he squirmed, staring at my neck. "What happened to your neck?"

I rubbed my burn. "This? A branch scratched me on the way to school. Is it bad?"

"Yeah. I'd hate to cut my neck. Yuck. That'd hurt heaps. Gosh, I'm already shakin'—look at me." Laughing, his disgusted tone became bubbly. "Since you've been so brutally assaulted, what do ya want for lunch?" He opened the bag and began counting a heap of fifty and twenty-dollar notes.

"I don't know, it's your money," I shrugged, walking past the ute. "Aren't we gonna drive up?"

"Leave it. Like you said, I don't have my licence, plus there's no time limit for parking," he mused. "Let's go for a wander."

We strolled past roundabouts, cafes and hippie shops only to end up across the road from the pharmacy.

"How about The Bunker?" asked Cameron.

"No, too expensive. I don't want you wasting your money." I searched the shopping line. "Why don't you choose?"

"Me? I don't care what we eat, unless ya want a kebab?"

I rolled my eyes and noticed a familiar car parked outside the pharmacy. "Damn, almost forgot. I gotta get Mum's pills."

Cameron sighed. "Well, if you're goin' in there, mind pinching some DXM?"

I frowned, raising my left brow.

"What?" Cameron scoffed.

I crossed my arms. "You know I don't do crap like that. I don't!"

Cameron took a step closer, grinning. "But you have."

"I'm not doing it, Cameron!"

Glancing towards the pink entrance of the pharmacy, I saw something that made my brain numb. Cameron soon got bored, finding another distraction.

A tall, dark-skinned guy, all bony-like, yelled Cameron's name and the two shook hands in between the passing people. They were talking about *Kev, New Kev* and something about how business was *booming*. Everything they discussed faded as I concentrated on two blue eyes that were across the road.

Below, I noticed that the owner of the blue eyes had the most perfect lips. Her light brown hair was still tied up in a high ponytail, and she was standing without a care in the world.

Cameron, I guess, finished his chat with his associate, and nudged me.

"What are ya looking at?"

A cold sensation ran down my spine, making me shake. "Hmm?"

"What are you staring at?" he insisted, examining the other side of the road.

I stopped acting dumb, scratching my head. "The um ... new girl in our year. She just started today."

His eyes locked onto Amberley, and he grinned, "She's cute. The heck, why would you stand outside a pharmacy like that? She doesn't look sick." His eyes met mine. "Wanna put bets up?"

"On what?" I was interested, I'll admit. But damn, I wish I had never asked.

"I'll give you fifty if you go an' talk to her. What do ya reckon?"

Smirking, I put my hands in my pockets. "And why would I need that? I'd talk to her anyway."

"No you wouldn't. Come on, it's money. Free money, all you got to do is talk to her. Ask her what she's doing. It's easy."

"No." Turning away from Cameron, I glanced at my shoes. "She could just be waiting for her parents. What's in it for you? Like, what if I don't do it?"

"If ya don't, you have to get me that cough syrup."

"What? So you and Haley can use it?"

"No, no, no, it's for something else. Don't always assume shit." Cameron pointed at the pharmacy. "Either way, you're gonna have to go down there—just talk to her. Don't be a bitch!"

I stared down my options and braced myself, handing Cameron my laptop. "Fine, but it's not for the money. I want to go down there."

Cameron smirked, saluting me as I marched across the busy crossing.

My heart was racing faster than it had been this morning, and thank the stars, Amberley hadn't seen me yet. *Who am I kidding? She doesn't know who I am. Maybe the uniform? No, Amberley wouldn't notice me.* Heck, with the way she's holding that plastic bag, I don't think she notices much.

At the end of the crossing, there was a bloodwood tree nestled between the pharmacy and a small Westpac office. Beneath the tree's dry leaves, an elderly man sat playing his guitar as if he had the power to make the clouds go away.

I squatted next to the street performer as he started to play *Tears in Heaven*. His voice was brittle, and against its sombre tone, I saw Amberley's parents leave the pharmacy.

Taking out my wallet in the hope that it would distract me, I found a dollar eighty. I threw it into the performer's golfer hat, hearing the clash of coins, and awkwardly nodded to him.

When I glanced up, Amberley's eyes were peering through me.

I scoffed as a cold sensation burnt my insides. Quickly, I returned to my shell and stared at the sidewalk. I approached her like it was the last thing I could do to save my miserable life, took a deep breath and said two words.

"Excuse me."

I steered clear from any eye contact as the shadows beneath her feet staggered. All three strangers moved out of my way.

Finally, I entered the blue interior, and Amberley's mum uttered, "Sorry … Hmm, honey. That boy's from your school."

Damn, I hate when people do that!

I shook it off and ventured into the first aisle, overhearing another conversation.

Amberley's mum, all high on spending money, began to raise her voice. "Now, we haven't forgotten, but I want you to get the antibiotics."

Amberley's voice was rather mellow, like she was expecting the conversation. "Sounds good."

I peeked my head around the aisle, and we did that awkward eye tango again.

Amberley looked away first. "Look, I'm fine with getting it, it's just ... Aren't I too young to go and get it?"

"No, no. It's prescribed under your name. It doesn't matter that you're not eighteen yet—you need it. And if ..." Amberley's mum sighed. "If it gets worse, you'll need to be able to get it yourself if your dad and I are busy."

"Okay, Mum! Can we not talk about it, *please!*"

"Sorry, honey. Just hand them this and if they ask you anything, answer honestly." The two moved to the back counter.

Searching the aisle, I read bottle after bottle, finding the DXM on the second-lowest shelf. However, before I could take one of the bottles, a voice startled my quick hands.

"Hey, kid. You know any good places to eat around here?"

Standing next to me was a wealthy man in his business attire and a perfectly done-up tie. It was Amberley's father, who searched the shelf with me. He had the same ocean-blue eyes as his daughter, spiky hair neatly combed to the side, freshly shaven cheeks and a perfect smile. Although he reeked of cologne, his suit was fresh like he'd had it dry-cleaned this morning.

I apologised, and being a little bewildered, I listened closely when he repeated the question.

Shrugging, I stared at the ground. "The Bunker's okay. And Thai Square has a lot of variety. Noodle Paradise is cheap! That's where I'd go. There's a nice Indian place in Glenbrook and lots of choices near the Lapstone Hotel. Besides that, I've never really gone past Faulconbridge. There might be something nicer up the mountains."

He laughed and said thank you, making me twitch.

But that didn't bother me. No, something stuck out more than his suit and his relaxed mannerisms—it was what he said afterwards.

"What's a boy like you doing here? You don't need this." He picked up a one-hundred-millilitre bottle, inscribed with *Dextromethorphan*, and shook his head. "You have so much to live for and this is what you're doing with your time? Don't take it for granted." Then, throwing me the bottle, he smiled, "Enjoy!"

When I was alone, I paced back and forth, thinking about what he had said.

Placing the syrup on the shelf, I swindled a second bottle from the fourth shelf and strolled to the back counter.

The waiting area at the pharmacy was so sterile. It had a sharp smell that made my nose flare, and the carpet was disgustingly stained with shoe scuffs.

As I stood beside an old plastic seat, taking out Mum's prescription papers, I noticed Amberley in the corner of my eye. She stood tall, placing her papers on the counter, and smiled.

She almost learnt the pharmacist's whole life story before saying, "Can I get this? Metrond—Metroni Dazole, please. Thank you so much."

The second pharmacist asked me if I needed help.

I showed her Mum's prescription, but of course, she didn't believe me.

"Look, it's for my mum. She's been on it for a while. We got a new doctor. I don't know, the GP just sent us to him. Our old one ironically just passed away." I pushed the prescription closer to her. "Please, she needs them. I can't go home without them, she'll go skits!"

She didn't take my sarcastic tone too well, but Samantha— according to her name-tag—went searching for Mum's pills.

Both pharmacists came back at a similar time, and at that moment, Amberley and I both said *thank you*. I turned my head, seeing that her ponytail was now undone.

Grinning, I nodded to her and went back to admiring the carpet's patterns.

At the front counter, Amberley's father stared at me as I paid for the medication with some cash I had previously gotten from Cameron. The girl at the register insisted on checking my bag, and yes, I showed her its contents.

By the time her register clicked, and the floor became familiar, Amberley was behind me, laughing with her mum. *What a lovely family.*

I walked to the exit, and Amberley's dad kept shaking his head at me.

Biting my lip, I rubbed my burn and ignored the floor. I looked Amberley's dad in the eyes and went to shake his hand.

"Tyler, by the way," I told him. "Just letting you know, you stare a lot. And, in case you want to *report me*, I'm here for my mum."

"Nice to meet you, Tyler," he shook my hand with a firm grip. "The sarcasm's a nice touch. And thanks for the recommendations. We might visit some for lunch this weekend." Letting go, he smiled. "What year are you in?"

"Twelve. Why?"

Amberley's mum appeared right behind me. "You're the mumma's boy," she said. "You're doing a great service. Coming all this way. And here! Golly, I've been to a lot of pharmacies, but this one's a little … wild, huh?"

I smiled, gulping at the ridiculous situation. I hated these people, and I regretted shaking that hand. It was so cold! But, to my surprise, it was about to get a little worse.

Amberley stood behind her mother.

I scratched my frizzy hair and slumped my bag over my shoulder. "Anyway, I better get a move on."

Stumbling outside, I stared right at Cameron on the other side of the road. He watched me as I turned back to the brooding father, the optimistic mother and the curious girl that made my head all bothered.

Even as I glanced at them, the door swayed and stayed open, and I felt nauseous.

"Nice meeting you all." I waved to Amberley. "Oh and ... hey."

Turning around before she could reply, I went to fetch my old shy self.

When I reached Cameron, he was clapping his hands like I was some sort of street performer. He gave me my laptop. "Wow, you said *hey*. And for a second, I thought you had pussied out. Here." He ripped out a fifty-dollar note.

"I don't need it," I pushed his hand away. "I did it 'cause I was interested, not 'cause of that ... Actually. Here. Thought I owed you for last time." I grabbed the bottle of cough syrup and tossed it to him.

Cameron lit up like a glow worm and pinched the DXM from the sky. "I knew you could do it. My man! Now I have to give you the fifty."

I argued, but he insisted, stuffing the note into my pocket. Sighing, I held my laptop, and Cameron went on one of his tangents about Haley.

"She's gonna love this man ..." On and on he went, and before I knew it, my friend finally made up his mind. "Let's get some Thai. I'm really craving it. Do the chicks from school still work there?"

"Yeah, why?"

"I don't know. Time I get someone new in my life."

Now don't ask me what was up with Haley. I'm not even sure. But heck, we kept walking as Amberley's father drove past us as if what just happened never actually did.

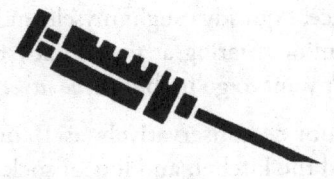

Home

It had gotten dark by the time I arrived home.

Cameron was gone. After our Thai, he stormed off, telling me that he was going to stash his money in the usual spot. So again, I was left alone, walking down the dim-lit road of Colourless Avenue. It was a quiet street, littered with used plastic bags, slouched jacarandas that hadn't bloomed in years, and a charcoal road that was riddled with potholes. The mailboxes decreased from thirty to twenty as the sun swayed below the crumbling exterior of a hobo's shack near the cul-de-sac's end.

On the right, a steep hill ventured towards the train station, and on the left was number sixteen. My home!

It was another rundown house like eighteen and twenty, however, it oozed with the scent of incense. Beyond its front lawn, the shack had a shattered front window, a timber veranda and a makeshift plastic sheet that was meant to keep the rain out.

I pushed through a flimsy metal gate and noticed that a cheap-looking van was parked on the driveway. On its left side, it had the imprinted words, *Beau's Hardware and Plumbing*.

Damn! That dumb van makes my teeth grind.

I hopped onto the veranda. An ashtray was full on a single table that stood next to the type of seat you'd find at an old English auction. Dust and rotting cut-timber took up most of the space next to the table, along with a duffle bag. Fortunately, for me, the bag was more of a tripping hazard as it had been left right outside the front door.

23

Losing my balance, I quickly caught myself, and yanked out Mum's pills just as a precaution. Staring at the mouldy doorknob, I braced myself. I really didn't want to go in, but *home sweet home … right?*

I opened the door as conservatively as I could. The television was blasting beyond the kitchen and lots of sock fluff was sprinkled between the creases of the patterned cream carpet. The lounge room was thankfully closed off, yet, for some reason, I continued to tiptoe into the dying kitchen. The steps creaked, the roof was practically crumbling, and behold—more papers and cigarette filters were snuggled between the litres of cough syrup, Panadol and many dark blue pills that covered the kitchen bench.

Empty and partially full bottles of wine lingered all over the joint; empty canisters burnt my vision and pill packets clawed at my feet. But no matter what Mum had hoarded, there was still this ember that ignited inside my belly.

After I placed her medication on the table and opened the fridge, I wanted to scream. I couldn't explain why. It was more annoying than any powder, any medication, any type of bottle filled with poison.

It was my pizza!

The six slices I had left in the fridge, just in case I came home, were gone.

All that was left was half a pepperoni, a note that said Tyler's, don't touch! and a grey cardboard box, left empty on the fridge's middle shelf.

After everything that had happened today, I had treated myself to a can of soft drink that was hopefully still cold in my bag and a new writing book, confident that those six pieces of pizza would be there when I got home.

I slammed the fridge's door and screamed the culprit's name.

"*Mum!* Are you kidding? You ate my pizza, you mother…"

As I hauled open the lounge room's sliding doors, Mum was *laughing*. Ignoring me, she plunged deeper into a drunken abyss.

I yelled her name over and over, but she just sat there, sunken between too many bottles of wine and expired food. The room reeked; the lounge had become nauseating, and the stupid television hadn't been turned off in days. It was showing more static each time I walked inside to argue.

Mum's nose was red and blistered. She wasn't sick, no! She was simply enjoying the moment. The old *Alice in Wonderland* movie was playing. But before I could give it any attention, a loud shrieking sound made my arms tense.

"What is it now, Tyler? Piss off will ya, you're ruining the show. Did you get my pills, sweetie?" Transforming from furious to suddenly kind, Mum turned to me.

"You ate my food," I reiterated. "The food *I* paid for, with *my* money. Don't touch my shit; I was saving that."

"Did you get my pills? Tyler, did you get them?"

"No!" I crossed my arms. "I told you this morning, *don't eat the pizza*. I even said please."

Mum raised her voice, "*Pills, Tyler!* Where are they?"

"Just listen to me—for once. Then I'll tell you."

While she was having her tantrum, Beau's forearm moved away from behind Mum's neck. They were cuddling like usual—him being a big douche-pillow—and between mum's loud nags and my argument, Beau stood from the rotting lounge.

He was a big man. Bigger than most, with broad shoulders—heavy-duty kind of shoulders—that'd knock anyone down. His beard was unkempt, brown from his cheekbones to the wrinkles below his neck. Honestly, there was more hair on his chin than on his scalp! His flannel shirt was crinkled, his hands were bruised with chipped dirty nails, and his jeans had fallen below his waist, held lightly by a crappy leather belt.

Yet, despite his intimidating stature and hefty chest, not to mention that tradesman's manner, I didn't retreat and hide behind a filthy cupboard. I wasn't scared—well, I wasn't as scared as he thought I was.

He clasped his knuckles and stared me down. With my chipper ol' face, I was surprised Mum's enforcer hadn't moved earlier.

While she was screaming, Beau said the daftest thing.

"Shut your gob and give her the meds, Tyler! God, you're the worst, ya know that? Just stop whinin'!"

I dropped my shoulders, feeling the insides of my pockets. My spine was so curved, it was ready to pop. "Don't talk to me!" I pointed at Beau. "And stop buying wine and coke and all this shit you keep shoving into my house. Look at her, dickhead, she's ——"

A wine bottle flew past me, exploding behind my head. As it shattered, the shards scattered all over my left heel. The glass felt cold.

It was a surprise for Beau, but for me … *Heck, I'm not sure anymore.*

"*Don't talk to us like that, you shit!*" Mum screamed. "Get me my pills, Tyler. After everything I've done for you. I've given you a great childhood, haven't I?"

Beau lost his smile, crossing his arms. "Do what ya mother says, boy!"

Scoffing, I stomped into the kitchen, and returned, pegging the pills at Mum.

I glared at Beau. "Don't talk to me. *At all!* Can't you see what you're doing to her? … I'll be upstairs. You happy now, Mum?"

Mum didn't respond; she just went back to watching the movie.

I moved quickly. Beau wandered to the door, but luckily the staircase was right behind it. Halfway up the stairs, I put my middle finger up at him.

"What's wrong with you?" he demanded.

I stood my ground, "*Everything!* She's just using you. You're nothing to her—so leave while you can!"

"*Enough!* I'm sick of your crap, Tyler. I love her!" Beau pointed at the lounge. "Your mother's a very broken woman, but I'd sacrifice everything for her. So stop being so ungrateful."

"*I'm* ungrateful?" I laughed. "Surprised! I'll see you at dinner—wait! I cook my own food, I wash my own clothes, I clean my own things, I work, buy food, deal with the welfare and donations. But you're right! I'm the ungrateful one. Who do you think pays for her medication? Piss off, Beau."

I stormed off, ignoring the rest of his comments, and found the one clean haven in this rotting mess.

My room is my home! I'm glad there's a lock on the door. It's a lot quieter than the rest of the house, and the floor's a nice grey, not as dark as it is downstairs. When I flicked my lamp on, my heart stopped beating so fast. I'm like a neat hoarder with all my belongings stacked above shelves and on top of desks and cupboards.

Strolling in, I loosened my tie, slipped off my shoes and dumped my bag against my desk. My forehead felt swollen, and my eyes were so sore. I had only enough energy to sit at my desk and look at the newspapers I had collected. Each one had circles over the things I would like to buy. Some were just ideas, others were necessities—and yet I didn't have enough money to buy any of them. *A mini-fridge, a car, a house or an apartment.*

I only left the papers there to remember that things were going to get better. But, as each day passed, for me, that notion became a bigger lie.

Pulling out my laptop, I searched online. I looked at apartments for sale, anything cheap I suppose. Then I searched for jobs with decent pay.

I was just wasting time.

After a while, I took off my tie, opened my window and crawled out onto the rooftops.

Metal sheets, planks of wood and the occasional nail guided me towards a small handmade balcony.

Atop the roofing, a shitty clothesline I had put together dangled against the back wall of my room. I took the clothes hanging over the rundown wire. They were still damp but dry enough to wear again. One was a towel, which I flung over my shoulder.

It was a windy night; the stars were up, and the streetlights were foggy.

Leaping into my room, I folded each of my shirts and pants. I rested my blazer over my bed's end and pulled out a chopping board from beneath my mattress. This was for my desk, so I could cut the tomatoes and cucumbers I had bought using Cameron's fifty.

Taking some spreads and a loaf of bread I had stowed away in my cupboard, I made three sandwiches—one for breakfast, one for lunch and a snack for whenever. I wrapped them up and left them in an empty drawer. Sure, it wasn't a fridge, but the wooden desk felt cool enough. Hopefully, nothing goes off.

I would use the fridge, but not after what just happened. Not anymore!

I took out a toiletry bag and some shorts and unlocked my door. Opening it, I saw what was on the other side. My room was part of a three-door hall with two doors on either wall and one at the hall's end.

I snuck over to the end, passing paintings and family photos. The one facing my room was the worst. I walked out and its frame was the first thing I would see. Dad, Mum and I, all happy.

Enjoying what we had. Mum could be cruel sometimes but keeping a photo of Dad was torture.

It makes me sick!

Mum looked less tired in the photo. A lot of people say we have the same sage-green eyes and olive skin. Yet now we're both a pasty creme. Her honey hair was clean, and her perfect smile was soothing. But nowadays, I don't think she knows how to smile.

Dad, funnily enough, had much darker hair than Mum and me. It was almost black. His nose was large, but it was a nice round button like mine. *I really miss him.*

I entered the bathroom and noticed that I had a blackhead on my nose, a big bag under my left eye and a new swollen burn across my neck. It was worse than I thought. It didn't sting, but now it was browner, blending between the creases of my skin.

Undressing, I folded my pants and underwear and turned on the hot water. Waiting for the shower's glass to turn grey, I then cooled the stream.

People always draw something in the fogged-up glass with their finger. But me, I just place my hand over the grey wall for a moment and lift it to see my handprint. This time, when I moved my hand away, the see-through handprint had drops of water trickling down its palm as if it were crying.

Instead of cleansing my body and washing my hair, I sat under the waterfall and let it dampen my back. Water dripped from my eyes, yet not all of it was from the showerhead.

I guess I was reflecting on today, on how sad it was. I still wished that the rope hadn't snapped. I wanted to die!

What's the point? I know it's not okay, but I keep on living, and things keep getting worse.

When I glanced up at the shower wall, the handprint was gone.

*"Some changes look negative on the surface
but you will soon realise that space is being created
in your life for something new to emerge."*

ECKHART TOLLE

What Makes You Happy?

It was the last day of January, an unspectacular Tuesday. Now that school had been on for a week, I kept to myself, and accepted the mundane flavour of my day-to-day life.

During my recess break, I could hear lots of mumbling, some juniors screaming, and a bunch of kookaburras chirping atop an oak like it was sunny. For some reason, I wasn't in the mood to eat. So I sat in my spot, watching ants move around my leather shoes as if they were two mountains. Scratching my neck, I realised the rope burn across my skin had faded.

That's when I heard a depressed sigh.

The seat to my left, the one next to the bush and its concrete urn, had a new visitor. I lifted my head so fast that everything lingered in a blur. Scoffing at my light-headed high, I examined the green leaves next to me. They were a sage, all subsiding against the breeze with little red extremities piercing from their roots. The branches became thicker the deeper you looked, and when I reached the centre to see what was on the other side, the leaves clustered tightly, caging up any image.

Yet between the cracks, the small pours of sunlight revealed a girl.

Her hair was pulled back in a ponytail, her head was slouched on her tender palm and her knees were pressed together, protecting her skirt from the vicious wind. Though I'll admit, it was better than watching ants, I had to stop. It's wrong to stare for so long. Heck, I'd be creeped out if some dude was observing me from behind a stupid shrub.

It was Amberley. If you wanted to know—she was weird, judging by what I had seen and heard. *Maybe weird's not the right word. She's different, that's it! Different.*

Today was the first day she had caught the bus. We're on the same one; I get on at the second stop, and she gets on at the fifth. For the last week, I had seen her sauntering around minding her own business. Her face always looked calm, but her posture was kind of nervous like she was trying to not fall over.

The boys, of course, introduced themselves. Jacob, with his short hair, flicked to the side, pumped out his chest as though it was gonna burst and introduced himself like a *proper gentleman*. Crouchy was by his side, holding his binder tightly. He smiled to be nice and asked Amberley if she liked Extension Maths.

Xander, who doesn't always hang out with that group, ended up tripping over himself, making everyone laugh. He talked to her the most. I haven't said a word to her since the pharmacy. Heck, I don't think she would recognise me.

In the beginning, she sat with different groups. The popular girls seemed to be her favourite. I guess none of us really knew her yet. *Maybe she was really annoying or perhaps she's a bit gross. She could be the opposite of what she looks like. Maybe she's confident, or maybe—just maybe—she's like me.*

See, I'm different—unique, in other words. I've changed in the past few years. I won't get into it, it's *personal*. But I'm not new, so people don't exactly treat me super kindly.

It's strange though; you'd think Amberley could be whatever she wanted. She could lie a thousand lies, and no one would have the slightest. But instead of sitting with Bronte and Katie, she decided she wanted to be alone. And I couldn't blame her. *It's fun sometimes to be alone.*

The bell went. As I stood, my head turned towards Amberley's. I didn't mean to do it; it just happened. Our eyes met, and we stared at each other. My gut clenched.

But unlike me, she smiled and waved. It was a small wave and a big smile, but deep in her eyes, behind her tanned skin, she was lying. Her hands next to her upper leg were grasping at the seat. Her arms were stiff and straight, and some strands of her hair dangled in front of her temple.

I grinned and avoided any further interaction.

Pacing towards my math class, I watched more ants with each step I took.

Nuts! I have Society and Culture. My timetable said it as clear as day, so I took a detour around an old demountable.

It took a few good minutes to find the classroom, and when I overcame the staircase and glanced ahead, I saw Amberley across the hall with Xander.

"What's up, Tye?" Xander asked.

I shrugged, yet Xander kept talking. "He's always pretty quiet—kind of like you. Have you guys met?"

Huh? He put me on the spot. Of all people, *Xander* put *me* on the spot!

I played with my bag straps. "Yeah, kind of. Hey again."

"Hey yourself. You two coming in?" Amberley had already jumped into the doorway. It was like she didn't care, acting all smug. The whole lesson she kept ignoring me. She was the opposite of what she was at the seats.

We had a double period, so Sir let us start our majors.

Each student had ideas for their topic, their focus questions, their main aim and so on, however, Xander's was quite a mouthful. His project was about homeless people and whether they have access to services. It would be rough interviewing a crap-ton of homeless people. And with all the ethics behind it, what would you even ask them?

See, mine was simple. It was to find out whether people are happy or not. Obviously, there were complications, but you get the gist. On my laptop screen, I had a few draft questions. I don't think the questionnaire had changed in a week, but when

Sir came around, it seemed as though I had done a marathon of work.

That flashing black bar, teasing me to type, was the only thing that moved.

"Do you know any homeless people, Xander?" Mr Taccori asked.

Xander, with a smile as big as always, laughed. "No. I'm sure I'll meet one sooner or later. I'll just ask around, go to a Salvos or somewhere, they'll know."

Sir nodded. He continued with the class, telling everyone to make their main aim more narrow and less broad.

"I have a feeling he doesn't like your main aim," I said. It was more like an exhausted breath, but Xander got the point.

"Why do you say that?"

I leaned in closer, lowering my voice. "Just how Sir talks to everyone else about their PIPs, it's different when it comes to you. It's like he looks down on you. I don't know, maybe I'm full of crap."

"You're talkative today." Xander grinned, "Full of crap could be it. Eh, I couldn't care. You're meant to pick a topic you want to do. And I want to do this." He leaned over my laptop. "What makes you happy? ... Hmm, I have an idea. You wanna help?"

"With?" I raised a brow.

"I'll do your survey and interview if you do mine. You just have to pretend to be homeless—well, when I actually have a survey and interview for you to do. What do you think?"

Before answering, I stared blankly, watching Sir as he talked to Amberley.

They discussed her project's main aim. It was to find out whether people who were diagnosed with terminal diseases felt content. It was pretty dark, and Sir had many worries. He was voicing his concern, particularly when it came to ethics, but

Amberley said it was fine. She already had a focus group planned at the hospital.

The one thing that stuck with me was when she said, "It's okay. I always need to visit the hospital. So I might as well use that to help my PIP."

Xander kind of ruined the flow, so I had to redirect my attention.

"I like it, Xander, it's a solid idea. I'll get Cameron to help, he's pretty much homeless."

Getting excited, Xander went in for a fist-bump. I almost ignored him.

Knocking his hand, I continued watching the black bar as it flashed on my laptop screen.

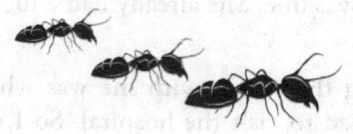

Watching Ants

It was the first of February, a warm day to begin the month. I didn't have Society and Culture, and unlike yesterday, I felt a little more empty.

I was eating another shitty sandwich and studying the ground's imperfections. Amberley, for the fourth time this week, sat on the opposite chair. She always stared forward or around or even at her phone. Yet every time she looked at her phone's screen, a sigh would come. She was consistently hugging things, whether it was her bag, her food or her chest.

Now, I wasn't watching, I just noticed a few quirks.

With the bushy plant between us, something peculiar happened: I got a message! It made my stomach twist.

I pulled out my phone to see Cameron's name.

I'm coming to pick u up from school, my home-screen read.

I typed, Don't worry about it, but I never pressed send.

Chucking my phone away, I sighed like it was the last time I could.

Could, should, needs to be. Different words, same meaning. It doesn't mean I don't want to end it. I do! I can't even explain it to anyone. I write things down, all these thoughts, and I never feel good. Or nice. Or ...

Why me?

Everyone else smiles and acts like they're fine. I can't be the only one, but in the back of my head, something pleads to just end it. It thinks of different ways, and all I can do to calm its cries is to write, or walk, or lay in bed and do nothing.

And as these thoughts rushed into my head, making the world seem like a dark balloon of black and grey, someone said something that made the voices stop.

With her hair in a high ponytail, Amberley grinned, tilting her head to the left. Her bag dangled from her weak shoulder as she stood with the most perfect posture.

Amberley asked me one simple question. "Is this seat taken?"

I looked up, hiding my tears. "Are you talking to me?"

"Yes. Can I sit here? You look a little lonely."

"Yeah, go ahead." I moved my laptop aside, and boy, was she an organised sitter.

Her posture never swayed as she leaned and rotated almost a hundred and eighty degrees. Her bag fell as soon as her bottom touched the timber, and unlike when she was on her own, she was less tense next to me, pulling out food from her bag.

You should have seen the stuff she had. A container with pre-cut steak, mashed potatoes, boiled veggies—and it all steamed when the lid popped off. I hadn't smelt anything so nice in such a long time.

"Cool spot," she murmured. "Have you always sat by yourself?"

I leaned back, keeping my distance. "No."

I guess she wanted more detail, but my damn body churned.

She fixed her bag between her legs. "Fair enough. I guess it's nice to be by yourself. Just you and your thoughts in the quiet. Do you want to hear about something that happened to me the other day?"

I shrugged.

"Well, I might as well tell you," she said. "I met this little girl in the hospital last week. She was really lovely. She just had a stroke, and one lasting effect was that she was now deaf. Poor thing. She um ... She liked ice cream, showed me the sweetest one in the little cafeteria they have there. But it's funny. Even though she knew she was never going to hear again, she'd watch these videos—which mind you, they had noise. But she'd watch them and read the subtitles on her mum's phone. And she showed me this one because she thought I looked sad. Do you want to watch it?"

Amberley was staring at me, right in the eye—there was no way I could say *no* to all that excitement.

"Sure."

Pulling out her phone, she started typing like a crazy person. She mumbled to herself, trying to figure out what the video was called. And finally, she found it.

It is Impossible to Tell if Anything is Good or Bad — Alan Watts. That's what she read to me, and that's what I saw on the YouTube bar.

It was a two-minute video about a farmer who had really annoying neighbours. Anyway, these bad things kept happening to him, like his horse ran away, and his son broke his leg, and so on and so forth. But every time something bad happened, something even greater would be the end result. And this Alan Watts, what he talked about, it really got to me. We really don't know how things are going to end up, even when the consequences seem to be good or bad.

Of course a little girl would like the video; it was colourful, and the cartoon placed a good picture in your head.

Once it finished, Amberley said, "It's interesting, hey? ... You're not a big fan of talking, are you?"

"You are the first person to ever say something like that to me." I sniffled, "I've just made mistakes, that's all."

Amberley smiled, and because of that, I'm glad I spoke. She licked her lips. "I get it. I used to talk a lot. But things change, people move on, something bad comes up. It just seems that everyone has someone ——"

"Thanks for rubbing it in!" I scoffed.

"No! I didn't mean it like that. I had a point. It just looks like you've given up—well, not given up, but maybe, you don't want to bother anyone."

Chuckling, I shook my head. "No, I like being alone."

"Oh, okay … I have a question then, if you don't mind?"

"Go on," I said, dropping one of my brows.

She leaned in closer. "Why do you stare at the ground like all the time? I don't mean to be rude, but I can't remember seeing you once have your head up when you sit here."

"I uh … I watch the ants. It's not that I'm looking down, I just like watching them all scatter around with food."

"True. I'll watch them with you." Amberley faced the ground with all this *happiness*. It was making me nauseous.

I pulled myself back and rubbed my forehead. "Why are you sitting here?"

"Wow, he asked a question!" *Great. She's sarcastic too.* "I already told you. You looked lonely. I've talked to everyone else here, all the boys and girls in our year, and not once have I seen any of them outside of school, except for you. And I don't know why, but it bothered me. And then I'd see you here by yourself. And everyone knows you, some people mention you in passing. And I don't get it! Inside, I feel so vulnerable, so bad for you. But it's kind of nice because I don't have to worry about myself!" Amberley frowned, tapping her knees together. "My mum thought you were really sweet, by the way. She thought what you were doing for your mum was kind."

I sat there, frozen. I've never had anyone be so honest with me before.

I grinned, "Thanks. But you don't need to worry about me. I'm always like this."

"I will though. I worry too much. I don't even know you, but I'll worry. You're not special, okay! I'm going to the hospital this afternoon and it's going to be a nightmare. That little girl, I'll be worrying about her. The nurses and doctors, gah. I'm just a worrywart." Pausing, Amberley looked away from my eyes. "Oh, look. The sun's out."

We both gazed at the sky, and for the first time in weeks, the sun echoed from beyond its hold, lighting our seat with a light blue gaze. The grey was gone!

I looked away first. "I worry sometimes. Like your dad, for example! He's an odd unit. He made me worry at the pharmacy 'cause he was all over the place—just putting it out there."

Amberley laughed, "He's like that. He likes to talk to people and get to know them. What were you two talking about? He wasn't sure about you, said you were funny."

"*Funny!*" I shrugged, "He just wanted to know where there were good places to eat."

"Is that it?"

I nodded.

"Cough it up. Where do you like to eat?" I was startled by how confident she was. She went through her bag, placing textbooks and other random junk in between us. "I'm going to write it down so I don't forget. And make sure it has nice food in case I want it to be my *last meal*." She placed a book and a ripped piece of paper over her skirt.

I lowered my voice. "A bit dark, don't you think?"

"Let's just say it's like living in the moment!" Amberley smiled. "And I don't like two things: mushrooms and bananas."

I leant back. "Right! If you and your parents want a really good *last meal*, just have pancakes. They're my favourite. There's a pizzeria in Blaxland. They have pastas too and a whole bunch of other stuff."

"Yay, pancakes! And who doesn't love pizza." Squishing her eyelids closed, Amberley groaned. "Crud, what's the time?"

I shrugged and pulled out my phone. "Twenty-two past one."

Standing, Amberley threw everything back into her bag. Her textbook must have been heavy 'cause once she wrapped her bag straps around her arms, she was out of breath.

"Sorry, I have to go, Mum's waiting. I have an appointment! We'll do this again some time. It was fun. Bye."

I'll be honest, I zoned out. She strutted away, catching everyone's eyes, including mine. *She was weird!*

But once she was a shadow in the distance, I examined my phone's dark-blue screen. There was another message from Cameron.

I'm here at the archway. Ready to pick u up lad.

That idiot, I don't want to get picked up!

When I searched for Amberley's silhouette, she was gone. All I could muster was a sigh, and as my eyes rolled back and returned to the ants, next to my leg was a packet of pills. They were slightly open with long words imprinted on all sides.

In a yellow sticker under the title, *Metronidazole*, there was a bold name. *Amberley Gibbon*. It must have been the medicine she bought the other day!

Snatching the cardboard packet, I jumped from my seat. I yelled Amberley's name, but it was too late. She said she was going to the hospital; was that for the appointment she mentioned? I shouldn't wag school, but there were only two periods left, and I had a free.

I read the leaflet inside the packaging to see how badly she needed her medicine. If they weren't that important, I'd just give them back tomorrow, but if they were serious, I'd have to reach the hospital somehow.

Damn! She needs to take it three times a day. Whatever infection she's got, it's certainly killing me. I need to piss school off and find her. *Why am I putting so much effort into this? It's not like she'd do it for me or anyone else for that matter.*

The bell went, however instead of going to English—which, is a subject I actually like—I journeyed to the archway.

This better be worth it! Let's just hope Cameron knows how to get to the hospital! 'Cause I sure don't. What am doing with my life?

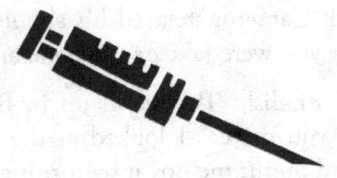

To Think and To Know

I past some juniors who were having a thick-headed conversation about shoes—they were so damn obnoxious, not letting me through.

Stumbling out of the archway, I noticed that Cameron was leaning over some Year Ten girls. They were pretty, and of course he was talking to them, but it was time we left before a teacher caught me still signed in.

In front of me, there was a dark green barricade that protected the students from passing cars. A crappy turquoise Corolla was parked beside it, stalking the school's front garden. I was surprised none of the teachers had done anything about the car.

All of the juniors were in their sports uniforms, so I stuck out like a blood blister.

Cameron, in his expensive-looking, white collared-shirt, hooked his thumbs into his hoody's pockets. He had hazel eyes that sparkled yellow when he flirted and small front teeth. Like, I mean *super* small.

Jumping, I landed on his back.

Cameron grunted, wobbling his body as he tried to grab me from behind.

I went from side to side, hanging on for dear life —it was like riding a bull! I'm sure those two girls were having such a *fun* time as he bragged about how rich he was.

"Piss off!" he scowled.

"Calm down. It's me," I laughed, sliding off his back.

Turning around, Cameron relaxed his shoulders. "The hell are you doin'? Thought you were Jake or someone annoying."

"Everyone's got English. They're all up in Building B. How'd you get here? Did you drive?" I looked at the girls. They smiled awkwardly, and kind of put me down by turning away.

Cameron stretched his back. "I didn't drive. Kev did! Well, New Kev. It's confusing."

My brows dropped, "What happened to Old Kev?"

"Old Kev's dead, or retired, or in Afghanistan ... Or skiing? No one really knows. We just have *New Kev* now." Behind Cameron, some kid got knocked down by a basketball. It smacked him silly in the face.

"Right. Why's he called New Kev then?" I asked.

"Because he's corny!" Cameron shrugged. "I don't know. It's like the boss' title. When there's a new boss, they're the New Kev."

"Wasn't the other guy actually named Kevin?"

"You mean Kevali?"

"Who?" I rolled my eyes. "We'll figure it out later. I don't have time—we have to get to the hospital. Where's the ute?"

"Aren't we getting food?" Cameron's face sagged, "Why do ya want to go to the hospital? Which one?"

I didn't think about that. Amberley's parents are pretty wealthy-looking. "I'd say Nepean Hospital, but I could be wrong, but I don't think I am."

A teacher, Mrs McCoy, went to check on the little Year Seven who had fallen over. She doesn't exactly like Cameron and me, so I pushed him forward to get a move on.

Cameron heaved back. "Fine, we'll make a detour to the hospital. Well, I would, but I'm not drivin'. You're gonna have to ask Kev. You don't have an appointment, do ya? 'Cause I wanted to hang out for a bit."

"Sorry, Cam. I ... I have to go, it's important." I put my arm around him, shielding our faces from Mrs McCoy's view. "I can't tell you why, but maybe another time. Nothing bad's going to happen."

Cameron smiled, finally walking towards the school's driveway. "True. Actually, I think you'll like New Kev. He's really keen to meet you. See you ladies later." Cameron winked at his two *fans* and escorted me to the Corolla.

It was stuffy inside. Everything was cramped and smelt like cigarette ash. The floor had a weird powder on it, circular stains covered the roof, and the seats had stuffing peeping out from their upholstery.

Between Cameron and I, there was a dirty syringe, brown from the inside out. Holding my laptop and bag on my knees, I sat next to a giant teddy bear, which was atop the middle seat.

Secret

"Sorry that it's so cramped, Haley and I have been meanin' to clean it—but man, I just don't have the time." Cameron closed the car door. After he got comfy, adjusting his seatbelt, he examined our driver. "I almost forgot. Yo, Kev, this is Tyler, my friend from school."

Kev was a large dude, and not *large* as in fat—his head almost touched the ceiling. He had oily black hair that slithered down his collar. His eyes were wide open—it was like he had never blinked, not once, not ever.

Through the rear-view mirror, I could see that his eyebrows were incredibly thick, his nose was cursed with a purple bruise, and his mouth had a raw cut sliding down his upper and lower lip. He also had really good skin. Like, top-of-the-line kind of skin, a model's skin if you were to place a picture in your head. Heaps shiny and smooth with no pimples, but it wasn't perfect, there were still wrinkles below his eyes, and when he raised his eyebrows, his forehead crinkled.

His hands were on the wheel, and he smiled at me through the rear-view mirror. "Nice to meet you, Tyler." His accent was different, maybe South Asian, but I couldn't place it in my head.

I waved, and then something horrid spoke. *Gosh, she gives me the biggest headache.*

"Tye-Tye! How have you been buddy? It's been ages."

I didn't answer her right away. Haley was the kind of girl you give a few seconds before answering. You got to let her think about what she's said.

She was the size of a twig, fiddling around with Kev's knee. Her skin was rather pasty, her hair was all knotty, and she had the largest bags beneath her eyes. *Her voice was the worst!* All crackly and raspy. Lighting a cigarette, she opened her window. Her brown eyes stared at me as she revealed a set of stained teeth.

She had been a schoolgirl once. No different than the two Cameron was talking to before. But now, her black shirt was covered in stains, her skin blemished in oils and scars that certainly weren't her own, and her eyes were slightly bloodshot from the misfortune torturing her life.

I grinned, "What do you mean? You saw me on Saturday."

"Was that you? Really?" Haley snorted, "I was out of my head! Cute uniform, by the way. I knew you and Cammy went to a posh school, but I never thought it'd be this nice."

Some smoke tickled my nose, so I wheeled down my window. The car started and we began to move.

Cameron leaned forward, "Hey, Kevali?"

New Kev—or whatever his name was—nodded.

"I know I said Tye was going to come with us an' do some rounds—I told you he's cool, but can ya do him a favour? It won't ruin our plans or anything, and we're not doin' much except the usual. Do you mind?"

Kev, with his deep voice, replied, "What kind of favour?"

"It's no biggie. He just needs a lift somewhere."

"Where to?"

"Um ——"

I butted in, "A hospital. Nepean, I think."

"Are you sure? *Think* is not the most confident word." Kev stared at me, dead in the eye.

"No, I know! Nepean. Do you know how to get there?"

Kev remained silent, and Cameron's face was now white as he bit his teeth together.

"That's fine, Tyler," said New Kev as he focused on the road. "You're a friend of Cameron's. And I go there often, it's not a problem. Consider this as a kind gesture. Nothing more and nothing less."

I dropped my head. "Thanks. What were you guys even doing today?"

No one responded.

After a couple of minutes of silence, Haley got all excited. "Kev, look! It's Beverage."

Before we left Springwood and merged onto the highway, I spotted the Indian guy Cameron was talking to a few days ago, standing by the kerb and admiring the sky. He was near the golf club, waving to us as we pulled in close. Kev obviously knew he would be there as he was already slowing down.

Beverage's bony black elbows leaned on Kev's windowsill, and he peeped his head inside, analysing the car. "My man, Kev! How are we today?"

Everyone knew everyone except for me, so I kept out of it. They talked about this, that, about Beverage's grandmother, and afterwards about Kev's merchandise. Haley went all sweet, calling

Beverage *baby* every ten seconds. I was surprised Cameron didn't get angry.

Then, with the click of his thumbs, Kev ordered Cameron to get Beverage's order. The teddy bear between us was unzipped and conveniently filled with all kinds of liquids and powders that weren't regular stuffing.

Pulling out a little vial that had in a monochrome script, *Morphine,* imprinted on it, Cameron began to hesitate.

"One sec, Bev. Just lookin' for the icing ..."

Searching the backseat, Cameron fiddled inside the bear and shrugged at me. What was he looking at me for?

With no other option, he snatched the dirty syringe between the bear and me. No way! As if he'd give the guy that crap. Who knows where it's been?

Cameron looked at the syringe, confronted some sort of demon, and the rest was history.

Kev gave Beverage his purchase, and along came two hundred dollars. But the skinny idiot wasn't done talking.

"I'd watch out, Kev. Coppers on the highway, down in Blaxland. RBT I think."

Kev growled, "You think, or you know?"

"There's definitely cops, that's all I got. Just warnin' ya." Beverage saluted New Kev. "Have a good one. See ya, Haley. Cam."

When we were back on the road, Haley called Beverage a dumb prick. She was glad he was desperate enough to buy from them. I don't know why.

I guess Kev was in a good mood. He gave everyone in the car a fifty dollar note each. I clutched the note, not knowing whether I should say thank you.

Instead of going via the backstreets to avoid the cops, Kev drove right through.

"Zip up the bear, Cameron. And Tyler, don't say anything, just look forward!" He was serious. Like, so serious, my heart started to rush again.

I guess for the others, the car was monotonous. But as we slipped further and further in, blue and red lights flashing all around, my left eye began to twitch. There were only two cop cars, four sirens and three boys in blue, but I felt like jumping out.

It's not the worst idea. Kev would surely kill me. But isn't that what I want? Well, it is. But he would be mean about it. I would rather do it on my own.

It's amazing how a few seconds can feel like hours. We drove by without getting stopped or asked for ID and finally reached the hospital without any other distractions. It was a nice drive. Cameron's phone was connected to the AUX, and I don't mind his music because he's into the same music as me.

The clouds were distant, and the blue sky came back, relishing the radiance of something I have no need to describe.

It's a pain to park at the hospital, but Kev's a surprisingly good driver. He reverse-paralleled into a spot not too far from the main building, and I thanked him as gangster-like as I could.

He smiled at me and shook my hand. He was actually pretty nice for someone so powerful in his profession—if you can even call it that.

Cameron walked me up to the main building.

"You heard, we'll wait ten, and if ya don't make it, we'll leave. Sound good?" he asked.

"I'll try," I nodded. "But don't worry. I'll call you if I know I'm not gonna make it in time. Thanks. I'm sorry today didn't work out like how it was meant to. It's hard. We should just chill, you and me, some time."

Out of nowhere, I felt a warm rushing pain across the back of my head. It made me stand up straight as Cameron pulled his palm away from my side.

I took a step back. "What was that for?"

"You're an absolute idiot! I saw the rope," yelled Cameron. "It was half-snapped. Don't do that shit! An' don't think that I'm an idiot. I know what it was for. I know you. Okay? Promise me you won't do it again."

I raised my voice. "I didn't do anything!"

"Don't be a dickhead." Again, he hit me, and another rush of warmth burnt my shoulder. "Promise me, Tye!"

Watching my shoes, I sighed. "Whatever. I promise. Stop going into the garage. It's mine, not yours."

"It's your dad's."

I found the courage to look him in the eyes. "Thanks for the update. I didn't think my dad was so nice! You know I love talking about family."

Pushing me forward, Cameron wrapped his arm around me. "Stop being you. With the sarcasm! Seriously … Are you good?"

I nodded, thanked him for everything, for keeping my head straight, and walked away.

The Travelling Package

I placed the fifty in my wallet before entering the main building.

It was a weird-shaped building, a trapezium made from smaller squares that didn't look like bricks. Very futuristic, with glass panels that slid open when I entered.

From the minute I stood inside the foyer, I felt cold. It was like something was wrong.

There was a front desk lady—I think—behind a glass wall that had a hole the same size as my head near its bottom half. I strolled up, observing the panel.

"Hi. Can I help you?" the lady asked. She had short blonde hair and a really crappy cardigan.

I read her name tag. "No. I mean, yes. I'm looking for someone. She forgot something at school, said she had an appointment at the hospital. So I thought I'd ..." I looked away from Cassandra and shrugged, "You know."

She lit up like a bloody glow-in-the-dark wristband and smiled. She had really round teeth if that makes any sense. "Did you come all this way to give her what she lost? What a sweetheart."

She gave me some directions. It turns out she wasn't a receptionist, so I ventured deeper into the hospital.

The real one was at a black table that was the height of most of my body. She was a big lady who would probably whinge about having a headache or something stupid.

She was chewing gum when I told her the same story as I'd told Cassandra.

"All right, what's this girl's name then?" she ordered.

"Amberley. Amberley Gibbon. I don't know why she's here."

The lady typed on her computer. Her fingers were so quick, yet so fat. Like, I don't mean to be rude, but I think she was breaking the laws of gravity. *How is she even typing so fast?*

She mumbled Amberley's name over and over until a little grin replaced her frown.

"Gibbon. She's getting treated at the moment. I don't think you'll be allowed to visit—it's only family, I'm sorry. But she should be out soon. She's not sleeping the night."

Damn, this woman's making my head all bothered. Just let me see her!

Wait. Why do I want to see her so badly?

I grinned and rolled my eyes. "Can you at least tell me what part of the hospital she's in so I can wait in the nearby waiting room? I don't want to miss her."

The lady told me about the north block. I had to go down a corridor, up through an elevator, and something about the second level. So I went, listening to the obnoxious tapping of my shoes.

Why was I doing this? Like, I should've just gone home and given her the medication tomorrow. *Nothing was going to change; she was only getting treated, right?*

I continued strolling until I entered a warm room that smelt like soap. Searching for a quiet chair, my reflection in the glossy marble flooring teased me as I held onto the package. It's funny how I sometimes don't notice things.

After the escape from school, the intense car ride, the several conversations and the loud echoing walk, my right hand was boiling; it was strained as I clasped Amberley's medication. I hadn't let go this whole time, not even when I put the money away.

The box was all flat now, crumpled at its corners. I decided to sit and rest my hand, placing the packet on my lap.

I sighed, pulling out my phone and calling Cameron.

Our chat was quick. I made a brilliant excuse about how I had found Mum and how she was worse than what I had thought. He understood; he knows her moods better than anyone.

Apparently, Haley called me *weak* for not coming, and Kev was a little bitter. *I think he likes me.*

"Sorry, bro," I muttered. "If I could leave, I would, but Mum will need help. I'll call you when I get out, and … and …" I lifted my head in search of a more elaborate lie, but Amberley caught my attention. Yep, she stared me down with an IV drip hanging from her arm.

I ended my phone call, saying *bye*, and gulped.

It was like I had startled her. Her mum was baffled, but I don't think she remembered me. My chest was hot, my heavy breath was loud, and we stared at each other in silence. She didn't want me to be here. *I shouldn't have come!*

Looking away, I hid my miserable face and staggered onto my feet. It seemed as though someone had just embarrassed me and the box of tablets almost broke into two.

I should go up to her, say sorry, say something, anything!

Instead, I left, rushing to the exit and hiding behind a wall so Amberley couldn't see me—*Mr Pathetic.*

Before the elevator opened, I finally did something for myself. It hit me.

I realised that this wasn't for Amberley—even though it helped her—and it wasn't for the people who made me uncomfortable. It was for me! I came all this way to prove something to myself, and now I was here.

So, as my fingertip pressed into the elevator's button, I turned back.

Amberley had barely moved. I passed many doctors, nurses and other patients, and was finally face to face with her.

"Hey … You forgot these. You left them at school. Here … Amberley?"

Her face went white, her mouth quivered, and I swear she was about to cry. Her head dropped, staring at my shoes. Without a sound, she stomped into the next room, dragging her drip and leaving me in a horrible silence.

All I managed was a sigh.

"Don't worry about her," a voice said behind me. "You're that boy from the pharmacy. I didn't know you two were friends."

It's funny, I felt a little tender. "You remember me?" I turned to Amberley's mum. "I don't think we're friends. She just sat with me today."

"She does like to sit and talk. It's what makes her special!"

Amberley's mum had light brown hair that weaved back and forth like waves, and she wore a lot of pink and white. She had dark hazel eyes that would have hypnotised many guys back in her prime. A coffee cup was warm in one of her hands. With small gentle lips, she smiled, and offered to take the package.

"Thank you for coming. It means a lot. How is she? At school? Is she fitting in? The move was very sudden, but we wanted to leave."

I handed her the packet. "Good, I suppose. Everyone seems to like her, and … she looks happy. We don't talk much. But, you know, she's good."

"That's great to hear." Amberley's mum squinted at me. "Shouldn't you be at school?"

I took a step back. "That's not wrong. She just left them at the seat, and I felt bad. But don't worry, I'll be fine. Is she okay? I don't mean to butt in or anything, but what's … what's wrong with her? Actually, I ——"

"It's fine. You've come all this way." Amberley's mum sighed. She had a sweet voice. "You're a good kid, and I mean it. It's been hard for everyone. But she's getting through it. Look, I would tell you, but it's awfully complicated. And it's not my place to say. Please don't mention it too much, especially at school. She doesn't like to talk about it. Okay?"

I nodded. "I understand. I guess I should go. Tell her I'm sorry. I shouldn't have come." Again, I felt gross. It was like a chill in my stomach, consistently biting at my insides.

"You're okay," Amberley's mum said. "I'll let her know. Do you have a way home?"

I began walking off. "I'll figure it out. Thanks a lot. I'm really sorry."

As I strolled away, Amberley's mum spoke again. "By the way, how's your mother? Is she feeling better?"

It was like the question gave me a migraine. I turned my head and grinned, nodding to Mrs Gibbon. *I'll just pretend I can't hear her.* And I didn't want her to worry, especially about how I was getting home.

Gosh, how was I getting home? I'll just have to figure it out on the way. *What's the harm? I already feel like crap!*

Doctors and Parents

As I went to press the damn down button, the elevator opened.

The smell of cologne made me heave as I tried to push forward. Unfortunately, another migraine hit.

"Hey, I know you! You're that kid."

Mr Gibbon was blocking my path with his six-foot abnormal arms. He had a bizarre welcoming gesture as if I were likely to be as happy as he was.

I kept my head down and apologised.

"What are you doing here, Tyler?" he asked.

Eh, why bother? He was with a short guy who was wearing a red turtleneck sweater. Being a delicate person, the second guy didn't seem too happy. His parted black hair fell over his temple like he'd been surprised by something ridiculous. The bags under his eyes were so dark and almost swollen, and his stubby tradesman hands—hands that looked like they'd hammered a few nails—were clenched tight.

I tried my hardest to avoid them, but Mr Gibbon wouldn't let me pass. His receding brown hair flopped to the side as he smiled a perfect smile. Even his eyebrows were well managed as he welcomed me like an old friend.

Giving in, I backtracked alongside them. "I was just passing by," I said. "My mum had a … an incident."

"That's never good. I hope she's better now. There's not much joy in coming to the hospital, especially regularly. Isn't that right,

McNeill?" He tapped the small sweater guy's shoulder, and they mumbled at each other.

"By the way, Tye—*can I call you Tye?*" Mr Gibbon asked.

I put my hands in my pockets and hunched my shoulders. "No. Sorry, it's just weird."

"Understandable. Tyler. My fault." He escorted me further as I studied his shiny leather shoes. "We tried some of those places you mentioned. Not bad. And we're going to explore the upper Mountain's delicacies if you catch my drift." He started laughing, and before I knew it, I was standing in front of Amberley's mum again.

"Hey, honey! Doctor, I'm glad you could make it. I do apologise for making you come all this way, especially on your way home, but you're the only one she feels comfortable talking to." Amberley's mum focused on me. "Tyler what are you still doing here?"

Amid the confusion, Mr Gibbon stood as my guard. "He was visiting his mum. Yeah, we were just catching up. I wanted to thank him for his food suggestions. He's a funny kid."

Amberley's mum squinted, her brows low and curved.

My spine got all tingly until the good doctor pulled up his sleeves. "I best not waste anyone's time. And that includes my own, *Mr Gibbon*. I'm glad you decided to call me. She's getting better. I can assure you of that."

Beneath his confidence, the doctor whispered, "*I hope!*" I couldn't stop staring at him.

When he left, I watched myself in the marble flooring and waited for a *discussion*.

"His mother? Is that right, Tyler?"

I peeped at Mrs Gibbon for a moment, then kept my eyes on the floor.

She smiled at her husband. "Hun, he was here for Amberley. She forgot her pills again!"

"Of course she did. She needs to …" Mr Gibbon played with his forehead, trying not to groan. "Why can't she make it a habit? It would save a lot of time and money. God, she'll ——"

"She'll be fine. Tyler noticed them at school, he brought them here."

Whoa! Mr Gibbon just hugged me. Or maybe he picked me up.

"You smart kid. You came all this way for her. Look, I gotta know, why? Do you fancy her?"

"Hunter!" Amberley's mum slapped his shoulder.

"*No!*" I mumbled. "I mean, I don't know. She's … I'm weird. Okay, I'm a people person in a way. I just … I could see that she wasn't all there. And I felt bad. And I can't explain it, but there she was. And she was nice to me, and I really don't have many friends, and I don't know why I'm talking so much. *I never talk this much— this … honestly.* This is weird. I don't like this, I'm sorry."

Placing my head into my palm, I wanted to cry. My gut felt more empty than emptiness itself. I needed to vomit, but there was nothing there.

Then I felt a warm hand on my shoulder.

"It's okay." It was Mr Gibbon. "We understand. I won't twist your words or change my mind. You're a good kid." He let go to put his arm around his wife.

"You don't have a way home, do you?" asked Mrs Gibbon.

I frowned and avoided their eyes.

Amberley's mum sighed, "We'd give you a lift, but we need to stay here with Amberley. We won't be long. Do you want to stay? Just for an hour."

My heart started racing. "No sorry, I need to go."

Doctor McNeill came to my rescue. Holding his hands together, he smiled.

"Good news, the inflammation in her lungs is healing. Now, I can't get into the specifics, but she understood everything. Just keep to the prescription I gave you, and it should leave her system in a few weeks—a month at best."

"Your optimism's nice, doctor. But a month at best was a long time ago." Frowning, Mr Gibbon glanced at me. "Actually, can you do me one last favour?"

"If you insist." The doctor began to inspect his fingernails. "I surely do need to get home. My husband's cooking a roast. Lamb, I think."

"That's great, Doc. It's on your way home," Mr Gibbon grinned. "You live up in ...? Where was it? Linden?"

Raising a brow, McNeill froze. "Yes, why?"

"Well, this boy is a good friend of Amberley's and his mother's a little preoccupied, and we can't take him, you understand our situation. So, if you could give him a lift to the station, we'd be grateful!"

Before the doctor had time to speak, Amberley's mum said *thank you*.

With his cold brown eyes, McNeill stared at me and nodded. "I'd be happy to."

The journey to the basement level was a long elevator trip.

The doctor smelt of sweet perfume, something a lady would wear. He had pasty white skin like Haley, yet more moisturised, and thick red lips like he had eaten a chilli.

Standing next to him, I was just happy to never see that dumb perfect family ever again.

McNeill and I cruised around the parking lot, searching for his car in a thick void of darkness. It didn't surprise me that he owned a black Mercedes-Benz. Its door swung open, but not like a normal car. It was an expensive mess!

As we entered, McNeill asked, "How do you know the Gibbons?"

I shrugged.

"They're new in town and ..." McNeill examined me from top to bottom. "Have we met before?"

I leaned against the car door's armrest. "Maybe. You're a doctor. You probably meet lots of people, especially around here."

He smiled, "I suppose. It's not the best place to live, but it has its moments." As he started driving, we reached the exit, the sun gleaming against the windscreen.

McNeill gasped, his eyes widening. "Wait a moment! I remember. You're that kid with, uh ... You came here with your mother. And you wanted Doctor Edwards, but he wasn't available, so they sent me in. My god, boy. Are you good? Is everything okay at home?"

I ignored his face. "I'm fine. What's it to you?"

"I saw your mother. What's wrong with her ———"

"You're the doctor the GP sent us to!" Now I knew why he bothered me so much! He gave Mum a new prescription. I pointed at his dumb sweater. "There's nothing wrong with my mum. Yeah, she's delusional, but you can't say jackshit after knowing her for twenty minutes. And don't ask me if I'm okay. I get that you help people, but you don't care about them. So butt out of it!"

It was quiet for a moment. The car was almost silent; the humming of its engine whispered as if the world had become a frozen wasteland.

McNeill turned at a roundabout. "I didn't mean to offend you. It's just, I've seen someone like yourself in a similar situation, and how they ended up, it wasn't that great." He raised his voice. "But don't assume things. I care for all my patients, including that girl!"

"She's dying, isn't she?" I stared at the black asphalt below, listening to the doctor's sigh. No matter how much he slowed, the road never changed colour.

"That's not for me to say. You know, you're either a dumb piece of work or a bastard with a big heart if you continue talking to her."

I looked at him, dead in the eye.

He glanced away, concentrating while he drove. "'Cause I'll be honest, I'm no fortune-teller, but no matter what you do, I can't see a happy ending to this story of yours."

"You're a positive person. Aren't you supposed to be good at giving false hope?" I glared at the road again. "I wasn't even going to talk to her again, especially after that crap I pulled in front of her parents. I talked too much, just like I used to, and now I never, *never* want to see that stupid, happy, dying family ever again! How's my story look now, huh?"

He didn't say a word.

I asked him to drop me off and he did. It was lucky because, by the time I made it to the station, the train had arrived.

When I had returned home, the lights were on. It was unusual, they were never on, not when Mum was *relaxing*. I paced onto the veranda, smacking my foot against Beau's bloody bag. *Why the hell is it still out here and why at the front door?*

After hoping and recovering, I braced myself before entering. I could hear Mum talking about her favourite dinners to cook—meals she hadn't made in years.

In all honesty, I thought I was quite sneaky. I tiptoed halfway up the stairs before Mum yelled my name. It was a nasty screech.

As I sighed, walking into the kitchen, Mum's eyes were clear. She had a glass of wine in her left hand; with her right, she placed down a knife. *She was cooking food!*

"How was your day, Tye?" she asked.

I took a step back. "Fine. Why?"

Mum sighed, walking around the kitchen bench. "Your school rang today. Mrs McCoy told me that you jigged class. Is that correct?"

I felt sick. Mum was being *calm*. "Yeah, it is. But it's not what it seems, it's just ——"

With a howl, she exploded. "I have been worried sick since two o'clock, Tyler! I can't believe you're still hanging around with

Cameron. We talked about him; he's not good for you! I was going to ring the police. I haven't been able to stand up straight." She sculled the wine, and her eyes became soggy.

"Look, Mum, I'm sorry. I was trying to help someone."

Beau was in the corner, sitting on a kitchen stool. He shuffled, making his voice known. "Boy, don't make excuses. Were you doin' drugs? What ya got in the bag? Coke? Pills? A bit of weed?" He stood up and tried to trap me.

"*No!*" I yelled, pointing at Beau. "Don't accuse me of some shit I haven't done. Don't even come near me, Beau! Mum, I swear to you that I wasn't doing anything bad! I didn't do drugs, I didn't hurt anyone, I didn't do anything. I was helping someone. *A friend!*"

Mum put her wine glass on the bench. "Don't lie to me, sweetie."

"*I'm not!*" I glared at Beau. "Don't you dare come near me Beau, you're not part of this family!"

Beau sat back, letting Mum continue.

"LIES, LIES, LIES! Why do you have to lie to me, Tyler? Just be honest. Why did you jig school? Don't you care about your grades, about your future? You can make a better life for yourself. And I send you to that expensive school so you can do that. Don't ruin it, Tye! Think about your father."

I rolled my eyes. "If it wasn't for him, I wouldn't even be going to that stupid school. I hate that place. And you didn't send me there. You were told to because it's free for you. *And I'm not lying.* I promise you, Mum! I promise on Dad's goddamn grave that I am not lying to you! I am trying my best to get out of here, so don't you dare even mention Dad. 'Cause you didn't care about him."

Okay, I'll be truthful here, I did go a little too far.

Mum started screaming and bawling her eyes out, repeating the word *lies* over and over. As she got louder, she dropped to the floor, rocking back and forth in a ball.

I sighed, staring at Beau. "Beau, did she have her meds today?"

"What do ya mean?" He pointed at Mum like she was some sort of animal. "Don't put this on me, look at what ya did."

"Just tell me if she had her medication! It's important."

Beau kept quiet for a moment. "No. I don't think she did!"

I ran into Mum's room next to the front entrance and grabbed a white packet.

Kneeling next to her rocking body, I placed my hand on hers. "I'm sorry, Mum. I didn't mean it. It's my fault, okay. I'm sorry I made you worry. Please, just take these, and you'll feel better. The scary words and voices will go away." I clicked my fingers at Beau. "Pass me a glass of water! *Please*." Surprisingly, he did what I said.

I held Mum's hand and passed her two capsules. "Just take them. Everything's going to be okay. I know it's hard, and I love you."

Mum pulled me close. "I would rather wine next time!"

She swallowed the pills, and I pushed her off me. "I'm going to my room. Make sure she takes them *every* day."

"Ya know, why do ya have to be so rude to her all the time?" bickered Beau. "She's your soddin' mother!"

"I don't need to talk to you. Just look after my mum!" I stormed off upstairs and slammed my door. After I locked it, I finally had a moment to cry about how stupid I had been.

What was wrong with me?

Friends

After I cooled off, Amberley somehow got into my head. Because of her, I had to deal with Mum. *No, I shouldn't blame her.*

I tossed my laptop onto my table, my office chair stiff from today's stress. Why was Amberley still on my mind? I searched the video she had showed me earlier today. The video had a name at its end: *Alan Watts*. So, I looked him up.

There were tonnes of videos, some five minutes, others two hours. I watched a few, did some homework, and as the sun began to fall, I heard a knock on my window. Ignoring the sound, I was ready for bed, staring blankly at my laptop's screen.

A second thud echoed against the window.

I turned in my chair.

"Come on, Tye. Let me in!" a voice hissed.

I grinned, pulling the window open. "You could have called."

Cameron climbed inside, tripping over his own feet. "I wanted to surprise you. How's your mum?"

"Better now. Sorry I couldn't chill with you. It's been a long day."

Cameron jumped, my bedsheets bouncing as he collided with my mattress. "You look like shit. How's the laptop going? I chose well, aye?"

"Yeah, it's heaps good for school." I closed the computer's lid. "Thanks, but you didn't need to buy it!"

Cameron laughed, "It was a birthday gift, and you deserve a

break. Stop complaining. An' besides, I have more money now—I could buy a hundred if I wanted to!" He began to glare at me. "Was the hospital that bad? Come on. I'll prove it!" Before I could even argue, Cameron was halfway out my window. "No buts, Tye. Trust me. It'll be a little midnight rumble. No biggie."

I rolled my eyes. "Fine, but where are we going?"

After Cameron got side-tracked, going on a few too many tangents about how Haley doesn't do this, and how Indian food is better than Mexican, we began our *rumble*. In all honesty, it was just a quick train trip and a walk through the middle of nowhere. Finally, we arrived at a familiar garage.

Cameron sorted through his three keys and unlocked the steel roller-door, pushing it up and colouring the inside of the garage with the light of the moon.

"You're screwing with me!" I said.

Cameron walked in. "No, this is where I've been hiding it. I thought it was a good idea. An', you know, next time you try and kill yourself, don't leave half the rope tied up on the ceiling. Especially my rope, from *my* ute!"

I closed the door behind me. "Piss off. You shouldn't even come in here! I get that you wanna leave, but don't shove your dumb junk in here with *my* stuff."

"*Your stuff!* This place isn't yours," Cameron pointed at me, his voice now louder. "You gave me the spare key. You told me that I could lay low here if I needed to get out. And I don't need to do that! I'm stashin' the money here for both of us. So that I—*we*—can get out of here. Admit it, there's nothing in this shit-hole for you, nor me. We had a plan."

I leaned against the table. "That I hadn't agreed to yet. I don't care what you do. Sell whatever you want, make as much as you want, just don't take it all back here. Not *here!*"

Cameron scratched his head. "Look, I get that have a lot of attachment to this place. It looks like your dad put a lot of work in 'ere. And if I knew I was bringing back my shit, I wouldn't even think of stashin' it here. It's safe. An' you can put some in—from the pizza place. I know it's not as much as I get, but we both want to get out of here. I need to!"

I sat down in a crappy old chair, half-eaten by termites. "You're not good, are you?" I sighed, "What'd they do, Cam? Why are you like this?"

Cameron stared at the ground as if it was a way out. He held his breath. "You're right. I'm not good. I'm scared, Tye. I'm really scared. With this New Kev, Haley's gone all weird. I don't think I have much time left. I need out! And whether I'm with you or not, I don't want you to get hurt!" His voice was soft, and I could see his pain through his eyes.

I pushed my teeth together, feeling my temple throb. "Shit! … Fine. I didn't know it was that bad. I'll chip in when I get a shift. Where are you hiding it? The stash?"

Cameron asked me to get up, and he moved the chair I was sitting on over to the farthest left corner away from the door. He climbed up and moved an out-of-place grey brick.

"Have a look."

Behind it was a crack in the wall near the ceiling. I climbed up after him, and there must have been at least ten thousand in there, stacked up in a little square box with wooden planks surrounding it.

"That's a lot. How long have you been saving?" I asked.

"A few months now."

"Do you know how much is in there?"

"I'd say thirty thousand," Cameron squinted. "Maybe more, I haven't counted in a while." Climbing onto the table

The Stash

in the middle of the room, Cameron began to unravel the half-snapped rope.

I put the brick back and sat. "Are you sure you'll be fine for a few more weeks?"

"Never better, Tye." Cameron smiled, "Gosh, you know how to tie a knot, don't ya? This thing's tighter than that shoe-knot you got me and Crouchy to undo after P.E."

We laughed, and when the rope came down, I wanted to leave. Cameron kept saying he was fine, and that the money was only a precaution.

When everything was locked and closed, someone called Cameron.

As soon as he answered his phone, I could tell it was Haley. They talked like lunatics, and it sounded like she wanted to meet up.

After a long phone call and another train trip, we reached a service station at 10 pm.

Haley called me *Tye-Tye*. Yuck! The two idiots snuggled as we went inside to buy some things. I bought some bread and a six-pack of water. While I sorted through the spreads, I listened to the conversation at the counter.

"Can I get a twenty-five pack of Winnie Blues?" Cameron asked.

"That'll be thirty-eight dollars. Can I see some ID?"

I looked over, and Haley took charge. "I think we misplaced it. But you can tell Beverage that he owes us for the last pack. I think he'll understand that it's not *our* fault, Javier. Just give us the packet, and we'll be on our way. And tell Bevvy we said hi."

The cashier was sweating, his face as white as snow. He did what they said, no questions asked, and the two left.

I could hear Haley's laugh outside. "Did you see his face! He really thought I was gonna slice him up."

Walking up to Javier, I smiled, said thank you and paid for my food. I told him to have a good night, and the rest was history.

Friends

Outside, Cameron was kissing his lady. How disgusting!

"All right, we'd better head off." Cameron offered me a cigarette.

I waved my hand at him. "I don't smoke anymore."

Laughing, Haley put a small steak knife into her pocket. "Tye-Tye's gone all good on us. Good work, schoolboy. I'm kind of proud!"

Cameron lit his own smoke. "You'll be right gettin' home?"

I nodded. "Yeah, see you around. Hope that thing under your shoulder doesn't bite. Looks nasty!"

"Ha, ha, love you too," squirmed Haley

Waving goodbye, I left. I hated being near Haley—she was dangerous! Yet even though I knew Cameron was trapped, there was something inside of me that was excited. Something warm and tender.

I guess I was looking forward to tomorrow. *Weird!*

68

"Words can be communicative only between those who share similar experiences."

ALAN WATTS

Thursday

I kept yawning during second period. It was a Thursday, meaning the week was almost over, yet it was too early to celebrate. Celebrate what, you might ask? Well, I don't know.

I had been feeling this rush of excitement since last night, and it had done me well. Through first period, I listened to every word the teacher said. Now, being stuck in Society and Culture, all I did was listen. I evaluated Mr Taccori's stories, which were totally not true, but he played them off well. His warnings about how we needed to have our interviews done by the end of the month were tiresome.

I asked Xander how his morning was, and he ranted about how his mum won't let him go to the skatepark—he's in Year Twelve, and he needs to take school seriously.

I even tolerated Charlotte and Lucy whingeing about some stupid party this Saturday. And between it all, after I listened to a novel's worth of words, Amberley rocked up to the green and yellow room. It was halfway through the lesson when we were learning about the history of social theories like the conflict and functionalist theories.

Amberley practically fell through the door, apologising to Sir. She handed him an absent slip and stared at me. Well, stared is a little hyperbolic! It was more that we noticed each other awkwardly.

"Tyler? Did you hear me?" Xander asked. He was nudging my shoulder.

"Hmm?" I turned to him.

"Are you going to Harry's eighteenth?"

I raised a brow. "When is it?"

"Two weeks away. Were you invited?"

I shrugged. "I'll probably go."

Xander leaned against the couch. "You are invited, aren't you?"

"Yes, of course. I'm on the page. Weird! Eighteen," I sighed.

Eighteen was kind of a gross age. Xander thought it was amazing; he told me that Harry could buy alcohol, go to clubs, do whatever. *Eighteen*—an adult!

That's when all the excitement left my body. I thought there was a little green or yellow on the tabletops, but it was really just a dull blue.

Again, it was cloudy, just in time for recess.

I sat in my spot, curious to see what the ants were doing. As I rested, admiring the storm's oncoming darkness, a shadow blocked my view.

I glanced up to see Amberley standing in front of me with this look of innocence in her eye. Leaning back in my chair, I watched the empty basketball courts and smiled. Now, I knew she was here to explain something, and that something was genuinely fascinating, but it wasn't worth the hassle. She didn't *really* want to tell me; it was like she had to.

So, I spoke first. "You know, I looked up that guy you showed me yesterday. From that video, the one about the farmer. It's some interesting stuff. I liked what he thought about, like with the world, how it works and all. It's cool."

"Is that a smile?" Amberley gasped. "I didn't know you could do that."

As she sat next to me, I moved my laptop and placed it on top of my legs. "I can do other tricks too. Like, shake. I'm a little rusty though. Actually, I found a video that I thought you might like."

As I pulled out my phone, Amberley got all sour. "Why? Aren't you curious? Why aren't you asking?"

71

"Asking what?"

She froze, staring at the clouds. "About yesterday. About what's wrong with me. You saw, you saw everything."

I sighed, keeping my focus on the ants. "I didn't see anything. I just gave you something you misplaced."

She moved closer to me, like really close. Our legs were touching, and her foot was almost on top of mine. "You didn't talk this much yesterday." Her voice was raw. "It's okay. I just wanted to let ... I wanted to say thank you. For yesterday."

As she stood, I didn't say a word. I just stared into the bleakness of the ground.

But she didn't leave.

Instead, she moved in front of me, and like yesterday, kept talking. "You know, you should stop staring at the ground, or watching ants, or whatever. Because if you keep looking down, you might miss out on what's in front of you." She sounded angry, annoyed, unimpressed, ashamed; I could list a thousand words. But, *boy*, did it piss me off.

"The hell does that mean?" I spat. "Who says shit like that? Look, I don't mean to be rude, and you're really nice. I just wanted to show you a video because I don't like talking to people."

Amberley stopped in her tracks. "Why?"

"Because people get annoyed at me when I talk too much. I'm annoying! And more than half the people in this school have pointed it out. So I try not to talk."

She tiptoed back to the seat. "Why are you being so honest?"

I looked into her eyes. "Because like you, I'm sick! I'm sick of this town, of the same identical people, all the normal stuff. It's so boring. 'Cause no one else listens, I don't know."

Sitting back down, Amberley grinned, "I get you. I moved here because of my illness. I wouldn't say it's bad here and you don't talk too much. You listen, like really listen." Searching her surroundings, Amberley leaned in close. "I'll tell you about it. I want to."

At that moment, I wanted to scream at her, tell her to *shut up* and walk away. And I don't know why. I guess I didn't want the weight on my shoulders.

"Last year, I was diagnosed with sepsis," said Amberley. "It's an infection that damages your organs through your bloodstream. For me, it's in my lungs, and it won't go away … *I'm dying.*"

My heart ached, I felt like crying as goosebumps swelled up my legs. "I'm sorry," I mumbled. "I can't imagine something like that."

It was silent again, and the breeze swept through, pushing the space between Amberley and me. However, even after she told me the sad news, she continued to smile. "It's okay. Things like this happen. It feels good, though, letting it out."

"It can't be that bad," I mused. "It's not cancer. And that doctor guy said you were getting better. That's gotta mean something?"

Amberley began admiring the ants. "It's been four months since I was diagnosed. Six since I got influenza. It should have taken ten days to go away. But it won't go. I don't even think the doctors know what's wrong with me."

"Is that why you moved? To find someone who could help?"

She shook her head. "It wasn't to find help. I can't do anything, and it's not Mum and Dad's fault. I guess I wanted to move. So it was easier to say goodbye to everyone at home—so I could say goodbye, and no one had to worry."

It was so hard to process, 'cause every time I thought about it, I'd end up putting myself in her shoes. And it felt good to know that I was going to die.

I looked her in the eye. "That's kind. It's scary, dying. I just … I get it. You hide it well, I doubt anyone knows. Your secret's safe with me. And you know, I don't talk to anyone, so …"

Once Amberley said *thank you*, the bell went. I didn't want to leave her, but she acted as though nothing tragic had happened. She told me to do this with her at lunch, so she could watch the video I had found.

I agreed, and we both went our separate ways.

I had double English. It was a long hour and forty minutes. My vision was clouded, my hearing was off, and I ignored the people I sat with for no particular reason. I suppose it could be shock or surprise, but that excitement that had enlightened me last night emerged from the depths of my stomach and weaved itself throughout my daydreams.

And that's all I did.

I dreamt something—actually, I reimagined the conversation with Amberley over and over in my head. I listened to how desperate her voice was, I noticed the times she would stare at the ground, and then it would fade away because I'd think of myself.

I was so selfish for wanting to die.

And, as I thought, lunch crept up, said hello, and I left the building.

When I arrived, Amberley was already sitting in my spot.

She laughed at me. "That's a first. I beat you. Huh, is that another smile? Must be your lucky day."

"There's a first for everything." I sat next to her. "But I wouldn't count on luck."

"How so?"

"'Cause it doesn't exist," I said, placing my bag on the ground.

Amberley sighed, "You're such a pessimist. You have what you have, and maybe luck isn't the end-all, but it sure helps to believe in something. Like those videos."

"Ah," I jolted. "I was going to show you one. Here, I'll look it up." As I took my phone out and searched, I explained to Amberley that she could show the video to the deaf girl. It was colourful, motivational, there were words to read—and then I said the daftest thing.

"It inspired me, in a sense. Made me feel a little less crap, especially after yesterday."

At last, I found it: *Life is NOT a journey – Alan Watts.*

We sat, our foreheads almost rubbing against one another, watching the four-minute video. It was like it held the secret to living a better life—well, better than what we both had.

To summarise, it was about how life is expressed as a journey, where individuals work towards a destiny. And this Mr Watts described how that was a silly way of perceiving things because life is like music. *You don't work the piano; you play the piano.* That's how he phrased it.

By the end, the moral was that we shouldn't wait for this destiny of ours, we should instead enjoy the journey that takes us there.

I had trouble reading Amberley when the video ended. Her eyes focused on the floor, and to my awkward surprise, she exploded.

"*I love it!* That is the best way of looking at things. How'd you find that? Actually, can you like it for me?"

I fiddled with my phone. "It's a solid video, huh?"

"You made my day." Amberley smiled. "Can you um … Can you play music? Like an instrument?"

I almost coughed, she caught me so off guard. "I used to play the guitar. I still do sometimes, but I lost the damn thing. You?"

She sarcastically pointed at herself. "Me? You want to know about me? Well, I used ——"

"No, I was speaking to the …" I pointed at the bush behind her. "The shrub behind you. Yes, you *blondie!*"

"I was actually going to go blonde, but I don't know anymore. Maybe I'll get some highlights. Go ombre …" Pulling her hair, Amberley blushed and giggled. "Oh, the piano. I am a professional pianist. They say I'm the reincarnation of Mozart." I nodded, and she kept at it. "And violin. I'm not too good, but I can still play it."

I raised a brow. "Really? That's like me saying I can speak Japanese because I learnt it in Year Eight."

"Go on then."

"All right, fine," I took a deep breath. "So ka toe kimi no na wa."

"And what does that mean?" she asked.

"I was being sarcastic. I think half of it's actually a movie." I rolled my eyes, placing my hands in the air to surrender. "You win. This is hard, I mean … I was making a point ——"

"That you can't speak Japanese, and that I can play the violin? What movie did you watch in Japanese?"

"It was on Netflix, I think," I squinted. "It was a very emotional film. Okay?"

"Netflix is good," she laughed. "There's so much on it; I just finished *Vampire Diaries*. So good, have you watched it?"

"No, but my best mate watched it all. All for a girl, but you know. He ended up liking it, so win-win."

"I like that. It's cute. A lot of effort, though. There's like three hundred episodes." Glancing at the basketball court, Amberley's leg was right next to mine. "What are you doing this afternoon?"

I thought about it really hard. "Nothing. Why?"

"Let's do something. Go on an adventure!"

I grinned, "And what would that be exactly?"

"I don't know. I'm new here …" Licking her lips, Amberley bit her tongue. "Let's go on a bushwalk and see where it takes us. What do you think?"

"Sounds good." Then I sighed, "Wait. I have work!"

"What time?"

"Six."

"We can hang out from three to five-thirty. That's enough time to go on a bushwalk, and we can even get food."

I liked the idea, to do something other than going home, working or being with Cameron. And I'll admit—this was one of the best lunchtimes I'd had in years. We both kept talking and talking, and by the time it was over, I was wishing it had gone on for another five minutes.

Amberley ordered me to meet her at the front of the school where the archway was. I couldn't refuse, but as I wandered to maths, all the plants seemed a little brighter.

The sun was out, and I began to focus on the things that were in front of me.

The Changing Forest

Amberley forced me to catch a different bus today. I don't like change, and I know it's a bus and all, but I felt so out of place. Plus, it didn't help that the person who forced me onto the bus also decided to ditch me.

While I embraced the compact seats, and stood in the middle aisle, holding onto the coldest pole man had ever built, Amberley sat with a girl from the year below. Surprisingly, she didn't forget about me. She snatched my laptop from my hand and rested it on top of her binder. So, with two hands, I wobbled back and forth until the trip was over.

We got off at the fourth stop, and everyone kept giving me these weird looks when Amberley asked me to follow her. *Stuff 'em!* The Year Elevens who thought they owned the bus, being backseat bandits, joked about how I was a faggot.

Finally, Amberley and I began to waltz around in Woodford.

Wait a minute.

"Woodford? We're going on a bushwalk in Woodford?" I uttered, hugging my laptop.

Amberley was busy taking in the sights. "I've never been here, so I thought we could just walk around. My dad used to go mountain bike riding when I was younger. He told me that Woodford has some great tracks, so maybe we can walk down one."

"Sure," I said, admiring the oaks. "Bike riding's different. Your dad doesn't really seem like the man for it."

Amberley laughed, escorting me into the thickening bushland.

"He used to love it. It's how he met my mum. He used to ride down highways looking for different tracks until one day, my mum ran him over when she was learning to drive."

"That's a romantic story." I grinned, "I love being hit by cars!"

"Sure you do." Amberley rolled her eyes. "Do your parents have any hobbies?"

I knew I didn't want to mention my father, but there was something about Amberley. I wanted to talk to her.

"My mum used to write. Stories, poems—she loved it. They were beautiful! But that was a long time ago." I lost my grin. "And, my dad, he was ... musical. Piano, guitar—he played anything, really."

"Wow, talented bunch. Is that why you learnt the guitar?"

"Yeah. It's been a while though. I'll try and find it when I get home."

Amberley stopped as we entered a dirt track. The stones on the ground were different shades of orange, bubbling like waves between the fallen leaves. She grinned, "That's awesome! I wish we still had a piano. If you can find your guitar, can I have a go?"

"Sure," I laughed. "It'd be fun. Well, it's better than bushwalking."

Amberley scoffed, "Please. I'm the bushwalking queen! It's nice to enjoy the world ——"

"Whoa!" I raised my hands in the air. "I never said I hated it. By any chance are you saying bushwalking makes you *happy*?"

Amberley giggled, "You're not studying me for your major. Good try, though."

"How'd you know my main aim? I've only told Xander."

Amberley continued to laugh as the forest became brighter. The trees began to dance with the wind. "Sir told me. He was concerned that mine was too worrisome, and that I might get depressed studying terminal illnesses. What a nice guy! He said something like yours, a project on happiness would be more suitable. Have you started any of it, like the questionnaires?"

I froze, tripping over an unearthed root that wiggled across the path. "Kind of. I've typed out some questions, but I want to do a practice survey to make sure everything makes sense. I was going to get Xander to do it, but he's all over the place, and I don't think he'll be much help."

"Why don't you get your parents to help?"

When she asked this, my belly dropped, goosebumps climbed up my arms, and for a moment, everything turned blue.

"My folks?" I waved her suggestion away. "They're not great at helping. They're not exactly like your parents."

Amberley stood still. "My parents weren't always like how they are now. Things change! I'm sure they can't be that bad. They're your parents."

I rushed ahead, my voice bitter. "No, they're worse. I wouldn't even call them that."

Amberley raced after me. "I can have a look if you want. We can compare questions and referencing. The little things. I know it's not much, but I want to help."

She's too much sometimes. I smiled, "Thanks, it means a lot. We can do it tomorrow." Glancing away from Amberley's face, I focused on our shoes. Hers were still new and shiny. "You know, I got this odd question in my head. It's not about my major. I think it'd make sense, but I don't want to offend you and make you feel bad."

Amberley and I were side-by-side. Our eyes met.

"It's about my sickness, isn't it?" Amberley asked. "It's fine, ask away. No point in ignoring it."

As the path lost its width and the canopies above sprinkled a cool breeze within the sunlight, I steadied myself. "Do you have a bucket list? Like a list of things you want to do before you ... you know."

Amberley raised her brows as if I were a comedian. "A bucket list? I've never thought to make one. Isn't skydiving and bungee jumping a little expensive for a seventeen-year-old's part-time budget? It's not like I can suddenly travel around the world and see the seven wonders or backpack through Europe. Why are you asking?"

I unstrapped my bag and searched inside. "No reason. I just thought that if this was going to be a regular thing, maybe we could write some stuff that's a little more meaningful than bushwalking. We can share it."

I handed her a writing booklet that I had bought a few weeks prior. It had a collage on its cover: a field, a quoll, an old pair of glasses, a fire and a crying tree.

Amberley held it and tilted her head. "Are you okay? This seems really out of the blue. I mean, it's a nice idea. But ... I just didn't expect this."

I shrugged, "Neither did I. I just thought if I were in your position, I'd wanna at least try and do some of the shitty things I've always wanted to do."

"It's cute." She laughed at me. "Number one is to keep your eyes off the ground. You have to stop doing that. It's funny and all, and you're getting better, but this whole trip you keep looking down." Amberley cocked her head, staring out into the forest. "Do you hear that?"

I lifted my head and noticed all the birds, the branches weaving over one another, the leaves fading from green to yellow, and the sound of rushing, falling ...

"Water?" I mumbled. "It must be further down."

Amberley had that look of innocence in her eye again. Yanking at my wrist, she pulled me forward.

I succumbed to her strength, jolting at how cold her touch was. She almost made my skin turn blue. "Whoa, your hands. They're freezing."

She continued to pull. "And your arm is warm. Really warm. What do you eat?"

I raised a brow. "Eat? Normal stuff, hopefully. I don't know, maybe you're just one of those people with cold hands?"

Amberley let go, grasping at her fingers as if they were endangered. She played with them, rubbing them all over, and sighed. "Maybe. I think we're close, come on."

Around a few bends, over a fallen tree, which was now a bridge arching over a muddy evergreen creek, and down a rugged sandstone hill, Amberley lingered to a halt.

"Do you see it?"

I searched ahead and noticed a black-burnt cliffside the size of a bus. Beneath it, there was a cave no bigger than a crease in a bedsheet. As the clouds vanished, rainwater drizzled down the cliff, falling in front of the cave and landing on an array of rocks and a dirt path saturated with lush ferns.

"Number two … Explore the waterfall in Woodford with Tyler. Question mark. Only if he stops looking down. Can he do that? Hmm."

I glanced at Amberley. She was sitting, writing in the booklet under a large grey gum. She grinned at me and placed the book in her bag. "I don't want to keep you from your job. And *you* wanted me to write a bucket list. Doesn't sound too hard, does it?"

I yawned, "It's not much of a waterfall, but if you want to explore it, ladies first. I'm sure we can find some graffiti in the cave or on the rock somewhere."

To my surprise, Amberley giggled all the way down to the cliff's foot and asked herself what was on the other side. I shrugged, and like a laboured babysitter, I followed her footsteps, making sure nothing bad happened.

We climbed the mountainside to see where the water came from. It seemed to be part of the same creek we had passed over earlier. The water scurried over several clumps of dirt with plants sprouting from their centre.

A sudden chill tickled my legs as a splattering stain covered the left side of my thigh. It was like the water had jumped from the banks. Great, now my school pants were all soaked. *Was that Amberley?*

When I glanced at the goof, her right shoe was wet. She kicked the water again. I'll be honest, it was annoying—she made me all cold. But it was nice seeing someone smile at something so silly.

She had drenched my arm and tie by the time we left the mountaintop, so I splashed a handful of water into her face. At first, I thought she was offended, as though I had gone too far, but she continued laughing.

"You're lucky I'm not wearing makeup!"

I leapt back when she covered my face with twice as much water. I guess she was the one who went too far, but heck, it made me laugh.

As I tried to dry my face with my blazer's sleeve, we continued to where the water fell. Amberley had this idea that because she was covered in water, she didn't care anymore about being dry. So, of course, she wanted to see what was beyond the waterfall—if you could even call it that.

She put her head under, and it was like watching someone tolerate a slight sprinkle during a sun-shower. Wetting her hair, she asked me to join her.

My gut quenched as I climbed the rocks, trying to avoid the slipperiness of the mossy surface. And at that moment, beneath the droplets of rainwater from a creek that spanned too far in this ever-changing forest, I forgot everything. I actually felt *happy*. I don't know if it was Amberley or something in the water, but that second of happiness felt like it went on forever.

When it was over, Amberley peeped inside the cave. It wasn't anything exciting—no door to Narnia, just a Gatorade bottle with a hose pierced through its plastic, an empty cigarette packet, an old bag of chips and several lines of graffiti covering the dark walls of damp rock.

Amberley didn't seem fazed. We laughed at how crap it was, and after a few more minutes of listening to the world around us, I asked if she wanted to leave. She nodded and led the way; however, climbing down was a lot trickier.

Amberley slipped, misplacing her foot on the last step to the path.

I couldn't tell you why or how, but I leapt after her. Steading her fall, I grasped her hands and waist, feeling her cold body. She leaned into me, said *thank you*, and we both stood there holding each other.

I let go. My stomach twisted, yet Amberley just continued to be her usual self.

As we returned the way we came, we talked about where we lived, our houses, what we liked about them and what we didn't. Amberley sounded as though she lived in a mansion somewhere in the east of Springwood. She also told me about her old neighbourhood and how different everything was in the Blue Mountains.

When we reached the main road, I suddenly got all honest. "I'd like to do something like this again. Maybe when I don't have work."

Amberley was at my side. "What are you doing tomorrow?"

"In the afternoon?" I shrugged, "Nothing, I might chill with a friend, but I'm not sure."

"If you want ..." She went quiet for a moment, then continued, "You can come over to mine, and we can work on our majors and figure out this bucket list."

"Sounds good." I smiled. "Do you have any practice surveys done?"

She nodded. "Two. I might start my interviews soon, maybe Sunday when I have my next check-up."

"Cool. I'll try tonight then, to get one done, and we can compare stuff."

She liked the sound of that.

As we reached the station and waited for our train, neither of us stopped talking. She asked about work, and I told her about the pizzeria. I asked about her job; apparently, she used to work at Kmart.

By the time I was alone, inside the train at Springwood, I began to get excited about tomorrow. Amberley waved goodbye from outside my window.

I waved back and smiled.

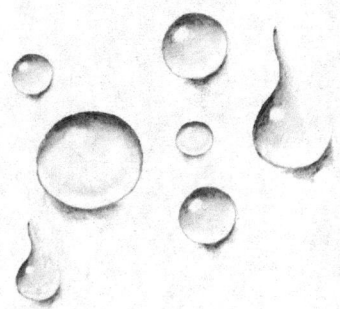

"As we are liberated from our own fear, our presence automatically liberates others."

NELSON MANDELA

Work

As I huddled over the gap between the train and platform, I searched my empty phone to see that I had roughly an hour before work. As I wandered upwards to the concourse, my mind felt light. Instinctively, I kept reminding myself to keep my head straight, avoiding any eye contact with the concrete steps below.

When I reached the top, I turned away from my house and towards the shopping strip, crossing the bridge that lunged over the highway. Near the local shopping centre, there was a timber seat and table where I unzipped my laptop case.

I opened my survey questions file and began to edit. I spaced out the questions, labelled them with numbers, added lines under the open-ended ones, and gave options to the close-ended questions. To make it look nice, I changed the words into the Helvetica font. Once I finished, adding a little ethical notice dictating that all information gathered was for my High School Certificate, the document was a page and a half.

Shrinking the writing from thirteen to eleven point, I voyaged towards the library. Gosh, it's an odd place. I only know it exists because there's a bush track near its backend that leads to a lookout with some caves. And if I'm not stoned, then I don't go near the library.

When I entered, all the noises, from the buzzing flies and the zipping cars to my idle footsteps, vanished. It was like I had entered a world where sound didn't exist.

The front desk lady looked as though she wanted to go home, but because of me, she remained seated.

I kept my strength and asked if they had a printer.

The lady nodded and told me it would be fifty cents per sheet printed.

After two dollars fifty had left my wallet, she came out of her office with ten pages, all copies of my questionnaire. As she joined me, her eyes perused my work. Smiling, the lady asked if I needed any help, and I refused. I don't know why. She could have been helpful with what to keep and what to remove. Instead, I left, placing the surveys between two A4 booklets.

When I returned to the station, my phone buzzed.

My heart pounded as if someone had just shot a gun, and I quickly searched its glass screen. It was a notification from Facebook; Amberley had sent me a friend request.

I felt all warm inside, smiling at nothing. But as I kept trotting forward, I whispered aloud, "I have Facebook! No way."

I'll admit, I made myself laugh, and continued home with only forty-five minutes before work.

At the top of the veranda, my big toe was met with pain. I hobbled, lifting my left shoe away from Beau's tool bag. *I swear to god, if he doesn't move the thing, I'm gonna chuck it down a cliff!*

Hopping inside, I rushed upstairs and clumsily got changed. Putting on my work shirt, I noticed that I had forgotten to lock my door. Strange.

I rubbed the dust off my black pants and jumbled through the insides of my bag. Between the neat pile of textbooks, my pencil case, some writing booklets and a folder for papers, I discovered that my questionnaires were still slim and neat. However, one of the corners was creased. *I hate when that happens.*

My heart began to race. I held two of my surveys tightly, unwilling to stand from my mattress. I read them over and over, wondering if it was worth asking or just leaving it for another day.

The carpet seemed grey as I stumbled toward the stairs, closing my door. I was shivering; my gut clenched, and my steps were sloppy like I was walking on ice.

The flicker of the television startled me as I tiptoed to the bottom floor, peeping through a crack between the two sliding doors. I exhaled, entering the surprisingly bright room.

Instead of grey, the carpet returned to its yellow hue from the sunlight outside. The program on the television was clear as the Panthers scored their second try against the Bulldogs. Mum had a clean face, and Beau, who was usually covered in gunk, had his orange sleeves rolled up with barely a smudge under his fingernails.

Neither of them noticed me until I murmured, "Hey, Mum. I ah—I was wondering if you could help me, with … my major. It's a, uh, a report, kind of, on happiness. I just need … Can you please fill out this questionnaire? If you want Beau, you can also do one." I handed the two surveys out, and Mum smiled. I hadn't seen her smile in so long, it was like I was staring at a stranger.

Beau nodded, reading the first few questions. "Looks good to me. Gotta pen?"

I slipped over myself, apologising, and ran into my room, stealing two pens as quick as I could. I handed them out, thanking Mum and Beau at least a hundred times.

Mum continued to smile. "It's okay, Tye. It's for school, and you've never let me down getting my medicine. I don't say it much, but I'm proud of you. We'd be happy to help."

I wanted to cry. And I almost did; her voice was so clear and nostalgic. It was like I had caught her before she started drinking, or snorting, or whatever else it was.

And as my eyes teared up, I laughed. "You don't need to say that. I know. Thanks again, guys, it means a lot. If you could write down some feedback on the back, like what questions you didn't like or any ideas for improvement, that'd help. Thank you. I got work, so …"

As I began walking out, I turned back to Mum. "I'll see ya later tonight. Just leave them on the dining table when you're done. It's due in August, but I'd be happy to show you what I find out."

Beau nodded, said it sounded *mad* and *well worth a read,* and Mum grinned.

Unfortunately, she would see me when I got home, but I wouldn't see her!

¶

With half an hour left on my shift, Cass asked what pizza I wanted. There wasn't much to do, so I took the bin out. It was a minute walk past the local pub, and when I reached the dumpster by the exit of the carpark, a familiar laugh echoed behind me.

I tossed a tied-up bag headfirst into the metal container, and behind my shoulder, smoking a cigarette was Cameron. He was busy staring into the dark olive of the trees, grinning when I noticed him.

"Doin' lad?"

I put my arms by my side, rubbing the crust off my track pants. "Just working. You?"

"Having drinks with the boys." He strutted over. "Got myself a fake ID. It's so good! When do you get off?"

I shrugged, "Twenty minutes. Do you want to share a pizza?"

"I'd love to. Just bring it into the back, where the smokin' area is. How're you gettin' home?"

I started walking back to work. We scurried past the front of the pub and across the road. "I'm walking," I said.

"*Walking!*" His voice was so slurred. "Nah, I'll drive ya."

"It's all good." I waved Cameron away. "I like walking. I got earphones; I'll be all right."

"No, I'm driving you. Don't worry, bruh."

I stopped him. "How much have you had to drink, Cam?"

Somehow, he couldn't quite catch his tongue. "Not much. Like two, three, maybe *seven*. Definitely not eight, unless you count shots?"

I rolled my eyes and began walking off.

"*What?*" he blurted. "We got paid today, an' I mean like *big* money, Tye!"

"Then why isn't it being saved? You want to get out of here, don't you?"

Leaping forward, Cameron covered my mouth with his palm. I could taste the sweat on his fingers. "Don't say things like that, Tye! Who knows who's listenin'? We don't talk about silly things like that … Do you want a drag?"

I pushed away, refusing his offer, and returned to work.

Cameron made a loud entrance behind me, screaming *Brando*—the chef's name—when I entered the kitchen's backdoor. Brando was surprised he'd come back, said it'd been ages since Cameron, *The Idiot*, had last worked a shift.

After a couple of minutes, Brando let me leave early. I grabbed my pizza and said goodbye to everyone.

When the pizza box was empty, I realised how crowded the pub was. Sitting across from Cameron and me, New Kev, with his brooding chin, pushed back his short, freshly cut, jet-black hair. Cameron chuckled with a fiery thrill in his eyes as Kev told us about his high school days.

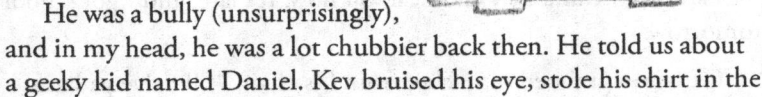

He was a bully (unsurprisingly), and in my head, he was a lot chubbier back then. He told us about a geeky kid named Daniel. Kev bruised his eye, stole his shirt in the change rooms and used to tease him, calling him ButtBucket and HalfNut. I asked him if he had seen Daniel since, and he snorted a laugh, telling everyone that he hadn't seen the kid since Year Eight. *Poor guy moved away because of him!*

When things settled, he ordered Cameron to get us another round of drinks. I refused, and Kev laughed. "It's on me, bud. I like this one, Cameron. He's modest."

When Cameron left, it became silent.

I sat, huddled as close to the ground as I could, examining the table. Kev had large, brusque hands with bruised knuckles, and on his right hand, there was a wedding ring around his ring finger.

He noticed my stare. "Surprised, I see. I am happily married. And no, they are not a fan of my doings. That's why I have two jobs."

I shook, staring at his hollow gaze. "That's quite a handful. Which job do you prefer? Do you enjoy this one?"

His eye floated above my head. "This is what I was called to do. Sadly. I enjoy doing it to a degree, but then again, I despise my other job. Though it makes my other half happy, and that's important. We all have to make compromises. Your friend, he does every day. He's an idiot, but a good worker. You should join us. He's told me that you hate school. Doesn't understand why you stay in it." Kev examined me from bottom to top. "But I get it—who you are. You're depressed." His grin vanished with a fierce eye towards me, and out came a rough, dark voice. "*Pathetic!* You just feel sorry for yourself. Boys like you are weak; you should man up. Make the world suffer so you don't have to."

My hands began to tremble, and I shoved them into my pockets as Kev's disgusted voice vanished. A calmness arose within Kev once Cameron laid eight schooners of Toohey's Extra Dry on the table.

I stood, "I think I should head off now. It's late, and I got school tomorrow."

Cameron grabbed his jacket from his chair. "I'll drive ya back."

I tapped his shoulder. "It's okay, Cam. You hang out with your mates. I just wanna be alone. I'll be fine. Thanks." I eyed down Kev.

Cameron put his jacket back and smiled. "I understand. We'll chill this weekend, yeah?"

I nodded. "Sounds good. Thanks, everyone, I'll see you all when I see ya. Laters Cam, love yah."

I tumbled out, strolling home with all these clustered thoughts in my head. I never looked up, only to cross a road, and the whole time I was worried for Cameron. *He was stuck with that monster! And there was nothing I could do.*

Day Two

I think I'm the eldest on my school bus—everyone else in my year had their licences. I did too. I had forged almost ninety hours of driving practice; I had to do all the maths, how much fuel, the works. Mum never took me on driving lessons, and for the most part, it was pure luck that I got my red licence in a manual. But, still, I didn't have a car.

After watching the road for a little too long, I noticed that Amberley got on. Instead of saying hi, I kept my eyes on the view outside.

When we arrived, I wandered through the bus bay. Before I could make any distance, Amberley stopped me in my tracks.

"Hey, what's up? ... Tye?" Her voice was rather raw.

I lifted my eyes. "Hey. Sorry, I just feel odd, weird, strange—you get it." I grinned. "Don't worry. It's not you, I think my tie's a little tight."

Her eyes sparkled and she grinned. "You weren't kidding when you said you talk too much." *Wait a second. Does she mean—what?* I swear my face turned red.

"I like it," she laughed. "It's cute. You shouldn't be ashamed. You feel weird, who doesn't? Are you going to Study Hall?"

I nodded as we walked together. "I think so. There's nothing really else to do, especially here. You know, I was thinking, what's the shortened version of Amberley. Is it Amber or Berlie?"

"My dad used to call me M.B." Amberley hugged her binder. "Why'd you ask?"

"Because you called me Tye. I'm not offended, was just wondering. *M.B?*"

"That's my name, don't wear it out."

I rolled my eyes, "How old are you?"

"Seventeen, I think," she winked.

We talked about birthdays. It turns out we were both born in September, and that she was twenty-one days younger than me.

We reached the Study Hall, a tall room where the ceiling was higher than most with fans that spanned a cool breeze that never reached a single person. Once inside, it was similar to the library. The world went quiet, yet here, it was desolate. I could still hear my footsteps and Amberley's yawn as she sat next to me.

I stared her down and frowned.

"Can't I sit next to you?" she asked.

I scratched my head. "No, I just … Don't worry."

She slammed her binder on the table. "Tell me. What's wrong?"

"Nothing. It's just … no one ever does." I pulled out a worksheet. "I'm going to write some maths now."

Amid my calculations, Amberley leaned against her palm and asked, "What maths do you do?"

"General. I'm not gifted, even though *most* of the year is. So, can I …?" I pointed to the sheet, which had algebra, triangulation, and derivatives pasted on different grids.

Amberley smiled, "Can I have a look?"

"Why? It's just maths."

"I wasn't going to come here." She paused for a moment. "And I like maths. I don't really have anything else to do. Do you mind?"

I lifted the sheet. "Sure. You any good?"

It turns out she was. She was almost too good!

We kept our voices low and spent the next hour talking about subjects. The ones we disliked, the ones we loved.

She told me about her art major and what she was planning to do. I liked the idea. It was awfully bewildering, but to summarise, it was about how different colours represent different emotions. Blacks, dark greys and blues were on one end of a spectrum, being sadness and grief. Then across the body of work, she planned to use green, yellow and orange, and finally pink and white at the other end of the spectrum. This represented pure and utter happiness. She had this whole plan about showing it symbolically through different landscapes.

Before the bell, we talked about why we had decided to do Society and Culture. I told her it was because of the six-thousand-word major. It was worth forty per cent of our overall mark and I liked to write. I couldn't say why, I just loved typing on a laptop.

She was shocked. "Really? I only did it because I want to travel. I want to understand the places around the world—you know, who lives there, what kind of secrets do they hold?"

I leaned against my chair. "And where do you want to go?"

Pulling out the booklet from our bushwalk, Amberley wrote down another addition.

#7. Backpack through New Zealand.

I read while she wrote. "New Zealand. That's interesting. A bit boring, isn't it?"

"Just to start with," she laughed. "Then Canada, Sweden, maybe the Czech Republic." She sighed, a silent sadness lingering around her mouth. I could feel the coldness of her breath.

"Are you sure?" I asked. "Do you really think you'll be aliv——"

The bell rang. It saved my stupid brain as Amberley frowned. Without saying goodbye, she stormed out of the room.

When I walked outside, the clouds dispersed, and the world became blue. The first two periods went on endlessly. I felt I had aged a whole century by the time they were over.

I waited on my seat, rehearsing what I was going to say. But Amberley never showed. My belly ached, my heart stung, and all I wanted to do was say sorry. I was shaking; my insides felt unwritten as if they were lacking any importance.

I didn't say a word during third and fourth period, and it didn't help that I had English.

Tom and Nic didn't shut up, but I ignored them, waiting anxiously for lunch. But the more time I spent waiting, the hotter my body felt. I was burning up!

There were four ants that stole the fallen crumbs from my sandwich. Four ants that avoided my mountainous shoes in hopes of returning home with a feast. It was like watching litter float in the ocean.

At last, Amberley sat next to me, placing her binder between us. She had another fresh meal that steamed when she opened its container; it smelt like butter chicken.

I swear I was about to apologise, but my mind lingered elsewhere. "Why are you sitting here?" I asked. I looked her in the eye. "Especially after what I said! Why are you bothering?"

She let the steam cover her face as her voice tightened. "You looked sad again, and I heard what you said. I gave it time. I may not have as long as you, but you're the only person who knows about me who isn't family." Searching around the spot, Amberley sighed. "If you want me to go, I will. I'm sorry!"

I gave it a moment, and before she stood, I cleared my throat. "No, don't. I should apologise. I shouldn't talk about that stuff. I'm sorry for being rude. I like being with you, talking. It's more fun than being alone."

Amberley grinned, "I like talking to you too. You get it more than most people. Just please don't say things like that. Okay?"

I nodded, "I promise. I just get anxious sometimes."

"Me too." She pulled out the bucket list and passed it to me. "Do you want to fill it out? It's not just mine. Oh, and there are rules."

I held the booklet. "Rules? It's a bucket list."

"There's only one," Amberley explained. "Everything we write down in that book, we have to do it together. No matter what."

I opened the booklet and agreed, reading through its nine points. Amberley had girly writing, very petite and round.

Writing number ten, I mumbled, "This is a little cliché, but I've never been on a rollercoaster before."

"Really! That is really cliché. Are we in a movie right now?" She made herself giggle. "Well, I've never watched a sunrise."

I cocked my head to the side. "That's all you got? In comparison to a rollercoaster, it's a little easier and cheaper. Smart thinking, actually! We can look up how to do all this stuff at your place. Got any other ideas?"

Amberley froze, squinting at me. "You still want to come over? Oh, are we …? We are, aren't we? I totally had a mind blank. It should be okay, my mum will be home."

"I got two surveys done and everything. So we can compare. And I went to work!"

Amberley admired me. "Look at you go. Who filled them out?"

"My mum and Beau."

"Beau?"

"That's my mum's current boyfriend," I rolled my eyes. "Surprised they've lasted this long."

Amberley went silent, staring at the bubbly clouds above. "So your parents aren't together? Must be hard."

I watched the side of her head, answering with a whisper. "It was once. Gets easier … So, whereabouts do you live?"

Orange Juice

A car honked its horn as we strolled past a block of houses, nearing the highway. I couldn't believe my eyes. Surely, it was cement or something other than marble.

Each window was framed with lacquered oak, each roof was covered in a family of asphalt shingles and each lawn was as perfect as its neighbour's. There was no litter, the road was silky smooth, and although Amberley lived twenty minutes away from school, it was as though I had discovered another planet.

Amberley hadn't said a word since we left the bus.

"What's wrong with you?" I asked.

She glanced at me. "Me? Nothing. I just had a peculiar thought. That's all."

"Peculiar? Odd choice of wording."

Suddenly, Amberley began to speed up, darting ahead. "Do you like anyone?"

I raised a brow. "Is that the thought?"

"No, I'm just curious."

"I like lots of people," I said. "It's not that I hate anyone, I've just made mistakes. I do have friends."

"Like?" Amberley turned to me, smiling.

"Like Cameron. He was with me the day I bumped into you at the pharmacy."

"I didn't mean it like that." Amberley rolled her eyes. "Oh, go on. Why do you like him?"

"Why wouldn't I?" We were side by side. "He's my best friend, and I may not like where his head is at, but I trust him. I trust him too much. Heck, he's been my mate since Year Eight. It may not seem long, but we've made a lot of good memories together. He wants to leave, join the army or something. But if he leaves, I wouldn't really have many friends."

"He must be important to you." Amberley stopped, "You have me! Are you sure you don't like anyone else? No crushes?"

I laughed, "How old are you again? Of course I don't have a crush on anyone. I can hardly stand our year group, let alone most of the girls. Everyone's so immature. Here, I'll tell you about the last week of last year. Two best friends since the start of Year Seven—five years in the making—ended their friendship over a photo of one of them kissing a boy. It wasn't that someone cheated. It wasn't that one friend had sex with the other's ex or whatever. Two seventeen-year-old girls got salty over a photo of a kiss that lasted five seconds. And it wasn't even the main focus of the photo. Like goddamn, grow up, get over it!"

"How do you know it lasted five seconds?" asked Amberley.

"Because I was at the party." I sighed, "I took the photo by accident. And I still get shit for it! I didn't even post it."

"Who were the girls?"

"Emma and Georgia." I squinted at Amberley. "Why?"

"Because I like Emma and Georgia. Emma's already filled in one of my questionnaires, and Georgia asked if I'd like to interview her." Glancing at the sun, Amberley smiled. "They're both sweet."

"So you like a lot of people then?" I asked.

"Yes, unlike you, I have empathy. Funny that."

I pushed my hand over my chest where my heart was. "Ouch. Feels bad. Do you like me?"

As the highway swayed in the distance, Amberley pouted her lips. "Something like that." She scurried off, and when I asked her what she meant, she informed me that we had arrived at her house.

It was half a mansion—half a bloody castle. It looked ridiculous!

It had dark wooden planks covering its walls; tinted windows, each with their own cream-like curtains; a real knight in shining armour standing by two ten-foot-tall bronze doors; and an immaculate back veranda that towered over a cliffside, adjacent to an abundance of bushland.

Amberley herded me aside, and as always, she had this innocence plaguing her. Immediately, as we wandered to the side gate, there was a warm feeling to the home. I accidentally slammed the gate right after Amberley told me not to. First impressions weren't always my strong point.

A little Maltese dog came running up to us, sniffing my legs. I flinched. *The damn thing could have bitten me!*

Amberley laughed, "That's Monte. He won't bite; he's almost twelve. Plus, he's missing half his teeth. So, don't worry, he's friendly!"

I kneeled next to Monte and his freshly shaved white hair. He sniffed my nose and lips, tilting his head. *Gosh, he's making me smile.*

After I patted his head, we continued inside.

The back wall was several glass panels, tinted so you could see your own reflection.

Amberley slid open the back door and yelled that she was home. I staggered behind, jumping inside to a cooler house. With a ceiling about a hundred feet in the air, two hanging chandeliers, and a bunch of random artefacts from different cultures atop shelves and cupboards, Amberley caught me in awe.

She placed her bag on the dining table. "That's the first time I've seen you look up. How do you feel? Are you light-headed?"

I dropped my head and eyebrows. "Really? It's just … you have a nice house. But I'm not a fan of these tiles."

"What's wrong with the tiles?" giggled Amberley.

"They just don't fit."

Sitting down, Amberley began fiddling with her bag. "Don't tell my dad! He built this house, like our last one and the one before."

I sat next to her. "He's an architect, huh? Wait, is that his job?"

"Yep. He's into making things himself. What does your dad do?"

I froze for a moment; it felt like I had half a peanut stuck in my throat. "He used to work in the city. Accounting, banking, almost got promoted to a manager once." I tried laughing. "Do you wanna compare surveys? Just to see what we've done? If you want, we could do each other's? It's extra data."

We spent the next two hours head to head, comparing, laughing, discussing, debating, joking and sarcastically acting polite. Towards the end, we listed sixty points in the bucket list. Apparently, my questionnaire wasn't too bad, but we both agreed it was a little long.

Annoyingly, Amberley didn't let me see her results. She folded up her answers and placed it inside the bucket list. She said she wrote feedback—a whole letter—but didn't want to see my face when I read it. *Confusing, I know!*

I said she could read mine, but she refused, and told me to place it into her *SOC* folder so that she could read it when the time was right.

Time flew as the sun set, glimmering with a yellow light behind a bubbly silhouette of gum trees. Monte continued to sniff my legs, tickling my ankles, and running rampant when Amberley's mum waltzed into the kitchen.

Before I had time to look away from my laptop, Tegan asked, "Amberley, do you want anything? I'm going to make dinner later tonight, so it's not cold for your father. And have you taken your tablets?" She paused as I glanced up. "*Hello*. We have a guest?" Staring at me, Tegan continued to the kettle, filling it with water.

I cracked a little, *hi*, but Amberley's mum did most of the talking.

"Oh, you! Tyler. How are you?"

"Good," I mumbled.

She turned the kettle on. "So, you two are friends. That's nice. I like this one, I really do! You know, you should have seen her ex-boyfriend. Do I even call Perry your ex? Oh, my bad! Do you want anything, Tyler? A coffee, tea, orange juice?"

I shook my head.

"No? That's okay." Tegan raised her voice. "Amberley, *tablets* … What are you two working on?"

I sat back in my chair, and Amberley sighed. "Okay, Mum!" Amberley stood. "Could you please pour me a glass of orange juice? You might as well get both of us some."

I argued, but Amberley insisted, standing and marching towards the kitchen bench. "Thanks, Mum. We're just doing our majors for Society."

Her mother poured the juice into two scotch glasses. "What are you investigating in your PIP, Tyler?"

I examined my laptop. "Let me tell you my main aim. Where is it?" I clicked on the document, and read it aloud, "*To investigate whether people are more happy or more content in the Blue Mountains and how these emotions are differently contained.*"

Tegan smiled. "I would love to read it afterwards, if that's okay? I used to teach Society and Culture, so if you want, I can proofread your PIP."

"Thank you." I couldn't tell if I was blushing or not. "Do you teach anything else?"

Amberley handed me an orange juice and downed two white tablets.

I focused on her mother, who was making a decaffeinated coffee. She poured the hot water into a mug. "I used to teach Art and Society. But now I stay at home to look after Amberley." Stirring the coffee, she lowered her voice. "How's your mother now? Is she feeling better?"

I paused and gulped, "Yeah. She seemed better yesterday."

Both Gibbons smiled, and I tried to avoid bringing up Amberley's sickness. I'm sure it was a tough time, so I mentioned normal things, like where the family used to live, if Tegan liked the Blue Mountains and, of course, the best places to eat.

Before I knew it, I was offered a seat at dinner. I couldn't refuse—I didn't want to. A home-cooked meal, it sounded almost too good.

Amberley got excited, packing her things and running upstairs into her room.

As I was placing my laptop into its case, Tegan suddenly said my name.

"Thank you," she said. "For being by her side. Even if you just tolerate it, she needs it. Ever since we moved, it's been getting worse. I know it, her father knows it, and well, I think she's getting the idea. You've lifted her spirit—I can't thank you enough." She sighed, tears wetting her cheeks.

I could hear Amberley searching for something in her room as Tegan stared at me.

I grinned, "I don't tolerate it. I have fun being around her. Don't thank me, please. You shouldn't. I think she's the one helping me." My comment made Tegan's face glow. She straightened her posture as she served me a bowl of curry.

Amberley leapt into the kitchen. She complained about how she couldn't find her charger, and Tegan acted as if nothing had happened. I said my thanks and enjoyed one of the best dinners I had ever eaten.

And from then on, time, life and every moment seemed to rush by as if they were the questions on a survey.

"How vain it is to sit down to write when you have not stood up to live."

HENRY DAVID THOREAU

May

In a week, Amberley and I had written countless new activities in the bucket list. From sixty to eighty to a hundred, to two hundred, five hundred and more, there were so many to pick from.

The most benign things, such as *taking Monte for a swim* or *watching a television show*, made me feel victorious. And the more challenging tasks, like *scaling a mountainside* and *going on every ride at a waterpark*, made me appreciate what I had. My favourite was *sleeping under the stars*.

As we crossed off one after the other, time flew by. In three months—a quarter of a year—we had experienced numerous changes.

I conquered number 117.

Tyler talking to other classmates in our year.

Amberley managed number 246.

Eat oysters and mussels.

And we both accomplished number 62.

Get munted at an eighteenth.

It was a lot messier during the situation.

Somehow, by the end of May, we had crossed off almost twenty pages with different points. Amberley got a job at IGA, and we went out for Mexican—Amberley had never tried it. We went to Luna Park, on a rollercoaster, on the light rail line, and Amberley's dad took us fishing.

We had teppanyaki, finished obtaining our questionnaires, had a campfire where we cooked marshmallows, and I even got my own car. It was Cameron's ute, Jess. He let me borrow her as long as I didn't hurt the thing. Plus, he knew I had my red licence, so she stayed at the front of my house.

vroom
vroom

With everything we had done, I had more good memories with Amberley than I'd ever had with Cameron. Heck, I didn't even see Cameron that often. However, there was this one time where Amberley and I bumped into him.

It was the twenty-fifth of May; the leaves were dry, turning yellow from the whispers of winter as they drizzled to the pavement. I had picked up Amberley from her house, and she had that innocence in her eye, smiling at an idea she'd had that morning.

She thought, now that she was a part of the community, that the two of us could drive to the Information Centre and stock up on brochures about the Blue Mountains. Even though we lived here, neither of us had ever done any of the touristy things.

So we grabbed several brochures about each suburb, from Lapstone to Bell. We searched for all the fun sights to see, the interesting places to visit, and the little bits and pieces that I didn't even know existed.

Amberley, like always, didn't shut up once she started talking to the front desk lady. They laughed, gossiped and I heard about half the woman's life, waiting for them to finish.

We finally left, and as I dragged my feet across the ground, shoving pamphlets into my bag, Cameron appeared on his tiptoes, examining Jess' tray in the carpark. At first, he didn't notice us. Orange leaves swayed around his legs, and some swung inside the tray, catching his attention.

Dropping flat on his feet, he noticed me, smacking the car's rear.

"Boy, oh boy, I knew this was Jess!" he blurted, walking towards us with welcoming arms.

I shoved myself in front of Amberley, instinctively guarding her. It wasn't that he was going to harm her, I just wanted to shield her from that part of life.

"What are you doing here?" I asked.

Cameron shook my hand. "I was going to ask the same thing. Business as always, Tye." He paused, leaning on my side and grinning at Amberley. "I get it. I was wondering who put that spring in your step." Amberley scampered to my side as Cameron waved. "Nice to meet you. I'm Cameron."

"You're Cameron." Amberley jumped, "It's nice to meet you too. Actually, I have a question for you."

"An' what's that?"

"Is Tyler always sarcastic?" Amberley asked the question with a suspiciously large grin.

I staggered, "What, no, I'm not that sarcastic."

Cameron put his hands in his pockets. "You get used to it. Trust me, uh ..."

"Amberley," she offered him her hand like it was candy. "I go to St Columba's now. Just moved."

"The College. Gosh, it's been a while!" Cameron shook her hand, almost snatching it from her arm. "Tye-Tye's lightened up.

He's not as bad as he was a few months ago. I almost knocked him out, he didn't stop with the damn sarcasm. Everything I said, every word, he'd be like *no way, really, that's so funny!*"

Amberley laughed, "Sounds like Tyler. What are you doing in Glenbrook?"

Cameron told us about how he works for a Salvos store. In his spare time, he also volunteers for St Vincent De Paul's charity run. He was terrific, cleaning the forests and parks in March, doing the charity van three times in April, and now, in May, he wanted to run the market stand in Glenbrook. Unfortunately, two other volunteers got there before him.

I clapped him on. "Beautiful! I don't know how you do it sometimes."

Amberley stared at me. "We can go to the Salvos to see if they have anything for Nathan's party."

Cameron batted an eye. "Nathan's eighteenth? Next Saturday?"

I nodded, and Amberley explained how we were going to get costumes for the 80s theme.

Cameron gave us a proud look like we had just saved his life. He pointed to Jess, "If you're going to Springwood, I actually do have some things I want to donate. I'll just grab my bag."

When we arrived, I did a crappy kerbside park on the rubble just past the blue Salvos building. Cameron fell out of the ute as I gave Amberley a hand exiting the opposite side.

Leading the way, Cameron mentioned what he was donating, how much I had changed, and how super grateful he was to meet Amberley. He left, walking around the building's side towards the donation bins.

Amberley laughed, "He's funny. You never told me he was into volunteering."

I eyed her down, shrugging, "Ol' Cammy's like a new person every time I see him. How was I supposed to know?"

"I want to live like that. Just enjoying life!" Amberley couldn't keep her eyes off Cameron. "Look how happy he is."

We entered the building, its doors sliding open. "Are you on something right now?" I asked. "Because you could have at least given me some."

Amberley began browsing through the different shirts hanging on a rack beside the side wall. "No, no. I've never ———"

"Never done a drug in your life, I know. You're fun, we get it!" I chuckled. "Which, by the way, I don't actually get that. Eh, Cameron's just …"

"Different? He's a lot like you, not as good though. And I am fun. I'm the most fun you've ever had. Drugs or not! I'm just saying, I want to live life daily, doing the things I know I enjoy—not crossing them out on a list. It's not the same."

I nodded, "I get you. And I'm sure one day, in a week, a month or a year, you and I will be doing that. But I wouldn't look at Cameron for inspiration. Drugs or not, I'm sure selling them isn't too enjoyable. Charity's just his cover story," I sighed. "He's part of the drug mob."

Amberley turned to me. "I was wondering why you were acting so stern. Reminded me of when we first met. Even though I'm not a big fan of what he sells, I still think he's nice. Just a bad crowd, right? And what he said had some truth to it: you've changed."

I pressed my palm over her forehead and eyes, gently knocking her head back as she began to smile.

We went into shopping mode, spending the next half an hour searching, laughing and disagreeing. Everything I wanted to get had to be up to Amberley's standards. I found these fluoro jumpers that had baggy sleeves, with a large black line pressed vertically through their centre. One was pink, and the other was orange. Amberley loved them and was certain the party was going to be cold.

On the other hand, she found me a brown afro wig and these rainbow track pants.

For herself, she fell in love with a chequered skirt and some black suspenders. She also fancied a pair of small retro red sunglasses that every girl wears at a festival.

Finally, Amberley picked up a pink scrunchy, and we carried it all to the front desk.

Waiting, we quietly listened to the two employees working.

One was a bigger man with jet-black hair jelled back, wearing a blue work shirt slightly unbuttoned around its collar. His muscular posture was very ladylike. I don't mean to offend, it's just, he really wanted to work those hips with his sausage fingers.

Palming his right hand against his broad chest, he said, "Really? What a bitch. I can't believe Tiana would do that!"

The man's co-worker, half his height but twice his age, had a crinkled face, curly blonde locks and a serious smile to complete her sassy attitude. She nodded and kept talking about a woman who was cheating on her boyfriend.

Amberley eyed me down, laughing, "Can you believe she did that?"

"And they were roommates," I whispered.

Amberley pretended to be shocked, gasping at my claim as the man turned to help us.

I stood still, holding everything with a tight squeeze. *It can't be him!*

With bruised knuckles, his rough voice and those pitch-brown eyes, Kev stared at me with a new face. The cut over his lips had now healed as Amberley nudged me to hand over the clothes.

"Tyler! We can't buy them if you don't give them to him." Amberley tapped my shoulder. "Tye?"

I shook my head, examining Kev's name tag. "Sorry about that … Kevali. Hmm, interesting name."

Big Kev began folding the clothes. "It's Pakistani. What are you two getting up to with these? If ya don't mind."

Amberley, of course, insisted on talking. "We have a party next weekend. It going to be 80s-themed. Pretty cool, huh? I was just wondering, how do I donate?"

"You guys are going to look so *cute* in these." Kev's voice was higher than normal. "With donating, it's easy, honey. You can donate different types of things, like clothes, jewellery, old movies, anything really, at the back in those little blue sheds. Or, if you'd like, you can go onto our website and donate however much you want." He paused and shoved everything into one large bag, pointing at us with an overly bent wrist. "Just wondering—I don't mean to be all grouchy on you two—but do I sense a new couple, honeymoon-stage kind of thing?"

My throat dried, clawing at itself and making me hurl. Kev kept smiling at us, all girly-like with his shoulders heaps high and his hands closed together.

Amberley and I stared at each other, shrugging and smiling; blushing, if I were to be perfectly honest.

I laughed, "No, we're just friends. And we just chill. I chill with heaps of people."

Amberley gave me a dirty glance. "He's spot on. Although he drives me crazy, I just use him for his money. He also knows the best places to eat and how to rub fake tan on, so why would I complain?"

Big Kev laughed and thanked us, calling Amberley beautiful.

I felt kind of odd, so I decided to just throw my money on the front desk, snatching our bag. "Twenty-two fifty, right? Sweet, keep the change, Kev! See ya 'round."

I pulled Amberley through the exit, and immediately she screamed. "What was that about? *You chill with everyone*, huh?" she mocked.

I frowned, "It was that guy!"

"Of course, you would discriminate against someone like him." She crossed her arms, trying her best to keep her eyes away from me. "He was sweet, Tye!"

"It's not like that. I couldn't care if he was feminine or gay or whatever. *I know him!*" I pointed at the Salvos. "He's not ... that's not him. It's not!"

"Maybe he's changed! Let's drop it, I don't want to argue."

Getting into the car, Amberley sighed. She searched our purchases and giggled, "Hey, did you end up finding your guitar?"

Sunsets and Break-ins

I was tuning my dusty guitar, ignoring the angry screams from Beau.

Changing the G string, I rubbed everything with a cloth that was meant for cleaning a pair of glasses. I found the silly guitar yesterday, right at the back of my cupboard, cramped behind a tennis racket and my Year Eight drawing of a gargoyle.

Not a bad drawing, to be honest, so I sent Amberley a photo.

A wall bounced from below. There was an impact, something fierce, and Mum's voice became louder.

Amberley replied with a *wow*. She said I was really good but not as good as her. I couldn't help but smile. Our messages went on and on, almost as if they were endless.

Replying, I mentioned that we should play tennis one day, and asked how her hospital check-up was.

Another thud came from downstairs.

"Are you kidding me, Sharron!" Beau screamed. "Forget the kid! He's almost eighteen, he can look after himself! Shaz. I don't hate 'im … I'm just thinkin' about what's best for us. For crying out loud! Sharron, listen to me."

Mum yelled over Beau's voice. "Why are you yelling? I'm his mother, I can't leave him. Stop yelling—am I yelling? Just let me think!"

Beau continued to scream at Mum, attempting to make her see his stupid view, and quite frankly, I was over it. I put the guitar down and went to calm the tide.

Beau swore his head off, telling Mum that he knew what was best; he would protect her, he had done all the planning, she just needed to leave with him. He had already made their connections with the town's pharmacy, the nearest bottle'o and and—shame on me for clarifying—the local drug dealer.

Mum screamed, saying he was crazy. She began howling *no* over and over, sobbing the faintest words.

But Beau dragged on. He asked her if she loved him, but there was no answer.

Mum shook back and forth on the lounge and cried an outlandish apology.

I stood between them, facing Beau's stubborn glare. "Enough, Beau! Don't talk to her like that! She doesn't want to answer you, so leave it be."

He revolted, staring at me with fierce eyes. "She took her tablets today. Why the heck's she like this?"

"Because that's who she is, no matter how many tablets she takes. Get out of my house if you don't like it! Damn, dude." I pushed past him and sat next to mum. "Hey, Mum, it's okay. He didn't mean it. He just ——"

"I want what's best for her," spat Beau. "Sharron, I want to spend the rest of my life with you, but not here. Not with …" He stared me down, "Don't talk to me like that again, Tyler, or I swear to God, I'll … I'll … *Shit!*" Punching the front wall with his bare knuckles, Beau screamed, "God, I'm trying, Shaz! I'm doing my best. I'll give ye time, I'm sorry! God*damn*. I love her, okay! Don't you dare tell her I don't!" He marched out of the house, leaving his tool bag on our veranda, and reversed out of the driveway.

When he sped off, I felt a throbbing pain in my head, wet tears against my shoulder and a subtle relief. I stayed with Mum for an hour and a half before she stood, kissing my weary forehead and telling me she wanted to go for a walk. Her eyes were swollen red, her hair icky from not showering and her black shirt all wrinkled.

I pleaded for her to stay, even offering to make dinner, to watch a movie with her, to do whatever else, but it wasn't enough. All Mum wanted was a glass of wine.

She shoved me aside, stomping out of the house and kicking Beau's tool bag when she left.

My heart was racing. I wanted to chase her, but the more I watched, hearing the crash of the front door, the more pointless it seemed.

Returning to my room, I tuned my guitar and added a little more research to my major work. Afterwards, I climbed outside my window to watch the sunset. Sure, I wasn't with Amberley, but my phone was the next best thing.

I didn't tell her about mum's condition, or about Beau—I simply mentioned that I was having a bad afternoon. I couldn't let her see my house, so instead of inviting her over, we FaceTimed before she had to leave the hospital. I think she was signing out with Doctor McNeill, who said his greetings through the phone. Since I had spent more time with him, I realised he was actually a nice guy.

As I waited for her to call me back, the sun began to fall. I relaxed on top of Mum's bedroom, playing an old tune with my capo on the second fret.

I strummed for what felt like five minutes, then something rustled beneath the purple sky. The vines that climbed the side of my house cried from Cameron's tug as he pulled himself up. Reaching the roof, he peeped his head past the shingles.

"I haven't heard that in a while. Do you even remember how to play?"

I lightened my strum to a pluck. "I can play; I just need to fiddle. I'm still a little rusty."

"Nah, it's good." Sitting next to me, he leaned against his arm. "Sorry I didn't text. Just felt like hangin' out. Getting away from … everyone."

I stopped playing. "Is everything okay? You're not in trouble, are you?"

Cameron laughed, "No … No, *me*? Never! It's just Haley's psychotic half the time an' Kev … Kev can be hard."

"Are you sure?" I insisted.

"Yes, Tye. I just wanted to hang out. We haven't done this for a while, just you and me. I miss it!" Looking at the sun, Cameron smiled, "How's that girl? Amberley, was it?"

I began plucking a C major. "Good. Real good. I can't describe it, but she's fun to be around."

Cameron paused, staring at the side of my head. "I'm happy for you. I like her, she's nice. And I think she's good for you."

"What do you mean?" I laughed.

"Look at you. You're playing a guitar outside, watching the sunset with barely a bag underneath your eyes. Compare that to when I dropped you off at the hospital a few months back, knowin' how the garage was; you were so glum all the time, staring at the ground. Bro, you barely spoke, an' when you did, it was just sarcasm or whining. But when I saw you with her, you seemed different." Stretching his arms, Cameron yawned, "Do you like her? Like, ya know, is she *the one*?"

My stomach slapped itself. I tossed the guitar to my side and leaned back with Cameron.

"Honestly, I don't know. It's hard to explain. I can't say much, but I'm trying not to get attached, especially with her."

"What? Come on, man," Cameron nudged my shoulder. "Why would you do that?"

"It's complicated. And like, maybe you have a point. Maybe I do look different, okay? But I still—in my head—I still …" I sighed,

"I'm just trying to get to know someone and enjoy being around them because they enjoy being around me. It's not about getting in, hooking up, having sex and moving on, or about falling in love. I want to spend time with her. And I feel like, at school, with your friends, with anyone outside of school, work, family, whatever it is, that's so rare to find. To actually have someone who enjoys being around you. To actually have someone who appreciates you. Like, of course, you're always someone who's like that, but she's on another level. I don't think of her as someone I want to have sex with—she's someone I want to enjoy the moment with."

Cameron sat, nodding to each word. He agreed with most of it.

The sun disappeared, and he said, "I didn't know you were so adventurous. If ya want, one day we could go hiking or camping. Just say the word." Standing, he waved me over to the side of the house. "I wanna tell you this game plan I got. For when we leave. That is, if you still want to go?"

I sat up, half dazed by his voice. If he was right—which, I don't think he was—Amberley was the only thing that was keeping me alive. And if I left with him, and she was still around, she wouldn't have me by her side during her death. *Makes me weak, thinking like that.*

I placed the guitar inside, and muttered, "Of course. I've been putting money into the stash every weekend." We climbed down the vines. "So what's this game plan?"

Cameron skipped down the driveway. "Soon. I gotta take you somewhere first. Can I drive Jess?"

Before I knew it, we arrived at a familiar place.

Cameron parked in front of a house I had never noticed before. We crossed the road to Dad's garage unit, which lingered next to an apartment block. The unit was the last on the left, number seventy-three.

"Here. Really?" I asked. "Why couldn't you just tell me everything at home?"

Cameron raised his arms. "This is where it'll start … and end, I guess—our journey. At the start, it'll be a bit slow an' rough, but towards the end, we'll understand where we're headed. You said you wanted an adventure, so I brought you here to go up there."

He pointed at the roof of the tallest building in the Blue Mountains. It was still under construction, the first high-rise, with temporary metal fencing grinding against the wall of Dad's garage. Even the pathway that travelled outside the fence had turned to rubble as the scaffolding began to sway in the autumn wind.

"The new apartments?" I scoffed. "You want to go to the roof? Won't we get in trouble?"

Cameron shrugged and wandered to the fence. "I'm not sure. I was putting money into the stash last night when I overheard a few kids. It was late, almost midnight, and well, I could smell bud, an' they were giggling behind the fence. If they're smoking weed in there, we might as well give it a look."

"Fair enough," I nodded. "I just don't want you to get in trouble with Kev."

"Tye, don't worry about me," Cameron shrugged off my concern. "Come this way, I think there's a gap somewhere."

I reluctantly followed until we found a gap between the fence and the gate where a lock was hanging on a chain. Cameron ducked under the chain, stopping halfway. "Don't worry. They expect kids going through here as long as no one gets hurt."

For an idiot, he had a point.

I climbed under, smearing dirt across my jumper. On the other side, there were metal plates, planks of wood and saws scattered around the inside of the apartments. Only the outer frame was finished. Walls were drying with plaster, and there were holes for the window frames. We didn't dare enter, and decided to scurry past the site's right side, searching for a staircase.

As Cameron wandered, I noticed that the bottom floor's right wall was made of orange bricks. *Huh, look at that.*

I stood to admire this one particular wall. I don't know if it was intentional, but the wall had been covered with several painted handprints, each a different colour and size. Green, yellow, pink—I could go on. Some were small, others large, all placed haphazardly around the brick wall with an empty centre.

Cameron backtracked to stare with me. He thought it was cool and wanted to place his own handprint on the bricks some other night.

I agreed, surprised that the tradesmen hadn't painted over it.

Leaving the wall untouched, we found concreted steps leading up to the ceiling with no railing for safety. It felt like the whole thing was bound to collapse.

When we reached the top of the ten storeys, sweat rolled down my temple.

A refreshing blast of air dripped past my forehead as the night sky revealed itself. I had forgotten how beautiful the Blue Mountains were. *Like no place on Earth!*

And even if Dad's garage was in the middle of nowhere, twenty minutes away from the station, and at least a ten-minute drive, it sure was a pretty neighbourhood.

We gazed at the valley, the trees below, each like blades of grass, and behind them, the staggering vistas of orange stone and black mountainside. There were barely any houses, and the canopies glistened with the hints of the city lights beyond. It was all nature and nothing more.

Cameron roared at the top of his lungs. He wasn't angry, just happy to be here.

After a *woohoo* and a *yeah*, he calmed himself and turned to me. "This is what I mean. Look at us. Two guys far away from any worries, with the stars over our heads, nature all around and silence. There's not a single sound. That's why I wanna get out so badly, that's why we need to leave. I hate this place, Tye. *I hate it!* It's like no matter where I am, ya know, unless I'm with you, I don't fit in.

I know I don't belong here. And the world's so big, an' there's gotta be somewhere for us. We just need to leave!"

He screamed again and continued to monologue as my phone buzzed.

"I just wanna shoot a gun in the air and scream, *screw you all*. Screw this town. I'm leaving. Bang, bang! Shoot it three times an' then leave, and never, *never, come back!"

I examined my phone, mumbling, "Yeah, oath. I can't wait." Amberley had rung me twice.

Cameron's tone turned sour. "It's that girl, yeah? Go on, answer it."

I put my phone away. "She can wait. I'm with you." I furrowed my brows. "What's wrong?"

Falling to the side of the concrete roof, Cameron leaned against its bannister. "Do you still want to go? Leave everything, school, your mum … her?"

I got closer to him. "Of course. We made this pact way before I met Amberley. It'll work out, trust me. We'll find a nice place that's far away with no dumb stuff, no stupid people, and we'll fit in and be happy …" I stopped myself, stunned by Cameron's tears.

Cameron wasn't sobbing at my words. No, he just couldn't hold it in anymore. "I'm scared. Tye, I'm so dead." He pulled up his long sleeve, and underneath, his arms were covered in slashes, bruises and swellings.

I fell to his side, putting my arms on his shoulders. "We'll get through it. I will *not* let anything happen to you. You're my brother, okay, the only person I'd risk my life for. You just need to hold on. Work the system, get on Kev's good side. You can sleep at my house if you need to. Just tell me. Don't keep it in or you'll end up worse. I am always here for you. Do you understand?"

Cameron began to shake. "I get it! I'm just so dead. I'm not okay, and I don't know what's going to happen. Haley is the only thing keeping me alive. If I don't suck up to her, pretend that I love her

… I'll leave you the money. If anything happens to me, Tye, the money's yours."

I mumbled excuses, but Cameron had planned this from the start.

"Stop whingeing for one second." He stood, towering over me. "Something will happen to me, Tye. And if it does, I need you to have the money. I have no one but you."

I didn't want to say yes, but I knew I had to. I nodded, "Sure, it'd be my honour."

We contemplated on who to go to. Cameron's parents had completely disowned him. I asked if we could visit the authorities, seeing that he was eighteen, but there was no solution; the situation just became more and more complicated.

We ended up hotboxing his car, not because I wanted to, but because Cameron couldn't deal with the stress of what he had told me. I smoked—for him—only one cone, and then drove us home.

He had passed out on the seat. I couldn't leave him in the ute, so I carried him inside.

His half-stoned self was heavy, but I soldiered on, placing him on my bed.

At eleven-eleven, I sat outside and called Amberley. And while my phone rang, I contemplated whether to lie or tell her everything that had happened. *I was so anxious!*

But as soon as I heard her sleepy, clumsy, annoying voice, it all went away.

The Party

I didn't get to sleep until three in the morning. Amberley and I just talked. And we would have kept going if school wasn't on tomorrow—I mean *today*, in like six hours.

I crashed on my office chair, listening to an Alan Watts lecture titled *What Have You Forgotten?* With everything happening so fast, it was nice to have a moment of peace. The lectures were like drugs, and I was hooked. Each metaphor, realisation, teaching—it made me grateful for the things I had. It didn't matter what would happen in the future, or what had happened in the past, the moment was now.

When I woke up, I was inside an empty house. Mum hadn't come home, and Cameron wasn't in my bed. I was alone.

I spent the whole day with Amberley. We sat at our spot at lunch and recess, talking about our favourite seasons and funny videos. We laughed when I discovered that I had misplaced one of my sandwiches.

After school, I went to her house and talked to her mum about what I wanted to do when I finished school. Her dad got home early, and we talked about bowling, fishing, and of course, food.

Unfortunately, when I arrived home, it felt as though nothing had changed. Beau's van was on our driveway, and again, I kicked his duffel bag making my way inside. Mum stared at the television with her nose blistered red, and Beau, right in front of me, snorted something I'd rather not talk about.

I locked my bedroom door, made tomorrow's lunch, finished chapter two of my major work and had a shower.

In the morning, I noticed that Jess' fuel was low.

I filled the ute up at a local petrol station, and got a large mango iced tea—Amberley's favourite. The front counter guy had dark skin and slender fingers.

"You're Cameron's mate, right?" he asked.

I took out my Visa card and our eyes met. *Wait a minute.*

"Hey, I know you," I pointed at the cashier. "Beverage, yeah? How's it going?"

Beverage scanned the tea. "Good. Tyler, right?"

"Spot on. Didn't know you worked here."

"How do ya think Cameron can smoke all of his cigarettes and still make dough?" Beverage tapped the register. "What number?"

"Fair point. Uh," I looked outside. "Three. By the way, I gotta ask. Why do they call you Beverage?"

"It's not a nickname, bud," he laughed. "It's my last name. Addermire Beverage. Look me up, aye?"

I paid him, taking the tea. "Of course. See ya 'round, Addermire."

That was odd. I barely knew the guy, but if he says hello, I'm not going to ignore him. Talking to people is fun. Now, I wouldn't go up to every stranger and say hello, but if someone greets me, I might as well see where the conversation goes.

There's no shame in talking.

¶

Amberley's house was like a second home. I knew it inside and out—where Monte laid on the couch, where Amberley's phone charger was, where the cutlery hid—and I could guess where the remote would be most times. We didn't do much today because Amberley wanted ample time to get ready for the party.

Sitting on the couch, we watched the fifth season of *Scrubs*, and it got me thinking.

"If you're so into living in the moment, aren't we just wasting our lives watching Scrubs?" I asked. "Like, it's a funny show, but shouldn't we be outside enjoying ourselves?"

Amberley dropped her head and looked at me. "It's on our list to watch it, and you put it there. Plus, we're not wasting our lives. You said it yourself, the show's funny."

"But we're just sitting here."

Amberley sighed, "Are you enjoying this? Being here?"

I stuttered, looking for an answer. "Of course."

"Tell me why. What's to enjoy here?"

It felt like I was being lectured. "Well, I'm in a nice warm house out of the cold." I grinned, "I'm laughing, I'm with someone I enjoy spending time with, I … I don't know. I'm having fun."

"Point proven then," Amberley continued to watch the television. "You can't be wasting your life watching TV or playing games if you enjoy it. You just pointed out the moment. Honestly, I'm happy being here, just doing nothing." Pausing, Amberley nudged my side. "How many episodes have we watched today?"

"Eight."

Dropping her jaw, Amberley gasped, "I think we should stop after this one—that can't be healthy for you."

Gosh, she makes me laugh.

We finished the episode, and it was about three-thirty in the afternoon.

Amberley decided to eat, and her mum insisted on cooking for us. I told her, like Amberley, that I was fine, but she went and did it anyway. I had never seen Tegan at work. She was always home, asking Amberley or me if we needed anything.

After we ate these amazing wraps with chicken, melted cheese, lettuce, aioli—the whole nine-yards—Amberley went into her room to get changed.

It was four, and for the next hour, I spoke with Tegan. I practically heard about Amberley's entire life, from when she was little, asking everyone if they were okay as soon as she could speak, to before she was diagnosed. She used to make her mum breakfast, go for walks, dance and so on.

Tegan sounded like a pretty awesome mum. She was always in an art class, from the moment she left university. She had, however, taught other subjects over the years, and ended up advising me and proofreading my major work.

At five, I threw on my getup, popping on my wig, fluro orange jacket, and rainbow polka dot pants that went up to my belly button. I was ready at fifteen to six, and Tegan told me I looked stunning. She was almost jealous, but then Amberley came downstairs, stealing my small parade.

She looked like she was from a movie, with her pink matching jacket and her hair puffed up behind a colourful headband.

"How do I look?" Amberley asked, smiling.

I bit my tongue, surprised by the question. "Uh … Cool. Good. Great, maybe?"

Amberley laughed, and Tegan took like a thousand photos of us in front of the fireplace, the front door and the deck.

It was six forty when we reached the party. My bag was heavy, and so were Tegan's worries. She was so concerned about Amberley, begging us not to do anything stupid.

Finally, she let us go, telling us to have fun, and that she was going to pick us up at midnight.

The party was already rowdy, with colourful clothes everywhere, and people drinking and talking. It wasn't late enough for dancing, although the music was loud. We said our greetings to the birthday boy, Nathan, and caught up with everyone else.

For an hour, I hadn't even seen Amberley. I got us drinks, and she would come by for another Cruiser, and then we would split up again.

I laughed, saw some stupid things at the side of the house, made friends with old enemies, danced for almost an hour, and it seemed that the alcohol made everyone very honest.

I remember sitting with Crouchy and Xander discussing how vomiting, while you're drunk, is simply a mind game. If you don't let yourself believe you're going to vomit, then ultimately, you won't vomit at all. *Magic!*

Crouchy's voice was slurred, and he eyed down the beer-pong table, telling me he was going to win because he wasn't drunk yet. I cheered him on, noticing how light my bag had become, and off he went.

Xander smiled, "It's a good party, huh?"

I nodded. "It's not bad. How's your major?"

"Best we don't talk about it, yeah?" He watched the dance floor and nudged me. "Hey, isn't that your girl? With Jake."

I glanced up to see Jacob all over Amberley, dancing with her and leaning in close.

"She's not my girl, Xander. We're just friends."

Okay, I might have stared for a little too long.

Xander chuckled as I noticed an ant on the dance floor. "Sure. Friend or not, she's—*damn!*" I could feel a warmth against my arm as Xander whacked my side. "You missed it, Tye. She totally dodged out of the way of Jake's kiss. Aw, now they're hugging. And they're back to dancing ... No, never mind. I think she's sick, dude!"

I searched the dance floor, and stumbling out onto the yard was Amberley, clasping her hand in front of her mouth.

I pushed past Jacob. "I got it, Jake. You enjoy the party."

He didn't refuse, laughing as he went back to cut some shapes on the dancefloor.

When I reached Amberley on the front lawn, she gagged into the side garden. It was quick and wet, and as she lifted herself from the fence, she turned to me with droopy eyes, cleaning her smile with her palm.

"Oh my gosh, Tyler! Where have you been? I missed you so much. I was just telling Jake about that time we went stone skipping." Her voice was funny, and she slipped into my chest, rubbing her head and hands against me.

I held her upright. "Are you okay? Amberley?"

She didn't respond.

"Please don't tell me you've passed out."

"No, silly," she murmured. "I'm just enjoying this." Lifting her head, Amberley smiled. "Are *you* okay? You're so worried but calm at the same time. Are you high?"

"No, I'm not high. What?" I laughed. "Do you feel dizzy?"

She threw her hands into the air, making an overabundance of gestures. "Before, yes, but now, I'm okay. Yes, okay ..."

Again, she vomited onto the kerb. She coughed and stood next to me. "Have I ever told you how great you are? You're so great, Tye!"

I rested my hands on her shoulders. "Do you wanna sit down for a bit? I'll stay with you, we can talk, and I'll get a bucket or something."

"But I want to talk *here*!" She stomped her foot. "Not where the music is."

I sighed, "We can get some seats and sit away from the music and talk. Okay?"

Thankfully, she agreed.

Holding Amberley up while getting seats and laughing at everything was hard! Desperately seeking a second chair, I held her in my arms as she blurted words into Toby's face.

"You see this Tyler? Love Tyler, he's the best. You two should talk more, you'd love him too, Toby. Toby and Tyler, double T with their big knees."

That didn't rhyme.

Toby smiled, agreeing with Amberley, saying that he already loved me.

When everything was still, Amberley dropped to the timber chair and admired the sky. "I think I'm good now. No more vomiting for me, Tye! Or is that even your real name?" She glared at me with suspicion.

I glared back, "How'd you know? My name's Tyler, not Tie—like bootie, that's so silly."

She laughed, "That's not funny …" Suddenly, Amberley lowered her tone. "I like being around Tye, even if he does stare at the ground sometimes. He's my favourite person. I'd even kiss him if I had the chance. But *shh!* Don't tell him."

I moved my chair closer to her side. "He likes you too. Says he's glad that you annoyingly forced yourself into his life. He would have been in a different place if it weren't for you." I looked her in the eyes, my heart rushing as I leaned in close. "Thank you, Amberley."

We were at the front of the party; there was no one around for another metre. But even if someone was near us, Amberley would have continued to cry.

Tears rolled down her cheeks. "That makes me happy to hear. But I'm sorry. I'm scared to hurt you. No, I'm really scared." She paused, her eyes so clear, I could see her soul. "*I don't want to die.*"

As soon as she told me the truth, I thought everyone was going to crowd around and support her; there wasn't a single person who disliked Amberley. But instead, she hugged me as tight as she could, bawling into my chest.

We sat with each other for the next hour, getting closer and closer, until I had my arm around her, and she laid into me like a pillow. Whether it was the alcohol or our growing friendship, Amberley told me things I couldn't believe. She was scared, frightened to leave her parents behind, and felt terrible for putting them in this position. She hated the hospital and Doctor McNeill because he always told her she was getting better. However, it had been a year since she was diagnosed with pneumonia which led to her sepsis.

The Party

I told her that she wasn't going to die, and that it wasn't her fault.

She drifted off to sleep, and I carried her to Tegan's car. Everyone asked if we were okay, and I nodded, not saying a word.

Tegan asked how the party was, and for Amberley, I told her it was one of the best and most strangely honest parties I had ever experienced.

Life

Life was good! To put it mildly, everything was going smoothly.

The orange of autumn faded, and there seemed to be a pink shade in the sky during the sunsets. I was rarely home, always crossing a number off in the bucket list with Amberley or avoiding mischief with Cameron.

Although Beau was back, he was more gentle with Mum. He started giving her her medication twice a day, replaced the front veranda's timber using the tools from his tool bag, and even took Mum on a few dates. When I got home, he would often greet me, and in the last two months, Mum hadn't had any of her outbursts. She did cry when Beau wasn't home, but the least I could do was watch a movie with her or talk about her day at the council—which is where she worked on Tuesdays and Wednesdays.

August was upon the horizon, and our trial examinations started on the sixth, so everyone was beginning to get anxious. It didn't faze me though; I was pretty confident with my subjects and their syllabuses.

Work was fine. I had started doing deliveries, and there was this one night when I was on my way back, after taking out the trash, and I saw Amberley's parents inside the pizzeria. They were proud that I worked at such a spectacular establishment—Tegan's words, not mine.

Amberley joined us after using the restroom. The Gibbons asked me for recommendations, and I tried my best to stay with them until Brando asked me to make a delivery. *That was a great shift.*

Cameron started to smile more. He wasn't smoking as much and had become less jittery when we went out for lunch. Sometimes he would sleep at mine, and I even got used to sharing my bed with him.

One day, he told me that he and Haley had rented a little apartment with a disgusting bathroom. It was mainly owned by Haley, but Cameron would sleep there most nights as he got better at dealing with Haley's mood swings and murderous spasms. *The key was to hide everything sharp.*

At first, I was in shock. I knew Haley was dangerous—but to the point of attempted murder night after night? I couldn't keep my jaw from dropping.

Unmoved by the pain, Cameron acted as if he was just watching ants. It was life, and that's what he had to do to get away from the world.

In June and July, Amberley and I crossed off two hundred points in our list. We went canoeing, did a three-day hike, finished watching Scrubs, drove around on go-karts, tried snails, swam in a lagoon, bought a two-man tent and camped the night away.

Afterwards, we cleaned the forests for a charity group, planted some trees, visited the tallest building in Sydney, went to an art museum and a local market, visited three different beaches, and jumped off an eight-metre-high cliff called Jump Rock. We even did some smaller things; for example, Amberley retaught me how to ride a bike on her old pink one, and I taught her how to play pool.

We went to a pyjama party and had lunch with Cameron to celebrate entry four twenty, and I apologised to Big Kev at the Salvos store for being *dismissive*. I also met Amberley's grandmother, Daisy.

Oh, and did I mention that I had taught Amberley how to play a few simple songs on the guitar?

To no one's surprise, Amberley and I hadn't kissed. Neither of us went for it, even though we had spent what felt like an eternity with each other. I could fart, and we would debate about whether it sounded wet or dry. She could trip over, and we would laugh about how cheeky the ground is. And unlike everyone else, Amberley wasn't afraid of the exams.

She did, however, spend way too much time studying. You see, our Society and Culture major work was due on the first day of the examination period. So we had to finish a six-thousand-word report, and have a stupid number of quotes memorised for the first English exam. Yes, for some reason, there were two English examinations.

Anyways, it was a Tuesday night on the fifth of August, and for the first time in about two weeks, I was trying to sleep in my own room. My major work was pristine, finished in a coloured print with a black binder holding its fifty-six pages together.

As I laid in bed, I decided to listen to a lecture by Alan Watts called *Let It Happen By Itself*. If anyone besides Amberley saw me do this, they would think I was a freak.

Yet amid the lecture's seven minutes, I forgot what the world was, and everything went black. Tomorrow was tomorrow and I couldn't change what was bound to happen. That was life, and I just needed to take it as it came, right?

On the fifth, Amberley had told me that her mum was going to give her a lift to school so she could properly prepare for the exams.

As soon as I arrived, alone in the school carpark, my body began to shake. Firstly, I went to submit my major work. In my hands, I held six months' worth of work to figure out that younger people were happier than those who were older. This was due to common experiences like the midlife crisis and an occurrence of depression that comes from age.

When I gave the booklet to Mr Taccori, signed the legal papers and walked outside, Amberley was still missing.

Curious about her absence, I sat at our spot and waited for her. The pink that seemed so familiar in the sky began to drift. Having trouble breathing, I couldn't help but look at the ground. When my eyes took in the concrete, the ants were gone!

Pulling a black pen out from my bag, I tapped it against my thigh in the hope Amberley would come.

She never did.

Before the exam, I searched for her, asking Crouchy, Emma, Xander and anyone else if they had seen her. No one had. My heart was pounding when we entered the exam room. Everything was noiseless.

My throat tightened, my legs shook, and my brain felt flustered. I was so cold.

After they told us about not having phones, and about the consequences of cheating, I faced the single table in front of me and thought one thing. *Where is she?*

After a creative writing short story, an essay and four short-answer questions that took a page to answer, I returned to the real world. The two hours of writing had drained everyone, and the many sounds outside tickled my ears.

Clouds had covered the sky, and as the blue regret of hindsight lingered in everyone's eyes, Amberley was still nowhere to be seen.

Jacob and Toby asked me how I went, and after all that writing, I felt pretty good about everything. I had finished the exam, answering all of the questions with enough persuasiveness in my writing, and I had used a handful of decent techniques.

The boys were pretty positive, and although I would have liked to stay and talk, I needed to go home. We were allowed to leave early during the exam period, so I left, trying to act like I wasn't in a rush.

Driving to Amberley's, I knocked on the front door until several bruises began to swell across my knuckles. But even though Monte barked at the door, no one answered or welcomed me inside.

I went home feeling an emptiness eating at my soul. Kicking Beau's bag on the veranda, I growled, swearing my head off. Mum was at work, so the house was empty.

I paced back and forth, thinking about what I could do.

No, I needed to study. That would do! To keep my mind off things, I could study for my second English exam.

For the next eight hours, I wrote and ate and watched videos and wrote some more, memorising quotes and their effects on the syllabus. I had messaged Amberley a few times asking where she was and if she was okay.

But, like life, it wasn't good.

At half-past six, my phone scared the living crap out of me, vibrating my entire table.

My body jolted at the sudden shock. *It was Amberley!*

I put the phone to my ear. "Hey, where have you ——"

On the other end, Amberley's father asked if it was me.

"Yes, it's me. What happened? Where's Amberley?"

His voice was tight and slow. "She's recovering ... Sleeping. She just got out of the ICU. The doctors are checking on her now."

My body was tense. "What happened? Is she ——"

"She had a stroke, went into shock ... Thank you for calling and being concerned, but, Tyler, listen to me. She'll be fine. You need to concentrate on your exams. All right?"

I raised my voice. "No, I-I'll visit tonight, and give you guys a break. I'm sure you're tired, and like you said, she'll be fine."

"Tyler!"

I began packing up my books. "I'll come right now!"

"*Boy, listen!*" Hunter's tone was now raw. "I understand you care about her, but let us look after her. We're her parents ... Come visit tomorrow when she's awake. Now's not the time. You have your Trials. Study! Goodbye, Tyler!"

Before I could argue, he hung up. Sitting back, I sighed as tears bundled around my eyes, but they never fell.

"Hospitals should be arranged in such a way as to make being sick an interesting experience. One learns a great deal sometimes from being sick."

ALAN WATTS

Visiting Hours

It had been over a week since Amberley was admitted into the hospital. So far, I had visited her every day, but with two exams left, both on Wednesday, I had to work up the courage and tell her that I wasn't going to be around tomorrow. My gut weighed an extra five kilograms, and my heart wouldn't stop racing. *What if she gets angry at me?*

In Amberley's private room, winter had lost its grip as the fragrance of flowers sprouted on the windowsill. I had never seen a hospital room like this one before. It was reasonably sized, with a panorama of a golden garden. Unfortunately, the view was useless as the window was always covered by a dreary blue curtain.

I stumbled in with … *Well, you'll think it's stupid.*

I was holding a bouquet of flowers as ripe as they come, with pink daffodils, roses and those yellow ones that have the big centres. I didn't pick it out, no, I just thought it would be a nice surprise.

Doctor McNeill poked his head up after he had readjusted Amberley's new drip. He smiled at me, "Look who's here. How many exams do you have left, bud?"

I held the flowers close to my chest. "Just two. Is it okay if I stay?"

He nodded.

Amberley was her usual talkative self. It had been a while since I had last heard her cheerful voice. The stroke had left her mute for a time, but now, she seemed almost as healthy as me.

Saying her greetings, she laughed. "Where'd you get them?"

I sat on the chair across from her bed. "The flower shop near IGA. *Stop laughing*—isn't it what you're meant to do when someone's recovering?"

Amberley and Doctor McNeill grinned at one another.

"*What?*" I insisted. "I gotta put them somewhere, aye? Where do ya want 'em?"

Amberley examined the room. "On my side table."

"I'll just move out of the way, Tyler." McNeill shifted to the bed's end.

Standing, I shuffled to the side table and placed the flowers down.

Reading his clipboard, the doctor paused, staring at us, then continued to read. He smiled. "Does that feel better?"

Amberley nodded, playing with her fingers atop her bedsheets.

"You should be out of here soon, M.B. Just a few more tests and we can send you on your way." Placing his note board on the bed's end, McNeill's tone became bubbly. "Lunch is soon. Apparently they have cheesy pasta today. It might be nice." He winked at me. "I'll go fetch some water for those flowers. Be back soon."

When the doctor left, I dropped onto a mocha-coloured chair next to Amberley's side table. "M.B? I didn't know he called you that."

"We're close." Amberley's eyes met mine. "It's also partially my fault for why he moved here. Guess who visited me about an hour ago?"

I glanced away from the ground. "Who?"

"Mr Taccori. He came so I could hand in my major work. We did all the paperwork, and he explained to the board why mine was late. They understood, so I'm finished."

"That's great. Do you feel good?"

Amberley shrugged, "I guess it's a relief now that it's over."

"Did you end up using my survey?" I stretched, cracking my back. "'Cause, in all honesty, I nailed it. Every question was worth a Band Six."

She shook her head. "No, I forgot. Actually, I knew I had it, but you're not a patient. How would it have helped?"

My jaw dropped. "Because I'm amazing. Look at me. Nah, I was just honest. It could have been an interesting perspective."

Amberley smiled, "Well, *Mr Amazing*, did you use mine? It was probably better than your crappy effort."

"Crappy?" I had to stand. "I'll have you know, I knew you hadn't used mine, so I didn't touch yours. No, I completely forgot. Lots of things have happened since we filled them in."

Even though Amberley grinned, her eyes lingered on the front wall. Before I had time to ask what was wrong, she said, "You seem happy today. Did something bad happen?"

"No. I just want to cheer you up."

A chill entered the room, and like a thunderstorm, the blue lights above the hospital bed began to flicker. The machinery inside became quiet, the glimmer of blue faded, and all I could see and hear was Amberley.

"You don't need to do that," she mumbled, her cheeks a burning red. "I'm as cheery as I was yesterday. I'm just a little scared, that's all."

"Don't say that, Am. I'm here and so are your folks. There's no need to be scared."

"And why do you need to say that?" she frowned.

"Because I get it. You have good people who love you. And everyone at school wants to come and visit you, and they won't stop asking me how you are."

Amberley raised her eyebrows. "You get it! How would *you* get it?" Her voice wasn't loud, it just remained firm. "How would you understand that a cold could get you here? 'Cause that's how it started. All I got was the flu, Tye. And now I'm here. I'm always tired, my chest hurts. I feel like I can't breathe! How do you get that?"

I gulped, "I don't! But I know you. And I know what you're feeling, that you're scared ..." Looking back and forth, I searched for my next words carefully. "Do you want to read my survey now?"

Amberley crossed her arms, tears bundling along the sides of her eyes. "It's in my bag, in my Society folder."

I knew exactly where to look. As I scrambled through her bag, she continued to whine about how on earth the survey was going to explain things.

I slipped out a folder, titled SOC, and noticed my writing.

"Enough, Amberley. Just read it!" Unfolding it, I handed her my filled-in questionnaire. "When we first started to make the bucket list, and you invited me to your house, I didn't know how to say things properly. I didn't know whether I wanted to ignore you or to piss you off, but something inside stopped me." I sighed, "Maybe it was because you were happy or because you wanted to sit with me when everyone else had already left. But Amberley, I'm weird, I'm not right. I'm ——"

She placed her freezing hand on my arm. "You talk too much. Let me read. Please?"

I nodded and read with her.

Question 1: Do you have a disability, if so, is it psychological, physical, intellectual or sensory impaired?

Yes, Psychological.

Question 2: What is your disability?

Depression.

Question 3: How do you maintain your disability? (Eg: Prescribed medication, Professional aid, Carers, etc.)

I don't deal with it. I guess I've gotten used to ignoring the bad thoughts and the negative ideas in my head. But I have never tried to deal with it professionally or with any aid. No psychologists!

Question 4: Is your disability one that may become terminal in the near future?

Yes and no. It has already been terminal in a sense.

Question 5: Do you believe your disability affects your ability to be culturally happy?

Of course. I get paranoid when I talk to people, like I can't express myself. I fear that they're going to judge me, that they're going to think that I'm annoying or that I talk too much. I can't stop looking down, and when people notice, it hurts. Looking at someone else's face just worries me. And every minute of every day, I feel empty. Like there's nothing inside of me! And I want to scream. I want someone to talk to and tell them all the thoughts built up in my head, but when I get the chance, I don't. I hold it back. Because I don't want them to be pushed down by me, by my selfishness. But I think it might be getting better. I'm not sure. But I am not happy!

Question 6: Do you believe you fit into society and the community you are a part of?

No. I feel lonely. Even with my friends, old or new, I feel like I don't belong. Like I can't be me!

Question 7: What makes you happy, and what do you think would help to make you a part of the community you live in?

Nothing. My best friend is losing his grip on a good life, my mum screams nonsense at me every day, and sometimes I don't think she even knows I exist. And don't get me started on her new boyfriend. I did meet this one girl though. Every time I am with her, I feel warm and maybe, somewhat a part of a friendship. She helps! Besides her, the only time I've ever felt relief or a sort of happiness was when I tried to kill myself. The first day of school and my second attempt at my life. With a rope around my neck, I jumped, and for a moment I was happy. There were no thoughts, no worries and no one around. Even if it sounds bad, Amberley, I wanted to tell you, but I never could. I hate my life! Please don't judge me after reading this. Since I have met you, I haven't had as many bad thoughts. Thank you.

Tears dropped onto Amberley's bedsheets. Her grip had tightened, shaking at the words I had written. "Why?" she begged. "Why didn't you tell me? … You're an idiot, you know that!"

I sprung up, arms wide apart. "I don't know, I didn't think. I … I just couldn't!" Trying to sit across from her, I stood up, and then sat back down. I felt sick to my stomach like it was about to implode on itself.

It was silent, and Amberley smiled. "You get me! I get it now. You do get me." She began to laugh.

Lifting my head, I looked at her cheeky face. "Why are you laughing?"

"You get me …" She wiped her tears. "It's funny."

I tried not to grin, but I couldn't help it. I was with Amberley.

Shrugging, I pointed at her nose. "Yeah, I get you."

"You get me. And I get you."

I pointed at myself. "Me?" To my surprise, I joined her crazed comedy, laughing at nothing. "You get me? We get each other. Am, why are we laughing?"

She put my questionnaire down. "Because we get it. It's funny because we're here. I'm glad you showed me this, Tye. Don't thank me, thank you!"

I leaned forward. "Are you on morphine? Why are you so funny?"

We laughed for what felt like an hour, and every sentence we said, we'd giggle like little kids pranking their parents. She told me she wasn't on morphine, *she hadn't had surgery, silly!* I laughed at that too!

But soon we had to return to reality as Doctor McNeill opened the door.

He was holding a plastic vase, staring blankly into the room. "Sorry. Is everything okay?"

Amberley rested on her pillow, folding the questionnaire. "Right as rain! We just got a new inside joke, that's all. Thank you for bringing the, um ..."

"Vase," McNeill noted. He filled the plastic with water from a sink that poked out next to my chair and handed it to me.

"Cheers, McNeill." I placed my bouquet inside as Amberley asked the doctor how his husband was.

"Good," McNeill grinned. "He's back into his old habits, but he's trying to avoid it. He's getting stronger every day."

Amberley rubbed her hands together. "From the way you describe him, he sounds amazing. I'm sure he'll get through it. To have someone like you in his life, he's bound to make it through rehab. He should come in if I'm stuck here, I'd love to meet him."

McNeill pouted his lips, "Sounds like a plan. I'll see. It depends on what he has on. He's absolutely bombarded with work, like myself, but with his two jobs and the hospital giving me night shifts every Friday, we barely have the time."

"That's okay, it was just a suggestion. But if you could spare some, could you *please* bring some of your cooking over? I don't want Mum to wear herself out, and Tyler can't cook."

"I can cook!" I spat. "And I've shared my pizzas with you since like the start of April."

Amberley nodded, "It's good pizza, but Tyler, you haven't had Sebastian's stir-fry or his husband's roast. And he makes the best schnitzel. Like, I'm telling you. *The best!*"

The doctor laughed at himself. "Thank you, Amberley. I'll make it a priority. I know as well as anyone how sickening the food here can be. Reminds me, Tyler, can I speak with you outside? Just really quick? It's about your mother."

I bit my lip. I had told him to back off, but instead, he kept on insisting and tried to bring Mum up whenever I was with Amberley. Although Amberley knew my mum had schizophrenia, and as a result, saw things other people didn't, McNeill did respect my request to keep things private.

Walking outside, I closed the door behind us.

McNeill tried to act casual, pointing at the door. "She cheers up when you're here. I haven't seen her smile since she was admitted. Look, I've doubled the dosage on your mother's antidepressants. Not because she asked, but because she's getting worse. And I don't want her to get reliant, but at the moment ——"

"Don't! Please. I don't need this," I sighed. "I get you're trying to help, but don't criticise her. She's had it hard ..."

McNeill raised a brow.

"Don't look at me like that—she's my mum!" I yelled. "And she may seem psychotic one day and crazy the next, but she's still my mum, and I don't need a doctor judging her, saying she's getting what? *Over-reliant?* The meds calm her down, and the other ones stop her visions. If they're helping her, then I'm willing to pay for them. Just put her back on her normal dosage."

As I turned back to walk into Amberley's room, Tegan waltzed down the corridor with a coffee in one hand and her handbag around the other. "Tyler! Gosh, I'm sorry I wasn't here earlier,

I got caught up in that little canteen they have downstairs, and Nikki was there, and we got to chatting. And, well … now we're here." She sniffed the air. "I smell daffodils."

My eyes widened, "You know what that smells like?"

"Of course I do. Well, I smell pollen. What? I like to have flowers in the house; gosh, it's like you've never been there before."

I shot McNeill a look of confusion, and he shrugged.

As she entered Amberley's private room, Tegan became overwhelmed by my bouquet.

"Look at those! I knew I smelt something. Are these from you, Tyler?"

I nodded, "Yeah, I thought it was a little stale in here. Bit blue and all."

Doctor McNeill stayed with us for another half an hour, informing Tegan about the fluids entering Amberley's veins and about her smooth recovery. As soon as he was finished, Tegan talked about where they used to live, The Northern Beaches.

McNeill didn't miss his old home. He did, however, think that it was better than the Blue Mountains.

When he left, I returned to the crappy seat across from Amberley's bed and rested my elbow on the sink.

Like a time-lapse, the morning left quickly, and midday turned to the afternoon as Amberley's father visited in his grey suit and navy tie. The night arrived with only an ounce of time left before visiting hours were over. No matter who strolled through the room, whether it was a nurse, a doctor, a little girl with plaited blonde hair or Amberley's folks, I sat, listening to what they said.

The blonde girl was named Kaitlyn. Her illness was not as serve as Amberley's, but she had lost her hearing after a recent stroke. This was the first day I had noticed her. She was discharged in March, and Amberley had told me that Kaitlin would visit her from time to time as she understood how sad hospitals were. She was sweet, and when her mother, Nikki, wanted to go home, the little girl, no older than seven, waved at me with the biggest smile.

When the nurses checked on Amberley, they would ask me if I wanted any water or coffee. Some of them even knew my name, like Cassandra, who was always behind the glass panel, saying goodnight or good morning when I came to visit. She was funny, always telling me that I was the cutest boyfriend she had ever seen.

I told her I wasn't anyone's boyfriend, and that I just cared about Amberley. Heck, lots of people kept saying that; I didn't know where they were getting this boyfriend idea from.

Every time I sat and visited the private room, we would laugh all day and I had fun.

Amberley's father told these great stories about when he was younger, getting stoned with his friends and going to parties every weekend. It sounded like the life. He grew up here, in the Blue Mountains—that's why they moved here.

Amberley's family was close. Her grandparents visited yesterday, and the other ones came the day before. In the past week and a half, her whole family had visited with gifts and cheery spirits.

At seven, I started to get hungry. Tegan was trying to convince her daughter that the pasta was yummy by chewing on it and (unconvincingly) moaning about how tasty it was.

"Come on, Am! It's delicious and it's getting cold. You need to eat."

"I know, Mum. Look, just …" Amberley sighed, "I promise I'll eat, but you standing over me like this isn't helping. And you need food too. When Dad comes back, you two should go home. You look tired, and I don't like seeing you like this."

"Amberley, I'm fine." Tegan rolled her eyes. "I'll sleep when this is over."

"I want you to sleep, Mum." Amberley held her mum's hands. "Coffee can only get you so far, and if Dad gets tomorrow off, we can spend all of tomorrow together."

Her mother nodded, "Okay, but I want to see you eat. And we'll visit at ten, that's the earliest they let us in. Hopefully Sebastian can sneak us in at nine, hmm?"

Laughing, Amberley shoved a mouthful of creamy pasta between her teeth.

Her dad marched in, smiling. "I can have the next week off and any more time I need. *We* need!" He turned to me. "You've gone quiet, Tye."

I lifted my head. "Yeah. Long day, that's all. Sometimes I talk too … you already know. I was just thinking about my Society exam."

"Do you two want time to talk about it?" Tegan smiled, "We know Amberley can't do it yet, but we can head off and leave you two alone."

Hunter eyed down his wife as she scoffed at him.

He gave me a thumbs up like a proud uncle on Christmas. "Of course. We'll come bright and early tomorrow. Society and Culture—you'll be right, Tye."

I grinned, and the two said their goodbyes, hugging Amberley and kissing her forehead. They waved at me, and Hunter shook my hand.

The door closed, and at seven-thirty, we were alone.

I stood, putting my hands together. "About that. I can't visit tomorrow. I have two exams on Wednesday, and I … y'know, need to study."

Amberley blushed, "It's fine, Tye. Gosh, you're so awkward. You've come here every day. A day off's not going to kill me." She pointed at the bouquet, "The flowers! Now, I get you."

"Don't start that again." I sat at the bed's end, next to her cushioned cold feet. "You know, I met this girl once. Weirdo started talking to me because she thought I was lonely. So silly, that! Even in the hospital, the girl told me a day off's not gonna kill her. And that's probably true, but it doesn't mean I'm not going to feel like shit. I like you."

She leaned back into her bed. "I like you too." Her breathing got heavy. "Study, Tye … I'll be fi——"

Amberley's body tensed, straightening as if her heart had just stopped. Her eyes fluttered back and forth at lightning speed and her chest shook as drool poured from the side of her mouth.

I jumped, trying to do something. *Anything!*

Hitting the emergency button by the bed's head, I threw the door open and screamed for the nurses.

When they came, I was useless.

All I could do was feel Amberley's cold hands. They were so tender; they made my skin turn blue as the nurses forced me out of the room.

The door closed, and my arms dropped to my side as my hair fell past my eyes.

Please, let her be okay. Please! Her hands were so cold!

Morphine

Whoo! I had finished all six of my exams.

I felt this weight lifted from my shoulders—Amberley was okay. They moved her permanently into the Rehabilitation Unit, so I have to wait 'til eleven to visit her. Last night I missed her for the hour she was awake.

I had the rest of the week off as the exam period was still on, so instead of sulking around the house, I decided to stay at the hospital and give Amberley some company.

Mum wasn't too fazed with me not being around, and work had given me some time off. Cameron didn't mind either. He knew from day one where I was, and he even told me that Amberley would be fine.

It was five past eleven when I struggled to find parking. Once I found a safe and empty area, my heart slowed, and I gradually parked Jess next to a kerb that protected a dry lawn. The trees around the hospital had begun to bloom, welcoming spring. I brought iced tea, chocolate and my guitar, which I kept inside a soft case that I flung over my right shoulder.

As I hiked to the hospital, I noticed a turquoise Corolla. My leg hairs stiffened, my nose itched, and a sudden lightness clouded my head. Just past the hunk of metal, Cameron sat on top of a timber fence, scratching his neck and picking at his nails. He turned to me. "There he is! Been lookin' for you."

Standing next to him was Haley, her brown hair in knots and her saggy clothes covered in stains. The two approached me, and as I staggered back, Big Kev stepped out of the Corolla. He placed his phone in his pocket, walking around the car's bonnet.

"Tyler! It's good to see you. How's the girlfriend?"

"She's not …" I straightened my posture. "What do you want? I'm kind of in a hurry."

Haley skipped to my side. "He's feisty today, Cammy. What's wrong, Tye-Tye? You look sad. Did something good happen at home or do I need to cut that angry frown off?" She caressed my cheek with two fingers, making my skin tighten.

I palmed her aside. "I'm going to the hospital. So obviously it's not great." I crossed my arms. "I'm fine."

"Calm down, jeez." Haley laughed, "You don't have to act like someone's dying. Unless …" She gasped, "No, I shouldn't say. But I do want to meet this girl of yours. Cammy and Kev have, why can't I?"

Before I could talk, Big Kev raised his voice. "Enough, Haley! Let the boy be. He's havin' it tough." Lowering his tone, Kev leaned against the Corolla's hood. "Don't mind us, Tyler, we were just wonderin' if you could do something for us? A favour! It'll be worth a lot of money, and well … I would be in your debt."

"Why me?" I spat.

Grabbing my shoulder, Cameron pulled me aside. "I think it'd be better if I explained it to you alone. Come, walk an' talk. It'll just take a sec; ya don't have to say yes." He waved at Big Kev, and Haley stared at us with a menacing eye.

Walking between two houses, Cameron's voice became raspy. "Tye, this is serious. He needs morphine! We wouldn't normally do this, but Kev's old source got angry, and they argued, and now they don't supply anymore."

I shrugged, "Why do you even sell morphine? Why don't you stick with coke or bud—*anything?* Why morphine, and why me?"

"Because of Amberley! How the hell does he know about her?" Cameron pointed at Kev.

"He works at the Salvos in Springwood," I shivered. "That's why your pay's always inside the donation bins."

"Obviously, that's why I have a key, you idiot!" Cameron frowned, "Look, she's a fine person. An' I don't want her in this business, but if he knows, I can't stop what he might do. He has connections everywhere. Including the hospital. Just listen to his plan, do what he says and get us a bag."

"No! This is nuts ——"

"Tye. Please! I won't be able to stop him from hurting you."

I knew there was nothing I could do.

We returned to Big Kev, and I agreed to his plan. The basic outline was about Doctor McNeill. Kev knew that he had recently moved to the hospital and that he was attending to Amberley. He said the doctor was an idiot, and that I could, through luck or skill, steal his identification card, locate the storage room, fill a duffel bag with morphine and leave without anyone knowing. Not to mention that I had to return McNeill's ID card and go home to wait for Cameron to pick up the delivery.

With each step Kev described, he knew each string to pull, and each one he did. If I delivered a full bag, he told me I'd be in his *good books*, that I'd be paid a wealthy wage, and that he would leave Amberley and me alone.

Cameron's eyes were round with scepticism.

I bowed my head and nodded, dumping the iced tea and chocolate into the duffel bag, and treading into the hospital's entrance.

As the doors opened, Cassandra waved at me. "Good morning, Tyler. I didn't know you played the guitar. Amberley's a lucky girl. You going to serenade her?"

"Kind of," I grinned. "I'd better get going. See ya, Cass." Laughing awkwardly, I stumbled into the elevator.

Once I reached Amberley's floor, I peered out for only a second and bumped into an excited Tegan.

"Tyler!" she cheered. "You brought your guitar? Amberley told me you knew how to play, but, well ..." She lost her smile. "Honestly, I just couldn't believe it."

"Well, I can play, I guess," I mumbled.

We laughed as Tegan handed me her coffee. "While you're heading in, could you take this?" She noticed my duffel bag. "You've already got a lot of stuff. Are you sleeping here or something?" Smiling, she nudged my arm. "No, I'm just playing. Just put it by the side table when you get in there. I have to help Hunter with the car. Amberley's been up a little more. We let her buy some new clothes online. And we wanted to surprise her when she wakes up today. We bought you some things too! I'll show you later. Be up soon." She frolicked away, the elevator closing as I took her coffee.

Inside Amberley's room, I leant the guitar against the sink, put the coffee on the side table and the duffel bag on the floor. Amberley had her eyes closed, sniffling little sighs in her sleep, as I unpacked the duffel bag.

Kev had filled the bag with more lollies and snacks. I guess this was his idea of being nice, or maybe Cameron did it. Either way, I was feeling nauseous.

Amberley's body was still cold; the aura around her arms was as icy as snow when I went to pick up Tegan's coffee. *Hold on, I just had the best, worst idea!*

McNeill always comes in to check Amberley every hour or so, and in between, he strolls back and forth checking on other patients. What would happen if I bumped into him?

I covered my usual seat across from the bed with the lollies. Zipping up the bag, I hung it around my shoulder and snuck out the door.

Amberley's face was so still, but deep inside, I knew she wouldn't be proud of me. I wasn't proud.

When I closed the door, Doctor McNeill was right on cue. "Tyler! Can I have a word? It's about ———"

"My mum, right?" I loosened the coffee's lid. "It's funny, I was just about to ask you something about her. She's—*whoa!*"

Pretending to slip, I threw the coffee at the ground, splattering McNeill's clothes. As I fell into his buttoned-up shirt, the coffee stained my shoes, smothering the floor in a brown ooze.

"I'm so sorry, Doctor!" I gasped. "Jeez, I didn't mean to get you dirty."

"It's okay," He leaned down. "It was just an accident; these things happen. Nurse, can you get some paper towels please?" The nurse came running, handing him a roll of paper towel.

I insisted on helping him clean, and as we rubbed the floor, I grabbed his arms.

"I'm sorry I got coffee all over you. I'm an idiot, I really am. Look at this, you're covered! Here, let me clean it off for you."

"*Whoa!*" The doctor swatted at me as if I were a fly. "Tyler, did you … did you just touch my arse?"

"*No!*" I hid his ID card in my hand. "What? Don't accuse me of … Amberley's my girlfriend, man! Girlfriend. Sorry, just …" I sighed, "I'm sorry. I just wanted to fix my mistake. You should go. I'll clean this up, you have patients to look after."

He gave me an uneasy look that made my stomach drop. "No, it's not your fault. I'm sorry for accusing you. I've been on edge lately, and I'm having trouble at home, which shouldn't affect my work. It's my fault." He handed me a second paper towel. "Here, we'll clean enough so people don't slip, then I'll get the janitor to fix the rest. You should be with Amberley."

I smiled, hiding his ID card in my pocket as we soaked up the coffee.

Chucking the paper towels in the bin, I skipped to the stairwell. "Gotta go. We'll talk later, I forgot something in my car."

He nodded, "Go ahead. Hey, what's with the bag?"

I scampered backwards and shrugged, "Lollies man. Girls love chocolate. And feta cheese."

Outside, Big Kev told me that the storage room was on level two near the children's ward.

I tumbled downstairs and snuck around each corner like an untrained spy. My heart was racing, my nose wanted to sneeze away all my anxious thoughts, and my body jolted at every little noise.

Surprisingly, the storage room was easy to find. I passed a janitor, who sighed after being called up to level three, turned a corner and found a grey door with bold letters that spelt *Storage*.

Out of breath, I threw on a pair of plastic gloves that I had stolen from the janitor's cart.

Pulling out McNeill's ID card, I chuckled at his awkward profile photo. His hair wasn't done, his clothes seemed uneven, and … *I don't have time to think like this!*

I examined the lock, tapping the card, pushing it under, and sliding it through. The door finally buzzed open, showing a green light. No, I should have looked around first. *I'm an idiot!*

Waiting at the door, I searched left and right—there was no one! *This is so stupid; they have camera footage.* Kev had told me not to worry because he was going to take care of it, apparently.

Leaping inside, the noise of my breathing guided me through the storage aisles.

It was pitch-black.

My vision soon adjusted as I passed boxes and fridges with different types of tablet packets, empty plastic drips and all sorts of machines. Finally, I read *Morphine* on a shelf.

My throat tightened, my legs almost gave way, and my eyes watered. *Let's do this! I've already gone this far.* It seemed like picking a handful at a time was taking hours, so I began to scoop the bottles out of the mini-fridge.

When the duffel bag was almost too heavy to carry, I closed the fridge and lifted the bag strap, praying the clattering bottles inside weren't too loud.

Opening the door was the worst. I didn't know who was behind it.

I tried listening in, and there were people talking on the other side. Two nurses, but they eventually moved, and it got quiet.

I pulled the door open. No one was there! *I'm either the luckiest person ever or I'm about to have a heart attack—this is too good to be true.*

Strolling into the main lobby, I threw the plastic gloves into the nearest bin and almost jogged out of the room. No one gave me a strange look, and no one eyed me down like a thief. In front of me was the exit, and my hopes were high. I hadn't seen Amberley's parents this whole time, and McNeill was all the way up on level three. I had done it!

Yet, as the sliding doors pulled away, Cassandra said, "You're leaving early today. What's in the bag?"

I turned with a waterfall dripping down my forehead. "The bag? Clothes. I'm not leaving, I'm just taking Amberley's old clothes to her house." I laughed, "She is my girlfriend, and that's what a good boyfriend does. So, I'm not leaving, I'm just putting some things away. I'll see you soon." I waved at Cassandra, who nodded with a smile.

Once I was free, I sprinted towards Jess. I threw the duffel bag off my shoulder and sat at the wheel, feeling like I was missing something. I checked my pockets for my phone, and instead, I found Doctor McNeill's ID card.

Damn! After the weird coffee spill, he'll know I stole it.

I ran back to the hospital and told Cass that I had forgotten my guitar, sprinting past her without another word.

As I walked from the elevator to Amberley's room, a sickening pain hit my stomach like I shouldn't have come back. My fingers shook while I turned the doorknob to her room, searching for McNeill, left and right.

Shit!

He was already inside.

"Tyler!" He looked at me. "Did you find what you were looking for?" Besides Amberley, we were the only ones in the room.

Avoiding the doctor like he were a plague, I snuck behind him. "Yes, I did. It was easier to find than what I had thought."

He smiled, "What do you mean by that?"

"The walk," I laughed. "It wasn't as long as I thought it was." I made it to the side table, and the doctor and I were millimetres from touching. Leaning back, the table reached just below my waist.

"That's good." McNeill's eyes followed me. "Hey, this'll sound a little rude, but did you grab my keycard before, or at least have you seen it? I seemed to have misplaced it."

I had the card in my hand, dropping it onto the side table. "No. No, we just had a weird moment. I, ah …" I shrugged, letting go of the card and moving away from the table. "I haven't seen a card, and I wouldn't even know what it looks like. Have you looked in here?"

He nodded.

Searching the room, I smiled, "I'd give it another go. I forget everything, like my car keys, they end up in the most …"

McNeill's eyes lingered on the side table. He threw his hands down, picking up the ID card. "There it is. Gosh, I am out of it today. It was right there. How didn't I see it? Well, I'm going to get a coffee. My break started four minutes ago, and I need a nap." He tapped my shoulder and left as if he had never lost the stupid card in the first place.

I sat next to Amberley for a moment. Home was far, but she was here.

Finally, her eyes opened, and she smiled. "Hey, you."

I must have been dozing off, because I leapt from the chair, smiling back. "Hey! You're up."

"Yep," she nodded, noticing the room, "And you brought your guitar. And lollies?"

"Cameron heard, so he brought some." Croaking, I unclogged my throat. "Now that you're up, can I tell you something?"

"Of course."

"You wouldn't believe the day I've had. And it's only twelve. But don't worry, you've made it better," I laughed.

"I know. I'm really good at sleeping. I like this," Amberley pulled herself up. "Just you and me, talking. It's a good life."

"Yeah, talking. Talking's good. Life's good." I rubbed my throbbing forehead. "I think after tomorrow, life's going to get better for both of us and we'll go to New Zealand after you finish your exams. And Canada."

"And Spain?"

"Yes, Amberley. And Spain." Pushing back my oily hair, I leaned back. "The whole world! Just you and me."

Amberley closed her eyes and smiled.

"I used to think the worst thing in life was to end up all alone. It's not. The worst thing in life is to end up with people that make you feel all alone."

ROBIN WILLIAMS

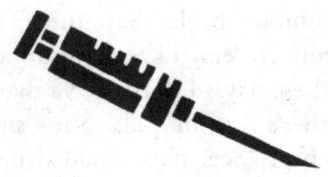

Empty

Amberley's parents spoilt her for hours. They got her all these clothes and gifts, and somehow, they managed to buy me a present. Two, in fact!

One was a framed photo of all of us camping, and the second was an olive jacket that was wind-resistant and warm. I tried it on, and it fit well. To celebrate, I played my guitar, and we all told stories until the visiting hours were over.

Amberley was so happy when we left. With a smile, she told me that the worst was over. There was no need to worry.

At eight-thirty, Colourless Avenue was pitch-black. Even the dim streetlights weren't strong enough to guide me to my front lawn. When I parked Jess, I rediscovered the duffel bag full of morphine bottles. *Right, I have to give these to Cameron.*

Throwing the bag over my shoulder, I held the framed photo in my left hand, kicking Beau's stupid bag on my way up the veranda. *This is the last time!* My heart was rushing and I was so hot-headed. After I groaned, I hopped inside, cooling off my sour foot.

Tiptoeing from behind the kitchen, Beau greeted me. "What ya got in there, pal?"

I marched around him. "Nothing much. Just some clothes … from a friend's house."

His voice was quick and his eyes seemed glassy. "Can I have a look, if ya don't mind?"

I climbed the first step, pulling the bag away from Beau. "Sorry, I *do* mind!"

"Fair call," he stumbled back. "Sure there's no drugs in there? I know you boy, you do 'em, like me and ya ma." He smiled, "Where do you go these days? I don't see ya that often—an' where the hell are ya mother's freakin' pills? She's snappin' like crazy." He pointed at the bag. "See, if you had drugs—'cause I know Cameron, I know what he sells—then those drugs would do her and I a-wonder, boy. They'd make me one happy stepfather."

I climbed another step. "Whoa! You're not *step* anything. Her meds are on her side table in her room. I bought them yesterday after my exams." I swerved the bag behind my waist. "And even if I had drugs, I'm not giving any to you or Mum. If you know what Cameron does, why don't you buy them off him? 'Stead of asking me." Sighing, I rubbed my forehead. "I'm going to bed; make sure Mum has two tablets before she goes to sleep. Goodnight, Beau!"

Beau's eyes remained fixated on the bag as if he had X-ray vision.

Falling asleep that night was hard. The morphine under my mattress had plagued my room. Listening to lectures, podcasts, music, whatever it was, it didn't help. I was awake whether I wanted to be or not.

After much consideration, I messaged Cameron at four in the morning, telling him I couldn't sleep.

When he responded moments later, he told me to forget about the morphine and to meet him at the train station. So that's what I did.

I left, sneaking out my window without a sound. Well, that's what I thought.

I wore my new jacket, zipping it up to keep warm. Then, I met an interesting Cameron, who was excited, thrilled, anxious, and for some reason, hooked on spending money.

"Look," I yawned. "The laptop was good enough. I know it may almost be a year old, but you don't need to buy me anything."

Cameron slapped my side. "But your birthday's ——"

"Two weeks away. Don't worry about it. Why are you so excited all of a sudden? You seem happy; what happened?" I asked.

Walking around me, he pushed his chest into the air. "Breakfast. We'll do that! Oh, ya know that bag under your bed, that's the key. Once that's all sold, we'll have enough to get out of here. To be free!"

I smiled, pushing his chest back down. "Calm your horses. Don't get ahead of yourself just yet."

"What? Don't you want to leave?"

"We're not having that talk again," I rolled my eyes. "I just don't want you to get your hopes up, that's all. It'll hurt if they're so high."

"I see. It's the girl—of course it's the girl!" Cameron crossed his arms. "Then I'll leave you here with her."

"No, Cameron," I raised my voice. "She's still in the hospital. When she's happy and healthy, and I know she's okay, then yeah, we can leave. But at the moment, I don't want to go. I still need to finish school, don't I? We have our final exams in October, and then we can leave after that!"

Cameron frowned.

We walked around for an hour and went to the first open cafe.

As we sat with our coffees, Cameron asked, "What happened to her? Amberley. How'd she end up in the ICU?"

"I'm not going to ask why you know half of that," I said, stirring my coffee. "She had a stroke on the sixth, and on Sunday had a seizure."

"How come?"

"I shouldn't say. I would, but it's not my place." I admired the ceiling. "Let's just say she's the toughest person I know. She's amazing."

"I'm happy you found her," he smiled. "Ya know, if you can't go, I'll split the money with you, an' you can spend it on her. It looks like she's already spending some on you." He pointed at my jacket.

I felt its crisp fabric. "I'm happy I found her too."

We talked about new games, caught up on school gossip and drug-dealer drama, and finally, left for my house. Delivery was due as we journeyed up Colourless Avenue. Unfortunately, there were red and blue lights that sparkled at the cul-de-sac's end. *Cops? Why would they be here?*

"Be careful when I give you the bag," I said to Cameron. "Don't get caught or like hurt yourself."

"Bro, this is my life. I'm used to it." Cameron laughed. "Ain't nothin' careful about a delivery; I just gotta keep my head down …" Slowing down, Cameron gulped, "What's the ambulance doing here?"

I glanced forward, and behind Jess was an ambulance, their emergency lights colouring my house. On the driveway, a paramedic was trying to calm Beau down. His face was so red.

My stomach dropped, and I began to sprint.

As I ran past Beau and the paramedic, Beau screamed at me. He didn't want me to go inside, it wasn't his fault. He was … *sorry!*

When I reached the veranda, I didn't feel any pain; there was nothing. There was no loss of balance, no shock to my toe, my foot was fine!

Instead of kicking Beau's tool bag, my shoe stepped over it. Since before I could remember, that dumb bag was always full of tools, but now they were gone. *It was empty!*

Beau's

Inside, Cameron stopped at the front door, telling me to slow down, and to have a look in the lounge room. I ignored his cries, marching upstairs with one thing on my mind.

Next to my busted bedroom door, there were several tools spread around the ground. My door hinge was bent, my lock had been smashed, and the timber door itself had a newly cut hole above its knob. I gulped, pushing past the broken doorway.

No!

The bag Kev gave me, the bag of morphine, it was empty! There were five bottles left! *Five!*

Beau had stolen them. *That idiot, he's stuffed me!* How was I going to explain this to Kev and to Cameron? *I can't deliver five bottles.*

Trembling, I held myself, dropping the bag and retreating. I couldn't even look up, not until I reached Cameron's side.

"Cameron, the bottles, they're ... they're ..."

Glancing up, I noticed that Cameron's eyes were watery. "I'm sorry, Tye. I'm so sorry." *That wasn't what I expected. Am I really that stuffed?*

Cameron stared into the lounge room, and I joined him, smelling death's scent.

In the room, empty bottles of morphine covered the carpet as a second paramedic readied his stretcher. Next to him, on the floor, Mum was unconscious. She laid with her eyes rolled back as frothy drool leaked from her mouth.

When the paramedic lifted her onto the stretcher, a horrible spasm cursed her body, making her arms jolt.

Please, no, not her! I don't want Mum to die. She could hardly breathe.

Running to her side, I kneeled down, holding back the tears that managed to pour from the sides of my eyes.

I asked the paramedic if he knew what had happened.

He told me that she had been doing *dangerous activities*. She was overdosing. Lifting the stretcher, the paramedic ordered someone to get his partner.

Cameron jogged to the front door, yelling out to Beau and the other paramedic.

I didn't know what to do; my body just shook and my face was so hot. Holding Mum's cold hands, I begged her to stay with me, to not die, to not go into the light.

The paramedics had no trouble lifting her down the veranda, over Beau's tool bag, through the lawn and up the driveway towards the ambulance.

As I marched with them, they began to administer medication into Mum's swollen, purple veins. Her skin was almost black beneath her eyes; her nose was blistered red and her arms had several scabs woven throughout. After they put a breathing mask over her mouth, they applied a drip, and her spasms stopped.

Closing the ambulance's doors, the paramedics drove away.

I was jittery. The one person I needed to blame was here, standing next to me. And he was as shaken up as I was.

As I walked inside with Cameron, Beau was right behind us. He grabbed his shoes and car keys; however, before he could escape, I blocked the door.

"What did you do, Beau? Why … Why is my Mum like that? Why didn't you stop her, you piece of sh——"

"*Enough!*" Beau's voice was raw. "It's your fault. I knew what was in that bag; you lied to me! Ya shouldn't have brought all that crap home, you idiot!" He pointed at the front door. "I care for that woman! I do. But don't blame me. They're from your stash, not mine. So move!"

"My fault!" I screamed. "You broke into my room and stole my stuff. *My. God. Damn. Stuff!* Who do you think you are? Look what you did to my mum! SHE'S DYING!" I lost my anger. "She's dying … And it's your fault! She wouldn't have broken into my room. No, she would never do that."

Beau stood tall. "Get out of the way, boy! Someone has to visit your mother—someone who she at least loves. She doesn't give a damn about you! You're nothing to us!"

"Nothing!" I was face to face with him. "No, I'm not letting you leave until you give me back the morphine. There's no way you and mum had a whole bag full. And she's my mum! I'm the one who takes care of her. You hear me? Now show me where you're hiding the ——"

A pain burnt and bruised my forehead. For a moment, my vision was blurred, and a ringing sound deafened my ears. Beau had hit my temple so hard, it throbbed the second his fist left my skin.

And he would have hit me again if it wasn't for Cameron.

Holding him back, Cameron screamed at Beau, telling him to go away.

When my vision cleared, I saw Beau get into his van. I ran to the front door and yelled, "I never want to see your face again. Don't come back, Beau. I hate you!"

He drove away.

"I … I …"

When I turned back to cry, Cameron was gone. I could hear him swearing upstairs. He must have found the empty duffel bag.

Joining me in the living room, Cameron held the bag and sighed. He stood next to Mum's drool, which now stained the carpet.

"Not good?" I whimpered.

"Not good." He picked up an empty syringe. "He took over a month's supply. Don't worry, I'll scavenge what I can from around the house. And when it's not enough, I'll explain everything to Kev."

"No!" I stood my ground. "You'll get hurt. I can't let anyone else get hurt."

"Don't worry," he awkwardly laughed. "Kev knows Beau. He buys from us every week. The whole thing's on him, he's a thief. Just tell me, do you really hate him?"

I shrugged, "I guess … What will Kev do?"

Cameron stared at me. His face was as white as a ghost. "Go. I'll deal with this. Visit your mum. Take Jess—just go. I promise you, no one's going to hurt you. Not Amberley. Not your mum. No one." He pushed me out the door. "Go!"

Birthday Gifts

It had been almost two weeks since Mum was admitted into the emergency department.

The first day was a mess. I wasn't allowed to see her, and once a doctor came and talked to me, I couldn't help. I offered to donate my blood in case she needed any for surgery. Heck, I would have given them eight gallons if I knew she'd be her old self again. Fortunately, the nurses told me I was overreacting.

I discovered that the doctors had administered a drug called *naloxone* into her bloodstream. I don't know what it did, but around half a day later, Mum woke up.

Although I never saw Beau, Mum did tell me that he had visited her most mornings when I was at school. What a douche—it was like he was scared of me.

Cameron sorted out the issue the morphine. Kev even gave me a visit to apologise and offered money for Mum's recovery, but I refused. I didn't need any more gifts from drug dealers.

School had gotten quiet, but once Amberley was discharged—a week after Mum had arrived—it seemed most of the students in my year had become lively.

See, I was turning eighteen tomorrow; the first day of spring. And as my birthday approached, Amberley and Cameron began to get ecstatic. They both acted as if it were a day to look forward to.

I visited the hospital for the one-hundredth time. Instead of going to see Amberley in the Rehabilitation Unit by myself, today, Amberley joined me.

"Hey, Cass. Guess who's back?" asked Amberley as we walked inside.

Cassandra lifted her head. "My favourites! Aren't you sick of this place, Amberley?"

Amberley laughed. "I'm visiting Tyler's mum. He said she's doing well enough now that we can talk to her. I'm excited. You look nice. Did you do something with your hair?"

"You noticed!" Cassandra played with her bangs. "Thanks. You're better than Tyler. Who, by the way, sees me every day for a month, and I don't think he's ever given me a compliment. Oh, I love you two, you're my favourite couple!"

Amberley glanced at me with a grin. "Couple?"

"Yeah, couple of ... of people visiting Tyler's mum," I laughed. "We're the ultimate duo, Amberley, the beautiful Cass knows that. Who wouldn't love these flowers we got Mum? So, Cass, there's a compliment."

Cassandra giggled, "You two are too much for me. Go on, visit your mum. And Tyler, work on your compliments. I don't know how you deal with that boy, Amberley!"

We strolled towards the elevators.

When we entered, Amberley leaned on the rail and wondered, "Couple ... Hmm, duo? What'd you say?"

I pointed at my chest, the elevator doors closing. "Me? Nothing. I never say anything. Barely speak. Unless you don't want to be a couple ... of people."

The elevator loomed in silence.

I smiled, "You'll like her. Mum. She'll like you too. She'll see how, um ... How amazing you are."

Amberley blushed, laughing at me.

Mum was in the same section Amberley was in before she was transferred into the Long Stay Ward. It was like a walk through all my old memories.

We journeyed past the bed where I sat for days by Amberley's side, where I first gave her the medicine she left at school, and where I now visited my mum. The smell of sanitiser and babies covered the walls; however, after all this time, I had never liked the stench.

Mum's room was warm in comparison to Amberley's private room. You could feel the healing inside of it, I suppose.

"Orange? I didn't know they had orange curtains." Amberley smiled. "They're better than the blue ones. They match our flowers."

I led the way, laughing. "You're right. It's warmer, don't you think?"

"Mmm, better. So, what do I say?" asked Amberley.

"You're asking me this now? She can probably hear us. I don't know, just be yourself."

Mum's drowsy body lay with her back propped up against a pile of pillows. She had machines monitoring her heart, tubes attached to her arms and pale skin—she was the spitting image of Amberley two weeks ago.

She smiled at me in her room walled by curtains. We couldn't afford a private one.

"You're looking much better," I said.

She tilted her head. "Hey, sweetie. I feel better. The doctor says I can leave tomorrow morning, hopefully." She pointed at the flowers. "Are those for me? You shouldn't have."

"Everyone deserves flowers." I blushed, "I brought someone with me. Someone I'd like you to meet." I moved out of the way of Amberley, who smiled and waved at Mum. "Mum, this is Amberley. She's ... Well, she was the one who thought we should get you flowers."

Mum seemed to tear up. "Amberley, that's a nice name. So, you're the reason why Tyler's been out so much lately. Come, come closer. Gosh, you're gorgeous. What school do you go to, Amberley?"

After Amberley giggled and said thank you, to my idiotic surprise, the two began to bond as if they were glue and paper.

After they talked for a while, I noticed they were so alike. I even discovered a few new things. Neither of them had left their hometown, not until they were seventeen, and when they left, they both wished they had stayed.

Mum laughed a dozen times; I hadn't seen her like this since she had filled in my questionnaire. She told Amberley several stories about me when I was little. There was this one where Dad and I would write down all the things we wanted to do in a booklet, and then during our holidays, we'd do every single thing we wrote down. If I was too young or it was too dangerous, we would keep it written down for the next holiday. I was seven when he passed away, eight at his funeral, and Mum couldn't help but cry when she told the story.

Amberley hugged me, and I felt a moment's rest.

We talked about having our parents meet, and I went to get lunch from the cafeteria. Before I could leave, Amberley stopped me and said she knew the best thing to buy, and that I needed some time alone with my mum.

When Amberley left, Mum whispered, "You like her, don't you?"

I nodded, "Yeah, she's great."

"Hold onto her, and don't let go. You never know what time's going to pull from your fingers or how long people last in that grip of yours. The memories are always there, but take them as they come, Tye." Mum sighed, "You don't want to end up like me."

"And what's wrong with you?" I examined my surroundings. "Should I ask her out?"

Mum smiled, "Do you know you love her?"

"I can't stop thinking about her, so maybe I do." I gulped, "I guess I wanted to know if you liked her."

"She's perfect." Laughing, Mum lowered her voice. "I know what it looks like when you like a girl. I'm your mother. And if I were to fall from the face of the Earth tomorrow, it'd make me happy to know you had someone like her by your side."

We hugged. I never knew Mum cared so much.

Amberley returned, and we spent the whole day with Mum, talking, eating, laughing and being happy. Mum knew my birthday was tomorrow. She said she had bought me a present and Amberley, the idiot, got excited.

When we were about to leave, Doctor McNeill told us that Mum could go home in the morning, and Amberley took it as a sign.

"Why aren't you excited, Tye?" She slapped me as we left the hospital. I didn't realise I was scowling.

"I don't know, Am," I shrugged. "To be honest, I can't remember a birthday that was good. So I don't look forward to them."

Amberley sat in the ute. "That's slack. Fine, I'll make sure tomorrow is the best day ever. It's your birthday ..." She laughed. "Are you still sleeping at mine?"

I started the ute's engine. "If tomorrow's going to be the best day ever, I might as well wake up next to you."

"Aww, do I make your day?"

I rolled my eyes. "On second thought, I'm going to go sleep in my own bed. Yours is hard and rigid."

Amberley continued to complain about how I had to sleep at her house and yada, yada. In the end, I wasn't excited because my gut felt really empty about the entire situation.

When I woke up, I smelt pancakes.

Amberley's parents wouldn't let me sleep in her bed, so like yesterday, I slept on her bedroom floor because Amberley wanted to stay up and talk to me. At midnight, she screamed happy birthday, making me feel like a startled sausage on a barbecue.

However, that morning when I opened my eyes, Amberley wasn't in bed.

The three Gibbons screamed happy birthday when I reached the kitchen. They even managed to put balloons up, decorating half the house and wrapping three gifts. I ate pancakes with Nutella and joked that it was the best last meal I had ever eaten.

Mr Gibbon got into a skin-tight suit and played with a bike helmet, holding my neck hostage with his arms. He called me Mr People Person and wondered if I would be interested in going bike riding with him.

After pancakes, we went out for an hour, just me and him, bullshitting about life. I fell over a few times, but he was a funny guy with his odd wisdom.

When we returned, I opened my gifts, went on a bushwalk with Amberley, and then had lunch with her and Cameron.

Cameron got me a present. Nothing special, just a *brand-new phone!* I didn't want to take it, but he forced it into my hands and told me he owed me from that time he lost my Year Seven Blackberry. He also gave Amberley flowers and a nice blue jacket. It looked expensive—had the brands and everything.

I promised Mum I would be home by seven to eat dinner. So, as the clock ticked, I sat with the two most important people in my crappy life, admitting defeat to Amberley. Today was one of the best days ever.

We talked, and that's what I loved doing. From midday 'til sunset, I had this growing, changing conversation with both of them. And when I drove Amberley home, leaving Cameron at the Salvos store once again, I couldn't stop looking at the sky.

"You were right," I yawned. "I do look at the ground too much."

Amberley laughed and bullied me for only just noticing.

When I dropped her home, I thanked her, saying *love you* when I sped off. I didn't even realise it.

Reaching my house, a sudden chill tickled my spine.

The lights weren't on inside, but why should I complain? Mum was probably planning on surprising me.

I walked over Beau's tool bag and stepped inside to feel an

emptiness again. The house was pitch-black; the fragrance of dust sent shivers down my shoulder blades.

Inside, the furniture was gone, leaving clean marks on the carpet from where it used to be, and behind it was only silence.

Opening the lounge room doors, I noticed that the lounge and television were missing. The kitchen was as perfect as the day we moved in, and by the steps, there were empty cardboard boxes. I was frantic as I rushed upstairs. The feeling became indescribable when I reached my busted bedroom door.

My room had been looted, its draws scavenged through, the taste of sweat from a heated rush, and on my bed, there was a letter. Shame on me to think that we had been robbed!

The letter was addressed to me. It was in Mum's writing.

She had left.

That morning, when she had returned from the hospital, she had packed her things and moved away with Beau to someplace near the beach. Without a word, she had left me alone to find ants marching on my bedroom floor. And the sad thing was, I wasn't angry.

I was just empty.

I felt a sudden urge to vomit, and in my desperation, I dropped to the ground and watched the darkness consume me.

That was her present—my mother's birthday gift! *Why did she leave? Why?*

Please, come back!

"The more you are motivated by love, the more fearless and free your actions will be."

DALAI LAMA

Good Company

I almost drowned in all the spit that was stuck to my throat. Scrunching Mum's letter in my hand, I felt every bit of ink as if it were as heavy as stone. The emptiness loomed in my stomach, and because my belly ached, I called the only cure I knew.

I swear, the phone dialled for so long. Its buzzing tune only made me more anxious each time it vibrated.

But then, I heard Amberley's voice. "Hello. Tye? Tye, what's wrong?"

With a mouth full of phlegm, my eyes gave way, and tears rolled down my cheeks. "I need help. Please! I really need someone. I-I'm scared. Amberley, I'm scared. I don't want to be alone."

Her voice felt nice on my ear. "Where are you? It's okay, I'm here. I'm going to come as quick as I can. Where are you?"

"My house. I'm alone in my house. And my mum ... She's gone ... I really ... I really don't like this."

On the journey to my house, Amberley stayed on the phone with me. She heard many things I wasn't proud of. I went through an aggressive fit and punched my bedroom wall until there was a hole in it. I questioned my existence, thinking that the world had abandoned me. And finally, I cried because I knew I was going to die alone.

Then I heard a car brake as Amberley's father parked in my driveway.

I sighed, realising I was now in the middle of the lounge room.

Amberley marched into my home for the very first time. As she stumbled in, I stood, whimpering like a dog. Glancing around, Amberley was in awe when she reached me. She was the only thing in the house besides its walls and lights.

I stared at the carpet, my legs quivering as I tried to hold back every bad thought that infected my head.

Hearing Amberley whisper my name, I could feel her arms around me, her head under mine, cradled against my chest, and a warmth that loosened my shoulders. I felt ... *full!*

Her smell, her heat, her everything made me give up what I was hiding, and I bawled my eyes out, finally embracing her. We locked in for a moment as I held her, not wanting to let go. Her voice healed my heartbeat.

"Tye, it's okay ... You're not alone, not with me. What happened?"

Tightening my grasp, I wept, "She's gone. Mum left, she took everything with her. The fridge, the lounge, the good pillows. They even took my stuff."

"Where did she go? I'm sure we can go visit her."

"Some beach with her boyfriend. That piece of crap, that bastard," I lowered my voice. "She's not well. She needs me!"

Amberley pulled away, staring at my bitter gaze. "I get you. But are you okay?"

I shook my head. "I can't sleep here. I can't do this ... She took everything. All I have is my bed, some clothes and this stupid letter. Like that's gonna help." I gave Amberley Mum's letter, and her eyes grew wider with each word she read.

She flipped it around to see the paper's backside and met my fragile gaze. "Come on, you can sleep at mine. It'll be like a really long sleepover. I promise we'll figure things out. Let's just take it slow for now and pack some things. Here." She offered me her hand, and I felt ridiculous taking it.

I used Beau's tool bag to pack my clothes and my school bag to pack all my textbooks; whatever else I could carry was placed into Hunter's car. It took three trips from the house to get everything, and on the last run, I found my guitar snapped in half. Its neck was bent with the six strings poking upward. I just left it.

Amberley, the freak, was so positive, she took it downstairs. She told me that we would fix it and that it'd be as good as new, and if not, we could buy a new one that was better.

Finally, we left. My legs felt like noodles, wobbling as I went to lock the front door. When I got into the car, it felt like my arse had sat on a blanket of needles.

Amberley's father examined everything with a wide eye. The house's walls were breaking, half the doors didn't close properly, the windows were either cracked or had a large dent, and the veranda was crumbling to pieces again.

The car trip was torturous—a deprived, bumpy ride that tasted sour.

Amberley's parents were nice, but I wasn't in the mood for talking. I didn't eat the food they offered, even though it smelt fantastic; I just couldn't eat!

Even Monte couldn't cheer me up with his cute little head-tilt and wagging tail.

As he sat by my legs on the Gibbons' lounge, Amberley drew a loud yawn.

"Do you want to talk?" she asked. "It's been two hours, and you've barely said a word."

I shook my head. "I don't want to burden you. I shouldn't even be here."

"Don't say that." She rushed to my side. "And you're not going to burden me. I want to listen to you."

I could hear crickets outside the window, creaking by a pond. "I'm good at that. Listening. But people would rather be ignored these days than to be cared for. Mum was like that. After all the times I stayed by her side, after I did what she wanted, she'd rather leave me and be hurt by her boyfriend. Or she'll move on, the idiot! Move into some other douchebag's house with his money and food. And he'll hurt her, and it'll happen all over again. Half the people at school ignore each other. No one ever asked me if I was okay, if I needed help, if I … if I was sad."

"I did," said Amberley. Her tone was clear as she towered over me.

"You said I looked sad; you didn't ask if I was."

Amberley frowned, shaking her head. "No, I asked if I could sit with you because you looked lonely. And when people are lonely, they are most often sad. Sometimes people ask those things in a peculiar way; you just need to be open-minded enough to notice."

"I did notice. It's why I went after you to give you your medicine at the hospital." I looked away from her. "Can I tell you a story? A little fact."

Amberley nodded, and I gestured for her to come closer. She sat next to me, and our knees whacked into one another.

"Do you want to know why I'm so sarcastic?" I asked. "I figured it out not too long ago with Cameron. It's funny what you can find on the internet. Like those videos that little deaf girl watches ——"

"Kaitlin! We watch them too."

"Yeah, we do," I nodded. "I searched *why are people sarcastic*. It came up with a bunch of stuff, but I only did it to prove Cameron wrong. I knew why, I always have … From the moment my father died, to Mum ruining herself with drugs, to the first nasty thought in my head, I knew why. And it just got worse. Everyone ditched me in school, they bullied me because I was weird, and finally, Cameron dropped out to do his trade. I had coped with all the unfair negative bullshit in my life by using sarcasm to hide the fact that I'm dead inside. To hide that I'm empty, that I'm depressed. And then you come along and tug on something that fills me up, but I'm still sarcastic. Not as much, but nonetheless … I'm sarcastic, and I know why." I stared at the carpet. "It's because I don't deserve kindness or good company. I don't deserve *you*. And your family and what you're doing for me. For some reason, I deserve to be alone."

Amberley burst into tears, grabbing my leg. "Don't say that. No one deserves that. We're here, together. And if I have to be by your side for a month straight, then I will … You're scared!"

"I'm not scar——"

"*You are!* Because I don't want to die alone, and neither do you."

We didn't cry. We only hugged, wrapping our arms around each other because we both knew she was right. She was always right.

Although our conversation settled as we discussed what to do with my house, Amberley asked me to tell her a story about my mum. My favourite memory.

She laid her head on my shoulder as we both watched a pitch-black flatscreen, and I told her something I hadn't thought about in years. As a kid, I used to have terrible nightmares. Every night I would have them, and I couldn't stand it any longer. And who better to ask than your mum, right? I was six and scared, and when I asked Mum, she told me the dumbest solution.

She said, *Tyler, tell yourself* no more nightmares *three times in a row and close your eyes, breathe slowly, and you'll never have a nightmare ever again.*

Ironically, I haven't had a nightmare since. Not until I woke up this morning.

And like that, it was twelve, and the end of my eighteenth birthday. Amberley had fallen asleep on my shoulder, and I sat there, unsure about everything.

No more nightmares, no more nightmares, no more nightmares! I hope it works twice.

Graduation

It had been over two weeks since Mum left. It felt like deja-vu, saying that.

Now that I had moved into their home, there were some ground rules the Gibbons had in place. But they were exaggerating—I wasn't planning on living with them for long. As soon as I got the money, I was going to buy an apartment or rent a house or something to get out of their way.

Hunter sat with me the morning after Mum left, and for the first time ever, he thought hard about what he said. He asked me all these dumb questions about whether I had been abused, if I had been fed, if I had been treated right, for how long I had lived in the house and all this personal stuff. I played along, and the more he learnt about my family life, the more awkward he became.

Nowadays, it's not too weird. The whole family knows about Mum and Beau and they only ask about them when I'm quiet.

I woke up to my alarm, its blasting tune amid a clutter of noises coming from the kitchen. It was ten to seven; the sun was beaming, my legs were stiff, and I was smiling.

As I opened the living room door, I saw Tegan cooking eggs in a frying pan.

"Morning, Tye." She focused on the pan as I walked out of the lounge room. "Are you excited to graduate?"

I took refuge on a kitchen stool. "Yes and no, I suppose. Huh, no coffee?"

"What do you mean by that, hun?" She turned to me, and I could see that the yolks of the eggs were like jelly.

I pointed at the empty bench. "You usually have a coffee in the morning. Did something happen?"

"Didn't you hear?" She laughed. "That's right, you had work. By the time we got home, you were fast asleep. It's Amberley. She's recovering. I'll let her tell you the good news. We're going to go and celebrate on Saturday and have a nice dinner. You better look your best, and get time off work, okay?"

I nodded, "Sounds great. So she's better now? Like, she's not sick anymore?"

Hunter nudged my shoulder, brushing past to get himself into the fridge. "Kind of. She's healing, healing twice as fast as before," he explained. "McNeill says she'll be right as rain by the new year, and by June, she should be as healthy as you and me." Pouring three glasses of orange juice, he offered me one and kissed his wife's cheek.

I took the juice and listened to the two joyfully chuckle over Amberley.

"It's almost over. Anyways, best I get to work. See ya, Mr People Person." Scrunching my bed hair, Hunter turned and leapt towards Amberley, giving her the biggest hug. *When did she wake up?*

She scratched her sleep-covered eyes as her father lifted his lips from her forehead and left. "Morning, Mum. I am so not ready for today. I have to put makeup on, and I can't be bothered."

I joined in. "I have to do my hair, so … Orange juice?"

She took my offer and glared at her mum. "Is Dad going to make it today? He's already had enough time off with me being in the hospital. Are you sure he can get the afternoon off?"

Tegan flipped one last egg. "Of course he's going to make it, Am. You shouldn't worry so much. Your father's work isn't going to care if he misses the afternoon to watch you graduate, and Tyler needs someone to walk him down." Putting two eggs on a plate, Tegan looked at me. "Are you driving today, Tye?"

I gazed back and forth between Amberley and her mother. "Probably. We're allowed to leave early, so we might get lunch."

I turned to Amberley, a warm feeling heating my chest. "So, Amberley, what'd McNeill tell you?"

She smiled and shrugged, saying that it wasn't important. But I knew she wouldn't be able to hold it in. She went on and on and ran out of breath a few too many times.

To summarise, the current prescription she was on was healing the inflammation in her lungs and kidneys, and the chemicals that had caused the problem were now finally dissipating.

After our eggs, I put on my uniform, and Amberley did her makeup. She didn't overdo it and she didn't have a cake-face like some of the girls back in Year Eight. Heck, she looked nice. Cute, even.

I drove us to school, mingled with Toby and Jake, and talked to Xander and a whole bunch of others. I think I spoke to everyone in my year.

We had crackers and dips and naan bread and all sorts of foods through periods one and two in Society and Culture—I didn't learn a thing. Mr Taccori gave us personal letters, and when the bell rang, I realised I would never have to sit through another school class ever again.

We had our final lunch with the teachers in the Presentation Space. The smell of ham was ripe, and after half a kiwi fruit, some photos and more talk of food, I stood away from everyone. Not because I was being annoying, I just liked the moments when other people were happy. Everyone was smiling, laughing, enjoying themselves, whether they were eighteen or sixty.

After I had taken a photo of Emma and Georgia with their PE teacher, Amberley bumped my shoulder. "I tried fish eggs; they were weird."

"Caviar? For the first time?" I asked.

"Yeah."

"They're nice in sushi. Hey, what do you want to do during the break?"

Amberley shrugged, "Don't know. What's everyone else doing?"

I scratched my head, squinting. "Cafes, I think. We got 'til three."

After the feed, the teachers prepared us for our final assembly. We all marched, two by two, into a herd of younger kids sitting in the chairs they had taken from their classrooms. After the school captains talked, we sat through a prayer, the principal's address and some other crap, then my whole year—one hundred and thirty-five young adults in uniforms—left under a human handwoven arch. Very anticlimactic!

Everyone said goodbye to each other like we weren't coming back in a few hours to properly graduate at the ceremony.

After a short drive, Amberley and I ended up at a cafe across the Nepean River. We walked and talked, and as I drank my soy cappuccino, Amberley shook her head. "You didn't have to buy me mine. I have money, you know."

"Think of it as a celebratory gift. For the good news last night," I smiled. "I'm sure the doc's happy he doesn't have to come in as often now."

Amberley stared at the river. "I don't think he really cares that much. It's funny what everyone says when you're not there though."

"What do they say?" I asked. "If it's Cass, I swear she's got something wrong with her."

Amberley cracked up. "No, silly. Well, at first, she said it. But Sebastian said it too, and they asked Mum about it."

We sat under an oak tree, overlooking the still water. The air felt fresh across my face. "What'd they say? You know, I think McNeill has something against me. I didn't mean to offend him when he wore that red sweater. Like, I just misspoke, and ..."

Amberley laughed a little loud, avoiding my eyes as she stared at her reflection in the water. "What's with everyone saying you're my boyfriend?" She looked at me, and when our eyes met, my throat tightened so hard I almost choked. "Because I don't recall you ever calling me your girlfriend or asking me if I wanted to be that." She squinted at me, grinning, but trying her hardest not to smile. "Have you been talking too much again?"

I pointed at myself. "Me! Never ... Well, I was thinking ... thinking about stuff. I'm a people person. Yeah! I was doing something, and instead of explaining how I knew you, I ..."

The sun was beginning to set below the water. Amberley tilted her head to the left. She looked at my lips and leaned in close, whispering, "Stop talking."

Before I could hold myself back, we kissed. My eyes closed, my head became thoughtless, and all I smelt and felt was her. Her lips were small but tender, and as shocked as I was, I rubbed my hand along her leg.

Although the kiss was great, she pulled away first. "I think we have to graduate soon," she said. It seemed three o'clock had snuck up much quicker than it did yesterday. "But I like that. You, being my boyfriend."

As my head recovered, I nodded. "I get you. That sounds great. You look great. We'll sit for another five and head off. So, we're doing this, right? We're ...?"

She laughed, "Yes, we're doing this. We're a couple. I'm happy! Are you?"

A tear fell from my eye. "I've never felt this happy in forever." I smothered her with a hug, laughing, "*I'm actually happy!*"

¶

The graduation ceremony took forever. Everyone's parents had to walk them into the hall at the beginning to initiate the proceedings, and it was a big hassle for the school and me to find a surrogate after Mum had left. Luckily, Hunter volunteered on my behalf.

We kept joking about different things. He always had some juicy stories back from when he used to smoke weed and pop pills, growing up twenty-odd years ago. We were by far the loudest people in line.

Still, once the ceremony started, teachers spoke, smart people got smart awards—it was always the same people every year—there were a thousand yawns, and then, it was done.

For some bizarre reason, they made my whole year stand in a giant circle around the families and friends in the audience with lit candles. After Mrs Mulhall congratulated us on graduating, my sorry arse led the foot of the circle's centre through the middle aisle. Two by two, we left the hall as graduates, unwrapping around the many watching eyes. It began raining as I left, and my candle didn't last long!

After some more photos, some goodbyes, and a lot of hugs, everyone in my year became anxious for the afterparty. Amberley and I went to her house to get undressed.

No! We weren't doing that!

The party was a gender swap, so I wore her uniform, and she wore mine. With a skirt, blouse and a tight-by-the-shoulders blazer, I somehow managed to walk with her to the party. It was only fifteen minutes away, but in that skirt, I felt way too free.

Soon, everything blurred together like a knitted sweater. I could always smell Amberley, no matter how much I sweated on the dance floor. I remembered hearing something smash, taking a pee in the middle of a forest with Xander, being lost in a carpark, rolling someone a cigarette. Ahh … Making a handshake with Ryan because we thought we were cool. Afterwards, I had some downtime, sitting on a log, far away from the music but not too far from the dancing.

I took a photo of myself to show Cameron how rare the party had been. As soon as I hit send, I felt Amberley hugging my chest from behind.

"What are you doing all by yourself?"

I leaned forward, pulling her up from the ground. "I'm not alone. I'm with you. My girlfriend!"

She managed to move around and sit on my lap. "That's cute. You must be in love?"

I laughed, "I'm pretty drunk, but ... love's a good way to describe it."

We kissed, and for the rest of the party, I was with her. Smiling. Happy. Alive!

Helping Others

My final exams for university were killing me. I didn't mean to be so pessimistic, but yikes, they were so important. Fifty per cent of our overall Year Twelve rank went into these exam marks, and I was only halfway. *I still had three to go!*

It was Sunday, the day before my Society and Culture examination. Amberley and I were rushing through Buddhism's history and how it had impacted the twenty-first century. Gosh, I was so sick of studying. For the last month, I had been writing, reading, rewriting and memorising.

When school finished, everyone worked. There were a few parties, I found our bucket list hidden in Beau's tool bag, and we celebrated Amberley's eighteenth—so not much studying happened in the first few days.

I went riding with Hunter again, which was fun.

As we climbed a dirt track, he shouted, "You still trying to get high off cough syrup?"

I staggered on my bike. "Cough syrup? Oh, you mean when we met? You know, I gotta tell ya, I don't do that. It's kind of gross."

"Then why'd I catch you stealing some?" he asked.

"My friend, he's in the drug business," I laughed. "Needed a kick or something. I have quick hands, so he asked if I could steal some."

"Well keep those hands away from Amberley! Quick hands … If I …" Hunter paused and began to ride ahead. "Are you two still camping at the beach?"

I shook my head. "Probably later, after the HSC. I think this weekend Amberley wants to visit some place that Kaitlin goes to."

"What kind of place?"

"Not sure. A company that looks after kids with disabilities," I shrugged. "It's like an hour's drive away. We'll get lunch, and she needs a break from studying. For someone who just found out they're alive and well, she's sure wasting it by studying all these hours."

Hunter rode up another mound. "You should be doing the same. Come on, I'll race you, Mr People Person!"

"I said that once!" I groaned.

Amberley's bike

The day after, Amberley and I left at eight. With a coffee holding my eyes open, I got lectured on where we were going. In hindsight, we were volunteering for a charity called the Starlight Children's Foundation. They helped sick kids by entertaining them and giving them a moment to forget about their illnesses.

Through merging traffic and my anxious driving, we made it to the head office at nine. Inside, it smelt like a playground. The waiting room was designed like an orthodontist, very clean and comfortable.

Amberley strutted to the front desk as if she was visiting a friend. I tiptoed behind, admiring the colourful walls; they had a happy hospital vibe. While she talked to the receptionist, Amberley mentioned that Cassandra had signed us up for the Starlight Express Rooms. From there, we were tossed into a van and driven to the closest hospital.

When we approached the main building, I whispered to Amberley, "You can't seem to get away from these places, can you?"

"Shush," Amberley smiled. "Maybe I want to help people. Especially those who are experiencing what I've been through."

"Amberley, what are we doing exactly?" I asked.

"You'll see. Trust me! It'll be fun."

The van stopped at the hospital's side and waiting outside was Cassandra. She gave Amberley a hug and was so glad that we had finally come to visit.

It turned out that on every Monday she finished work early to volunteer for this foundation. As she explained this, we followed her into a hallway, up a ramp and into a large playroom. It was filled with beanbags, televisions, tables with paints and colouring pencils, pillows, blankets, toys, picture books, drawings, a ukulele and all sorts of other fun things. In between the chaos, six little kids no older than eleven ran rampant.

As Cass introduced us, all of the kids said hi, except for one. He was a little boy with no hair and hazel-coloured eyes.

Amberley and I wandered around, talking to the children. I played FIFA on an Xbox with Maggie, a seven-year-old girl who had been in a wheelchair since last year. She told me that she loved soccer and would stay up every year 'til three in the morning to watch the World Cup with her father.

There was Lenny, who was six. He liked magic and decided to show me all these different card tricks. Poor kid had Tourette syndrome, so every time he would reveal my card, he would yell *bicycle*.

There was ten-year-old Jasmine, who was mute, and eleven-year-old Lawrence, who had juvenile Parkinsonism. Kaitlyn was there, showing the two how to draw a cartoon dog.

Behind everyone, the hazel-eyed boy sat alone with the ukulele, trying to play it. But no matter how many times he strummed its strings, there was never a single sound. I asked Cassandra if there was a guitar nearby. She led me to the adult's room, wondering what I had planned.

I shrugged, "I'm gonna teach the little guy at the back how to strum."

As I approached him, the boy glanced at me.

I waved. "Hey, can I sit with you? Is the beanbag taken?"

He pointed at himself.

"Yes, you," I nodded. "You look a little lonely." The boy squinted at me. "Have you ever played before?"

After a few awkward pauses, he told me his name was Harry. He was five, the youngest here, and it was only recently that Harry had lost his hair from chemotherapy.

I changed the topic and continued to play with him until our four hours were up. Although I was no professional at playing the ukulele, watching that boy smile when he could strum a C major was like nothing else.

Then it was time to leave. Harry said thank you and told me he would keep practising so that the next time I visited he would be just as good as me.

I kneeled down and smiled. "By the time I see you again, you'll be better than me, Harry."

"I'm going to practise every day, and for my wish, I'm going to get a guitar."

I laughed with him. It was damn hard not to cry. Finally, I stood and told him that he should always do the things that make him smile.

Amberley hugged me as we walked to the van. "That little boy really liked you."

I put my arms around her. "He did. Why'd you want to do this?"

"I already told you, Tye. To help others."

I rolled my eyes. "How'd we help those kids? I read one a book, played FIFA, drew, painted, and what? Played the guitar. How does that help?"

Amberley pushed me aside. "Because we went there to distract me from worrying about the exams. And instead of them worrying about their disability or dying, they were allowed to laugh and have fun. That little boy will never forget about what you did. That's why I wanted to come here. To help the people who are going through what I've experienced."

I held her again, stumbling into the van and sitting. "Fair point. Have you ever thought about becoming a doctor? You do bio and chemistry—you could practically be a lecturer at university if you wanted to."

Amberley shrugged with a smile. "I don't think I'm smart enough to be a doctor." Her eyes widened, "Crap! Bio! I haven't even looked at my biology papers. I'm so screwed for the exams."

"Don't say that, Am!" I rubbed her shoulder. "They'll be over before you know it. We'll pass them with flying colours. All ninety per cent, you'll see."

Finished

Argh, my fingers!

With a minute to go and two sentences left, my stupid religion exam was almost over! I was writing and writing, and the elderly lady at the front kept sipping her water. Finally, she said the magic words. "Pens down!"

Holy crap, I had finished. That was my last examination, and I hadn't completed my essay. It was the first test out of the six where I hadn't filled out every question. But who cared? I was done.

Amberley was in a second room, still writing away. I signed the last few papers, wrote my student number and exited the classroom.

Reaching the outside, it was like nothing I had ever experienced before. The noises of reality rushed through my ears, and I felt every sound blast against me as if they were a heartbeat pounding with no rhythm. But even though I had finished, I didn't feel that different. There was no weight lifted from my shoulders, no revelation as to who I was, and nothing life changing. I felt normal! Excited to sleep, sure, and to not worry about studying for tomorrow's exam, but something was missing.

I asked Alley and Josh how they went, and they were both surprised by how reasonable the test was. I agreed that it wasn't all that hard. But after thirteen years of learning, listening, writing and studying, I felt as though my time had been wasted.

As she approached me with a smile on her face, it seemed Amberley had experienced a different feeling. I spread my arms, and she ran into me like a bullet. Almost gave me heartburn!

As her head rested against my chest, she whispered, "We're done, we're done. We're finished, we're done!"

I leaned my head on top of hers. "How'd you go?"

"It was easy. I was so worried, but that was like the easiest test throughout the whole period." She paused, watching the sky. "What are we going to do now?"

I shrugged, and after talking to everyone else who had finished their exams, things kind of ended unceremoniously. It was like a deflated balloon that had been loosened over an emotional and elongated period that was hyped up to be something extraordinary. Or at least something along those lines.

When I drove Jess through the school's exit, I did feel a sense of relaxation.

Amberley lifted her left foot onto the passenger seat so that her knee was bent against her chest. She glanced at the windscreen. "What to do, what to do, what to do?"

"Do you have something in mind?" I asked.

She shook her head. "No, I don't. I'm a little overwhelmed, to be honest. Don't laugh, but I'm lost for words. We're finished …" She stared at the dirt beneath her chair. "Do you still want to visit your mum? Maybe, tomorrow?"

"Don't start," I spat. "I know she left the address and all, but she's moved on. Maybe we'll go sometime in the new year." Noticing Amberley's silent gaze, I couldn't help but smile. "Wow, you are out of it. And anyway, we have to see McNeill tomorrow to get your results. I asked your mum to rebook the check-up so we could go in the morning and do something afterwards."

"You did?" Amberley's voice cracked. "Thanks, Tye. Good thinking."

"I'm not just good looks, you know. I've got a brain. A real smart one."

"*Smart*'s a word I'd use softly," mused Amberley, her left brow falling.

I grabbed my chest. "Argh! You might hurt my feelings. Well, if you're so smart, what do you want to do? We have all the time in the world."

She leaned back in her chair. "Wanna go bowling? I don't think we've ever done that, and we can drop by the service station, get some snacks and go for a walk afterwards."

"Bowling?" I pondered. "Deal. We can get a discount from Beverage, if he's working, and go to some lookout nearby."

"Sounds like a plan." Amberley giggled, "Is Beverage that tall Indian guy with the spiky hair?"

"Yep, the one at Blaxland."

"Why do they call him Beverage? Does he always have a drink on hand?"

I shook my head. "No, that's his last name. He does love his bags, though!"

"Bags?"

"Cocai—ah, don't worry about it." I waved away Amberley's curiosity. "He's a cool guy. Once you're friends with him, he'll always have your back."

Amberley leaned on her palm, admiring the view from her side window. "Do you want to invite Cameron? I haven't seen him in a while."

"No, he's good." I focused on the road. "He's renovating his place with Haley. I'm going to visit him next week at my dad's garage."

Talking about Dad's garage got me thinking. Now, Amberley was a good person, and I would never put her in harm's way, but I wanted to do something thrilling.

I grinned at her "Do you want to do something stupid? It's not dangerous, but if it's still there, are you up for it?"

Amberley tilted her head. "And what would that be?"

Again, I laughed. "Don't worry. It'll be fun. I want to show you my dad's garage. He kept some cool stuff in there, and Cameron and I store a few things there too."

"Okay. I'm in. But if I get in trouble, mister, I'll ..." She crossed her arms, deep in thought. "I won't go near you for a whole month. Won't even touch you!"

"What does that mean?" I gasped. "No, Am. I don't believe you! You won't be able to—I'm too good."

"You would think that." She rolled her eyes. "But I can do it. You're clingy. And horny. You won't even last a week without me."

My mouth dropped as I tried my hardest not to laugh. "You're on. But only if I get us in trouble, which I won't. I promise. What's the worst that could happen?"

"To love is to recognise yourself in another."

ECKHART TOLLE.

Handprints

A full moon glimmered over Dad's garage as I pushed open its metal roll-a-door. The sound from its clatter vibrated across my arms as Amberley ducked under, stepping inside. *I swear, that girl was not afraid of anything!*

I followed her, closing the door and snatching up the papers that were still on the ground. They had been here since the day I tried to hang myself.

Amberley's voice echoed, "It's so dark in here."

I reached for a small rope and pulled it down, lighting the room. "Sorry about that." When I reached the centre of the room, I shrugged. "So ... What do you think?"

Staring at the walls, Amberley smiled. "I think you don't clean in here very often. It's ... cosy!"

"You really think so? I always thought it kind of smelt."

Amberley laughed, "It does stink! But it's got a humble feeling to it. We could get a cheap couch, maybe a TV, an old record player or a stereo, a big fish tank at the back, maybe a portable barbecue, some pans."

As she waltzed around the room, I stumbled onto my scrunched-up birth certificate. It was still staining the floor like a poison.

"I could paint the walls, and you could fix up the bricks at the back." Amberley looked at me and paused. "Okay, it'll take some time, but ..." I felt her hand around my wrist. "What's wrong? Tye?"

Lifting the certificate from the floor, I froze.

Amberley leaned over to investigate the paper. "Huh? Your middle name is Roger."

"Yeah," I sighed. "It's my dad's name. My folks weren't too creative when it came to names." I pulled the certificate away from my eyes and focused on Amberley. "I like the fish tank idea. We could get a really cheap big one somewhere ..." I turned to the exit. "Let's get some fresh air. We can come back and draw out where you want to put everything. Good idea?"

Amberley nodded, "Fine by me. We need some chalk though. Want to go to the shops?"

"Soon," I lifted the door. "I want to show you something else."

I didn't lock the garage when Amberley and I wandered down the sidewalk, passing the new apartments. She kept asking where we were going, if it was a surprise like a big fluffy teddy bear, or if it was food.

I shrugged, "It's something to remember."

She glared at me. "So I can take a photo of it?"

"If you want. I haven't seen it in a while; it might look nice. I just thought it'd be cool." The small gap between the fence and the gate was next to us, hiding in plain sight. I ducked under the chain lock. "Come on, this way."

Amberley took a step back, "What are you doing?"

I lifted my head from the other side. "Entering a dangerous construction site. Hey, don't look at me like that—it'll be fun! And I did warn you beforehand, so don't blame me, Am."

She was frozen still.

I began walking away from the fence. "You coming?"

With a stomp and some hesitation, Amberley ducked her head in a dramatic fashion. "Fine. But I'm only coming to protect you. I swear to god, if we get caught, I'm going to ignore you for a week!"

"It's better than not touching me," I chuckled. "I can live with that. Nah, I'll just annoy you."

"Ignoring means I won't go near you; I won't even respond when you ask me a question." I gave her a hand as she shimmied under the fence. "It's like you won't even know me!" she said. "I'll be a complete stranger."

I tilted my head. "Sorry, who are you? My bad, you shouldn't be here, this is a dangerous hazardous site. You could get hurt, little lady."

"*Little lady!*" Amberley folded her arms. "I'm actually the manager of this so-called hazardous site. So please, a little respect. I can get you fired."

I chuckled, guiding her to the wall of painted handprints. "Sure thing. *Pssh, manager?* I have a boss, Phil—I don't know no manager. You can talk to him, lady. I got man things to do, like you know, bricklaying and stuff."

Amberley reached my side with a grim stare. "You, doing man things. Look at yourself. You wouldn't even be able to pick me up from the ground. I'll have to talk to Phil and get you fired. That's a great—*Whoa!*"

Hugging her waist, I tossed Amberley over my shoulder. "I did it! See, I picked you up! All right, time for a little detour."

Amberley begged me to put her down, but I held on. She started giggling—I was just so *manly!* Finally, I made it to the wall and gently dropped her to the soil.

"Here you go, pretty lady. Hope you liked the tour. I've got five more of these in the next ten, so have a minute to catch your breath, and we'll be on our way."

Amberley caught herself and smiled, pushing her arms against my chest like she was some sort of monkey. A cute monkey! And as she pushed her head into me, I told her to look up at the wall. In all my time knowing Amberley, I don't think I had ever seen her light up so quickly.

The wall was covered in several-sized handprints, each a different colour. The hands were distinct, sporadically placed along the wall's patterned bricks, and for some reason its centre was empty.

While Amberley's jaw dropped, I found a can of white paint. And before she could tell me otherwise, I dumped my left hand, covering the whole thing in a white slush.

"Why'd you do that, silly?" Amberley laughed.

I looked at her and then the wall, the paint dripping down my wrist. "Why do you think, silly? Let's join in."

As I approached the wall, Amberley submerged her right hand into the paint. We stood side by side.

"I get you. It's pretty amazing," Amberley said.

I smacked my white hand onto the wall's centre. "I would have said cool. It's funny how all these people have snuck in here just to put their handprint on this wall."

Amberley placed her hand next to mine. "What? Like you and me? Huh, look." She pointed at the wall. "We're the only white handprints. Isn't it a bit rude to put ours in the middle? No one else did."

I sniffed, "You didn't have to put yours next to mine."

"I only put my hand next to yours because I was following your lead!" Her face went red. "I'm out of my comfort zone, okay? There was a lot of pressure an——"

"Don't worry, Am. I was joking. I think you've been hanging out with me for too long. You're talking too much." I grabbed her hand, pulling her away from the wall. "Let's go check out the view and find some water."

When we walked up to the building's roof, Amberley sighed. "Do you think they'll pull down the wall?"

"I'm not sure. It's kind of a big deal around here. I think a lot of people would get angry if they did. No one likes anger, you know?"

"I'm not a fan of anger." Amberley stared at the darkness behind me. "Look at all that room."

I glanced up to find the scaffolding of timber pillars standing tall, outlining the soon-to-be walls of each apartment. The smell of pine lingered within each room, each rectangular prism for a bathroom and each cubical for a cupboard.

I stumbled up a step. "They're gonna be pretty big rooms once they're finished."

"Maybe we could buy one. Together."

"Here?" I jolted. "I thought you'd be the kind of girl who would want a cosy cottage out in the middle of nowhere, near a dazzling waterfall. But not too far from civilisation, of course."

We exited the stairway, and the colours of midnight sparkled all around. Amberley took in the view. "You're not wrong. I'd much prefer a little house to call my own, somewhere in a field of happiness. Where I could have a garden, go for walks, maybe watch the snow in the winter. But for now—for Mum and Dad's sake—I just want to move out and live in an apartment. Hopefully the rent's not awful, but it wouldn't matter if my roommate was kind."

I leaned on a concrete bannister. "Who said you'd be living with a roommate? I thought that little *we should buy an apartment* was an invitation. That if we saved up for the next month, the next six, the next year, that maybe we'd have enough to move out of your parent's house. Be a little more independent, huh? I'd like that."

Amberley put her hands around my neck. "Who said it was an invitation? I love the idea." She paused, and the reflection of the stars shined in her eyes. As I smiled, those starlight reflections met my bewildered face. "I'm glad I talked to you, Tyler. You get me."

"I'm glad you asked to sit with me." I held her close. "The sad thing is, if you hadn't, I don't think I would ever be as happy as I am now. I don't even think I'd be here."

"I'm glad you're still here." She smiled, "Do you feel it? That warmness, that tender thrill inside of you. It's like a rush of excitement all at once, but when I'm with you, it's always there."

"I feel it." Resting my forehead on hers, I closed my eyes. "It hurts to not feel sad sometimes. I'm getting used to it though. Thank you." I grabbed her white-covered hand and laughed. "Amberley, your hand's not cold! It's warmer than mine."

Amberley tugged on my fingers. "Thank me? I should thank you." She giggled, "We talk too much. I love you, Tyler!"

My heart jumped. "I love you too."

We held each other, swaying under the stars above the handprints of the many who had fallen in love like us. And as we sat and admired our home, talking endlessly about nothing, I knew that I would never forget this night.

Summer Times

It was ten o'clock, and Amberley and I had been waiting for almost an hour. Apparently, McNeill's husband had an emergency, and he wasn't around when our appointment was booked.

When he finally arrived, I had already drunk two coffees. He took us aside, into a room that wasn't his office, and unfolded a suspicious form from his pocket.

"Sorry, I'm late," he said. "It's been a rough morning!"

Amberley ignored the papers and smiled. "We don't mind. Can I ask what happened?"

"It's fine, M.B. My husband's just a pain." McNeill looked over the forms. "He uh—well, I woke up to a phone call. He was in jail. I had to fill in paperwork and pay for his bail. It took all morning. So, sorry again. I know these results are important, but there's no need to worry. According to this, you're better than ever. One second." McNeill scanned through the details on Amberley's pathology report. He read each word as if he were a mind-reader at a circus.

"It's better than what I had thought." He smiled, "Your whole system's repaired itself; it's almost a miracle. I don't want to be too positive, but I've never seen anyone recover so fast from anything, let alone sepsis. Amberley, you're fine. Of course, we'll have to continue our fortnightly check-ups, but I'm happy to say you're perfect. My advice, get a good night's rest, a healthy lunch with Tyler and enjoy the next rest of your life. Don't spare a minute!"

Amberley was speechless; her jaw almost dropped from her cheeks. She hugged McNeill like an uncle and thanked him for the good news.

When they finished, I asked if I could see the results.

McNeill waved me away. "Not now, Tye. I just got them myself; they still have to be put into Amberley's file, sorted through, assessed—a whole process, you understand? But once I've finished doing that, you'll be the first person I give them to. I promise!"

I nodded, "Deal. Thanks for the good news. Same time in two weeks?"

"Make it for the new year." He pointed at me, "Have some time off—go on a holiday, enjoy yourselves. I'll see you in January."

We didn't see him until February, a whole three months after that check-up. And again, he said the same thing as if he was reading from the exact same results.

From the moment she discovered the good news, Amberley was almost a different person. She still had adventure deep inside her heart, but the way she approached things was off.

The end of November was Monte's birthday. The family got him a new chew toy that squeaked a hundred times a day. I got a licence to serve alcohol and ended up quitting the pizzeria to work at a bar. My first shift, Amberley's parents purposefully ate at the pub for lunch. I had to make them cocktails.

After that, Amberley and I went on a three-day hike, just me, her and a two-man tent. *Boy, was that a blast!* The last day, she slipped and fell, and when I helped her up, I could have sworn she had broken her wrist. After some X-rays, the doctor told us that she was incredibly lucky and that nothing was broken. Her arm did swell, but that was because she was still weak after recovering from her reliance on medication.

By Christmas, she was taking one tablet a day, instead of three to four.

Speaking of Christmas, the Gibbons have a huge Christmas tree, nine feet tall apparently. It took Hunter and me two hours to set up and another hour with Amberley to decorate.

We also had our Year Twelve formal. I don't remember when, sometime in October, maybe November. It was okay. The food tasted great and dancing sober was fun, but it was cut short so the conference room could kick us out by ten. I noticed how crappy people were at formally eating, not putting their knife and fork aside when they were done with their meals.

I sat with Amberley and Xander, who didn't have a date. He hung out with me for most of the night and was welcomed by the rest of our table. You could smell Jake's sweat when he stumbled to get his blazer. Everyone from my year group was smiling, and admittedly, I was going to miss every single one of them.

After the formal, Amberley and I went to Crouchy's for drinks and managed to make a cosy bed in Jess' tray. *Who knew what you could do with a second-hand mattress and a pop-up gazebo?*

On Christmas Eve, I took Amberley clubbing. We got smashed at this nightclub where the music was loud, and the bar smelt of vodka. Cameron was there with Haley. For some reason, Haley was really nice and not crazy; it was as if she had never done a drug in her life. Like, she called me Tyler, not *Tye-Tye*. She even took Amberley to the bathroom and held her drinks. And I couldn't have been that drunk, so I asked Cameron what was up.

"With Haley?" He shrugged, "She's trying to make a good impression. She really wanted to meet Amberley. But it's not just her. Hay's acting odd. She's trying to be, like, *deep* with me. She bought me a gift the other day! It's like she's actually being my girlfriend." He laughed, "An' get this, it's been two weeks since she last tried to kill me!"

"I gotta admit, I kind of like it," I smiled. "It's a good change. I'm happy for you. You never know, maybe she'll stay like this?"

"Maybe." Cameron sniggered, "Kev's more cautious now; he had some trouble last month with the cops. I think Hay's got her head out of the game. So maybe it is a Merry Christmas after all!"

Christmas Day was amazing! All of Amberley's family visited us for lunch, and there was a lot of laughing, smiling, eating, opening gifts and drinking. You could feel the joy from inside the house.

For Boxing Day, things remained joyful. Amberley and I met up with old friends from school, like Toby and Bronte. We spent the whole day relaxing in makeshift pools inside the trays of several utes and trucks, using plastic sheeting, ice and buckets of water.

New Year's Day arrived just as quickly, and instead of a party, Amberley and I went to a little gathering at Georgia's house. We mingled with the twelve people there and launched fireworks for the new year. One almost hit my face! Georgia's house had this fantastic view of the city in the far distance, and I was lucky enough to get a New Year's kiss.

Happy New Year!

January started with a bang—a warm bang. It was so hot we decided to visit a waterhole. Surprisingly, not many tourists were there. Amberley and I had the whole place to ourselves towards the end of the afternoon. Sitting in the hole, the water was freezing, but I couldn't get enough of it.

On the tenth, Amberley's parents took us on a holiday. We spent three weeks road-tripping, visiting white beaches with the most transparent water, and four-wheel-driving up sand dunes and rocky tracks. Every day was a day that I would live a thousand times over if I could.

Hunter and I caught this mighty big lizard the length of most of my torso. I learnt how to cook vindaloo curry and spaghetti with Tegan. It all tasted so divine, and afterwards, she showed me some old family videos. There were so many!

Amberley was struggling to get a new job. It's not easy when everywhere you approach seems to already have a hundred people employed. She had a lot on her plate, still learning to drive, needing money for a car and university enrolments. I told her I would pay for what she needed, but she refused. The good news was that we both had been offered university courses. We found out in December, but now it was official as I was completing my timetable.

There was so much paperwork, and I still had to do my taxes. Fortunately, Tegan helped with each step, finalising the numbers. On the downside, Amberley and I weren't going to the same campus. We still had similar timetables, and both our campuses were in the city, so we got to catch the train together every Tuesday, Wednesday and Thursday.

Once my taxes were done, and university orientation was over in February, things slowed down. The waiting room at the hospital was as despicable as always. Thankfully, McNeill wasn't late this time. He escorted us into his office with a smile as if he were excited to see us. But we knew where this check-up was going.

Amberley was fine.

After his little talk, he asked me to stay in his office.

When Amberley had left, I asked, "What is it?"

"Tyler, after all we've been through," McNeill grimaced. "I thought we were friends."

"Never said we were. It's just every time you ask to talk one on one, you bring up something that annoys me." I sighed, "It's about my mum, isn't it?"

He stared at the floor. "Sort of. You seem like someone who—through no fault of your own—ends up more deprived than others. I was wondering, that's all, but were you depressed before I met you? I'm not saying you are now—in fact, you seem happy. However, mental health conditions can stem deeply and may last subconsciously for years. I don't want you to fall apart if something were to break. Have you had any worrying thoughts, any moments where ——"

"You know, Doc, I consider your worries as enlightening." I picked at the sleep in my eye. "But you're no Dalai Lama. I'm sure if I were depressed or if I were having irrational thoughts that are worrying, you'd be the first person I'd tell. But I'm quite positive I can deal with it. Thanks for the concern, though, it means the world. Catch ya next month." I stormed out of the room.

I wonder what he meant by all that? I thought I'd hidden it well back in the day.

¶

The moments where you can just lay in bed are the best! Especially when you're next to someone you love.

It was nearing the end of February, a cooler period in comparison to the summer. Autumn was upon us and the leaves behind Amberley's curtain were turning red.

I rested my head on a cushioning pillow, smelling an all too familiar scent that made me tender inside. Feeling the softness of the bedsheet against my naked body, Amberley and I hid from the morning light. The sunrise was almost pink in the sky—a perfect day for later.

For now, I just wanted to hug the person who was next to me and never let go!

She always sniffled in her sleep like a bunny curious about a carrot. A weird way of describing it, I know, but similes don't do it justice. Before Amberley, I had no one, but now that she was here, I sometimes forgot how fortunate I was.

As I wrapped my arms around her, she clung to my forearm, opening her eyes.

"You're up early." She stretched, turning towards me so that we were face to face. I could feel her morning breath. "I had fun last night."

I grinned, "Me too."

"How long have you been up?"

"Half an hour."

Amberley gasped, "Why didn't you wake me?"

"'Cause you were too cute." I laughed, "I didn't want to disturb you. And I wanted to just lay in bed. Do nothing."

"Nothing sounds great!" She rested her head against me, watching the ceiling. "Tye, let's get away to the beach for a few days. I know it's out of the blue, but with university in a few days and the orientation, plus looking for a job, I'm buggered. Let's do nothing while we can."

I leaned against my elbow. "Okay, we can leave Monday, spend three days and come back. I just have to let work know."

"Is Monday the first?" she asked.

"Yep, a good way to start March. We can watch the sunrise; we haven't done that one yet."

Amberley giggled, "No, we haven't. We've been on a rollercoaster, but we certainly haven't done that." She stared into my eyes. "This is nice. Just laying here."

"Like I said." I smiled, "It's the best to do nothing. Nothing at all!"

> "It's better to have a short life that is full of what you like doing, than a long life spent in a miserable way."

ALAN WATTS

Nothing

The first day of March was—in no exaggeration—a perfect day!

You could taste the humidity as Tegan gave Amberley a big hug. She kissed her daughter a hundred times, acting like this was the first time we were going out by ourselves.

As a breeze swept through the Gibbons' front yard, Hunter asked me to take extra care of Amberley. For a second, they wouldn't let us leave.

Tegan hugged me. "Have lots of water and don't forget to fill up. Here, we'll give you sixty just in case."

I palmed the money aside. "Don't worry, Tegan. We'll be fine. I've got enough money to get us there and back safely."

She scrunched the notes into my hand. "Take it, Tyler. I insist. It's the least we can do. Everyone needs support. Isn't that right, honey?"

"You bet," Hunter straightened his posture. "You two have fun and take some nice photos. I want a panorama of the sunrise and the waves breaking on the beach."

Amberley and I dropped our eyebrows, surprised by the request.

"*What?*" Hunter said. "Our account needs a new cover photo, all right?"

Amberley laughed, "Don't worry, we're on it! Do you want me to write your names in the sand, really put you in the photo?"

Tegan rolled her eyes. "Ignore him; don't worry about us. Text me as soon as you get there. And don't forget to call. Gosh, I don't know what I'm going to do with myself."

"You know we went hiking like a month ago?" I frowned. "We'll be back before you know it. Here's an idea, why don't you guys go out for lunch while we're gone?"

Tegan smiled, thanking me for the suggestion, and it was finally time to leave.

Jess was packed, our shoes were on, and I was craving a swim. As Amberley's parents waved goodbye, Amberley screamed out the side window that she loved them.

We left early, so there wasn't as much traffic down the motorway. The air smelt fresh, we had a good playlist on, and the drive north was beautiful. You could really take in the scenery, especially the way we went.

We took a longer route around a busy road because I didn't like driving through heavy traffic. And without teasing me, Amberley supported my decision.

I couldn't explain why—maybe I was monologuing—but I began to talk nonsense. "That's one of the best parts about you."

"What do you mean?" giggled Amberley.

"You didn't argue just then," I said. "Most people would have whinged or forced me to go the quicker way so we could get to the beach faster. But you didn't."

"Tye, why would I? You've done so much more for me. You waited day by day at the hospital. Of course I'm going to respect your decision."

"I know, I'm just saying things." I smiled. "A lot of people aren't like that. It's one of the reasons why I love you. Like driving to the Foundation—'member that? I was so nervous; I just didn't want to tell you."

"Aww!" She put her hand on my leg. "When I get my reds, I'll drive you wherever you want to go."

I couldn't help but laugh. "You don't have to. I'm serious. I think I'm just feeling honest today."

"Honesty's the best philosophy!" Amberley mused.

I was caught off guard. "Is that really the saying?"

"Nope." She shook her head. "I changed it. It's weirder like that."

We arrived at Putty Beach just before midday. The sun was still beaming, the wind was almost perfect, and the water was pleasant. We had an esky full of ice with water, ciders and beer. As I carried it through the sand, tonnes of people and several dogs ran past empty campsites and dried seaweed. Finger-sized holes peeped from the driest sand and towards the water—where it was easier to walk— footprints lay scattered and confused.

We walked for ages, talking about nothing. My arm almost tore off from the esky's weight, but fortunately, Amberley found an empty inlet behind a mountain.

Amberley and I both wore white, setting up camp for the day. A subtle breeze caressed the cove from time to time, ploughing against my button-up. We didn't put up a tent and there was no portable cooker, just a crappy chequered mat and some popup chairs.

Weaving my feet through the cold shoreline, the water was beautiful. Even the taste of the salt seemed sweet when Amberley and I swam. And as we jumped the incoming waves, whether they were a metre high or a few inches, time disappeared with the tide.

To the left of our inlet, there were rocks between the crashing rapids. I helped Amberley with the climb as she was having trouble breathing again. We found several colourful crabs between several boulders, and there was an abundance of shells.

Amberley picked up the largest shell she could find—it was worthy of an ad—and put it against her ear. She giggled, waving me over. "Tye, come listen."

I joined her, holding the shell against my ear and hearing the serenity of a thousand waves.

"A souvenir?" she asked.

"If you want. Either way, I'll remember it!"

"I never said I'd forget." Amberley snatched the shell from my grasp. "I have a better memory than you. We'll keep it. It'll be in your bag, okay?"

I offered her my hand. "Let's reach the top. Could be a nice view."

After the shell was packed, I led the way up a rock face, and when we reached the top, the water looked so still. The sun was setting as clouds of pink confused the daylight. Many stars gleamed, and behind them, a full moon began to rise.

I sat, dangling my legs. Amberley joined me, our knees together, and our shoulders side by side. I wrapped my right arm around her.

"Smile!" said Amberley.

A flash stunned my eyes.

My hair was still sandy and stiff from the ocean, but even though I wasn't ready, Amberley's photo came out perfectly.

I pressed my forehead against her temple. "I can't be bothered setting up a tent—but we should probably do it. Get it over and done with, I agree."

Amberley laughed, "I didn't say anything to agree with."

"But you would have said something like …" I raised my voice, mimicking Amberley, "*If we do it first, then we can go do better things with our time afterwards.*"

"I don't …" She sniffled, avoiding my eyes. "Okay, that does sound like me, but we're up here at the moment. Worry about the tent later." She rested her head against my shoulder, "So this is nothing? Wouldn't life be nice if it was always this quiet? No due dates, no paperwork, no problems, no headaches, no worries … No knowing."

"What does that mean?"

Amberley sighed, "People know too much. They know about medicine, they know about art, societies and education; they know about many things. Sepsis!"

"Do you wish you never knew? About dying?" I asked.

She looked at me. "Sometimes. But then I would never have met you."

"No." I bit my lip. "I think we were always going to meet. If not in this life, then in heaven. 'Cause I know things."

Amberley whispered, "Like what? About dying? Heaven?"

"No, not heaven. I know that life isn't a journey, and that right now, I'm the happiest I've ever been. There's not a single bad part in my life. And my mum deserted me, my best friend's stuck selling drugs and I don't have a home."

Amberley lifted her head. "Do you need me to be your home? Because I can do that!"

"That'd be wonderful," I chuckled. "Come on, we gotta set up tonight's home before it's too late."

It took us almost an hour to return to the inlet. We had to go the long way, passing Jess so we could grab the camping gear. By the time everything was set up, I was two beers down, yet completely sober.

It was nine at night and the stars watched us watch them. I laid next to Amberley with her legs crossed on top of a mat. She played with her oily hair. "It's been a while, you and me. I can't even recall when you didn't talk."

"True," I laughed. "Just over a year now. When we first met, oh, boy! I thought you were the most bizarre girl. You were sad, but you hid it from everyone. And then how you said hey to me outside of class with Xander. You confused me."

"I confused you?" Amberley scoffed. "You were the biggest mystery. Everyone knew who you were, everyone talked about you as if you hung out with Jake and all those boys, and you always sat by yourself. And the most random people knew you—you got around! I only heard you talk once in class and it sounded like you were angry at everything." Amberley took a deep breath. "Do you know why I thought you were sad?"

215

I shook my head. "Nope. Was it my blossoming attitude?"

Amberley giggled, "Blossoming? No. I once—when things were really bad—I caught you staring at me. You had this fragile look on your face like the world was a burden to you. It was when I used to sit by myself next to that little hedge. I had found out that my illness was getting worse, and my old friends back home kept texting me, and I felt so bad ignoring them. I wanted my goodbye at home to be my last memory with them. Not a moment of farewell because I was dying, but a goodbye as in, *I'll see you again one day*. And being new in a place that's unfamiliar, it's hard. It's depressing! I felt lonely, even though I was surrounded by lots of friendly people. And when I saw you, I realised that you were the only person who knew what I was feeling. So I asked to sit with you, not because I could see you were sad, but because I ... I wanted to talk to someone who understood what I was feeling."

I was speechless. "I never knew," I uttered. "Gosh, I'm blushing. I don't have a story as to why I said yes. I didn't think; you asked, and I let you. The first few times, no matter what we talked about, I tried not to cry." I stood, letting the breeze cool my face. "But look at us now, Am! All that bad stuff, all the bullshit and unluckiness, I'm glad I went through it! Because if I hadn't, I would never have met you. And I would never have walked down that track and watched you smile under that waterfall." I dropped to her side, putting a hand on her thigh. My bent leg was between hers, our faces were now nose to nose, and my smile was as big as the cove we camped in. "Just seeing you makes me happy," I whispered. "And if I were to do nothing with anybody, I'd always pick you."

She leaned in closer. "For that matter, I'll need to tell you something silly. I like waking up next to you, it's a good feeling."

"What kind of good feeling?"

She bit her lips, and inhaled, "Love, curiosity, joy, thri..."

We kissed for a moment, not a single thought between us, only a warmness inside my belly.

Besides kissing, we talked more. Whether it was university,

work, Cameron, school days, regrets, ourselves—we never stopped. Even past midnight, the conversation continued as the stars began to fade. Heck, we didn't need the tent, we weren't planning on sleeping.

The sun was about to rise, and Amberley was telling me about her old hometown, the Northern Beaches. "We should visit," said Amberley. "It's only two hours from the mountains; we could go for a day. You could meet heaps of my friends. Do you want to do it?"

I widened my eyes. "It sounds great. I'd love to meet everyone!"

"Then it's official. Are you going to write it down?"

"Write it?" I asked.

"The bucket list, Tye! We're still doing it, aren't we?"

"I suppose. We haven't looked at it in months."

Amberley had a cheeky grin.

"*What?*" I laughed. "Did you bring it?"

"Yeah …" She lost her smile. "Oh crud, I left it in the car. You wouldn't mind—No, I'll go get it!"

I pulled her to the mat as she jumped onto the sand. "Don't worry, I'll run over and get it. I get you, even though that was out of the blue."

"I'm out of the blue—have you met yourself?" Amberley murmured. "Are you sure you want to go alone?"

"I don't want to miss the sunrise. If I run there, I'll make it back in time, and we can cross it off. It's a special moment." I kissed her, "I love you."

She returned the kiss. "Love you too. Take your time. I can barely see it over the horizon. Don't miss me!"

I winked, "Miss you? *Please.* Crap, what time is it?"

"Ten past five."

"Phew, we have plenty of time." I waved goodbye, "See you soon."

"I love you!"

Skipping down the beach, I started laughing, "I love you too!"

When I reached Jess, I was breathless. My whole body was on fire as I searched the front seat for Beau's bag. Behind Amberley's seat, the bag was already unzipped. I put my hand inside and heaved until the list popped out, closing the ute's door.

Hmm, something tickled my leg.

Searching for a fly, I instead found two pieces of paper on the rubble. Lifting them up, I realised it was one of my surveys. The lightness of the paper drew me in as I could make out petite and round writing. It was Amberley's response! I ignored its words and folded it neatly into my pocket for a later date.

As I began walking back to our inlet, the sun began to rise from behind the horizon. *Nuts! I better get a move on.*

Trailing my feet through the white sand, a squeaking sound vibrated like I was cleaning a window. Soon enough, I felt a stinging sensation in my abdomen, and decided to walk the last few metres.

For some reason, the inlet was still pitch-black, even though the sun was now a semicircle.

I looked away from the sky and dropped the bucket list. My insides cried as if my heart was being beaten; my arms went limp, and in that second of seeing Amberley gasping for air, I sprinted a thousand steps. I kneeled by her struggling side, holding her in my lap. She had tears in her eyes, and she was croaking. Her body jolted again and again. *Her illness. It can't be?*

She was suffocating!

I held in my sorrow, holding back my tears. "No, no, no. Stay with me. Am, stay with me. Breathe slowly, just breathe. Slowly. That's it. Come on, we can get through this … Don't hold it, breathe. I'll breathe with you." I tried to breathe like her, but nothing was helping. I grabbed her hands, hoping they'd feel better from my touch. "It's going to be okay; I have you. I'll protect you. I-I'm here! We're going to wake up tomorrow, and it'll all be as if none of this happened. I'm not going to let go! Breathe slowly. Amberley, we can do it. I'm going to get you to the hospital, that's it! I'll carry you there."

I tried to lift her, but she grabbed my arm, forcing me down to the mat. "Am, no! Don't do this! I can't ... I can't live without you." Tears fell from my eyes, staining the sand and making it dark. I was shaking. "You're going to live. We're going to visit your hometown and watch the sunrise together and buy an apartment, and we'll be happy. Maybe we'll get married—that'd be fun. You'll overdo it and have everything perfect. We haven't done that yet. And I can't if you're not here!"

She whispered, struggling to speak. "It's ... okay ... I'm ... not ... scared ... anymore."

I pulled her closer, holding her in my arms. "Amberley. Please, don't! I don't want to live in a world without you! You're beautiful, perfect, amazing, and you bring out the best parts of me. We still have so much to do!"

The croaking vanished, and all that remained were her fixated eyes and her heavy chest as it struggled to rise.

I had been crying so much, drool began to drip from my mouth. "We're going to be okay! No matter what, I love you. Please don't ... Am? Amberley! No, no, please, no. *Amberley!* Don't do this. Please! Wake up! Amberley, get up. GET UP! *I need you.*"

Her chest stopped. With one last breath, her head fell onto the sand, and she watched the sun rise.

I held her cold hands in my own and felt empty once again.

Like nothing, she was gone!

"In the short term, you'll see a thunderstorm. Once the thunderstorm is over, you'll see flowers."

MAXIME LAGACÉ

The New Boy

It seemed as though the world was weeping under a thunderstorm that never fell. The clouds were not bubbly, they were merely grey, covering the darkest blue sky and a trail of fog that surrounded the chapel's front garden. I couldn't bring myself to join the procession as numerous people entered through a timber doorway. There were murmurs of apologies, condolences that made my heart burn.

As I leaned on a garden wall, the most peculiar people arrived. Like myself, Xander wore his formal suit; same with Jake, Toby, Nic and Crouchy. Emma brought a bouquet, and her family sat with Georgia's. Kaitlyn sobbed into her mother's side, and Cassandra had to fix her running mascara. Even a few teachers, like Mrs Mulhall and Mr Taccori, followed the funeral director. Behind them, Beverage dusted off his second-hand blazer that had a line of stitching along its left sleeve.

Cameron came after the coffin was carried inside. He offered me a cigarette, but Haley glared at him, forcing him to join her inside.

Last but not least, I overheard Doctor McNeill. "Fine. Stay out, but do come in. I don't feel well today. And no, you don't have to come to the wake! I just … I need you by my side, so hurry along. I don't think I'll make it past the eulogy."

He strutted, alone, past the flowerbeds. "Are you not coming in?" he asked. "You'll get cold hands."

I watched several ants darting around a dried piece of black chewing gum. "Why do you care? It's not even that cold."

McNeill placed a firm hand on my shoulder. "It's freezing, Tyler. It's the first cold day of autumn. You should go inside, sit with Tegan and Hunter."

I lifted my head, catching his gaze. "Don't talk to me!"

"Tyler," the doctor took a step back. "I don't want you to regret not being there. She meant a lot to both of us ——"

"I didn't lie to her! Not about liking her, not about helping her, and definitely not about her illness!" I raised my voice, "So piss off!"

"Tyler, I-I'm sorry," McNeill gulped. "I didn't ——"

"Just go away. *Please!*"

After a moment of silence, McNeill joined everyone else.

The doors closed and the procession began. The tender breeze played with my hair as another familiar voice spoke.

"*Cold hands, uncovering rich lands, in the sight of youth, through dreams, it depends, on what is truth.*"

I turned to see Kev in an all-black suit with a red rose pinned next to his tie.

"'Til this day, I do not know the author of that poem," said Kev. "But it's one of my favourites. A little inside quirk between the doctor and me." He smiled. "My condolences, Tyler. It seems the whole of the mountains is here today."

"The doctor …?" I sighed, "And what does it mean? The poem?"

"For another time. Now I'm not going to say it, but I saw you with her, more than once. And the way you acted, the way you looked, she meant the world to you. At least say goodbye." Patting my back, Kev snuck into the chapel.

It sounded as though Hunter was doing a decent job with the eulogy, sobbing at every second word. I sat there, with no will to move and no need to look at the chapel's doors. I just admired the many ants as they ran with red rose-petals and dried crumbles of candle wax.

When the funeral was over, I was gone.

All I remember was seeing that photo of Amberley inside the information brochure that was being handed out. Her beautiful smile, her perfect skin, her deep blue eyes. All in all, her pure happiness. Gone, to be printed on a piece of white paper.

I drove past the river where we first kissed. My feet forgot to let go of the accelerator, I was so shaken up. My eyelids felt heavy, my back was sore, and my face was so wet, I had become a waterfall.

When I returned to Dad's garage, the sliding door seemed extra heavy. *I wonder how the wake is going?* Why bother thinking about it?

The unit was still rotten with damaged walls, unused tools and so much dust—a plethora proud of pity. Upon the floor, Amberley had left markings, outlining in chalk all of the renovations we were going to do.

I dropped to my knees at the furthest corner and huddled myself into a ball. Smelling my own skin, I tasted my tears and held whatever remained warm inside my cradled body. As I cried, I saw her in my head, her smile replaying over and over again.

And then Cameron forced himself through the steel door, shining the night-time light into my face.

Cameron's voice wasn't surprised, it was disappointed. "So, this is where you've been! You missed the wake. Eh, I can't blame ya … Do you want to talk about it?"

I stared at my feet. "Was the food nice?"

"Yeah, it was really good. Freshly made cakes and bread rolls; there was butter chicken, pizza, all sorts of stuff! Wanna go for a walk? Get some fresh air?"

I shook my head. "I don't know. Why are you here? Where's Haley?"

"At home. She's organising something with Kev. Something about what Beverage did today." Cameron pointed at the back wall. "I just popped on over to fill up the stash."

I lifted my head, holding Cameron's attention. "The stash. Let me help you!"

"Of course, just keep putting in half your money from the pub, and we'll be out of here by June." Cameron smiled, "Maybe, if we're lucky, May!"

"No, I meant I want to work with you. I want to make as much as you do and help you." I stood, begging with both arms. "I quit the pub; I don't sleep right, I can't concentrate. I haven't even tried going to university, and I need to do something that doesn't remind me of … *her*. Ask Kev. I'll come with you tonight."

He pushed me back. "You don't want to get mixed up in my world. If you start working with Kev, you won't be able to get out. You're not thinkin' straight, Tye. You've hit a rough patch. Just wait a few days. Do your course, see how it makes you feel."

"It makes me feel sick, Cam!" I stomped the ground. "I can't stand it. I don't own much, I'm a good listener, I'll do whatever you say, or Kev, or even Haley. And if I'm by your side, we can protect each other."

He raised his brows. "Dude, you're not thinking clearly, trust me. I get it's hard at ——"

"*Hard!* My girlfriend died, Cameron. She's dead! My own mum left me, I don't own anything because it's all with Amberley's parents." I dropped to my knees, pulling at his shirt. "If I can't get this escape, I promise you. I will try to kill myself. And you will come into this room to see my blood on those walls and my corpse lifeless on the floor. I can't do it anymore! It hurts so much. I'm begging you, man. Please take me." I took a deep breath. "I don't want to be alone right now."

Cameron swore his mouth off, lifting me from the ground. "But you stay with me," he said. "Don't leave my side, Tye. Kev likes you, but if you really wanna do this, he won't be the same around you. Things are going to be different, an' you're not going to like the stuff he makes us do." Cameron turned to the exit. "One warning before we go. Don't whinge. Don't even talk back or ask questions. Just do what they say. Got it?"

When we arrived at Haley's apartment, I was amazed at how clean the hallways were.

Once Cameron knocked, Amber—I mean Haley, screamed, *piss off, I didn't order anything.* There was a lot of commotion and banging behind the door, and finally, she opened it for us.

"What'd I just …" Haley's eyes widened. "Cammy! Why didn't you say? Hey, Tye-Tye, where were you today? You weren't at the food thingy after the funeral."

Cameron tried to force himself into the apartment. "No, he wasn't! Is Kev still here?"

"Why do you wanna know, hun bun?"

"Is he here or not?" Cameron reiterated. "I'm not in the mood to play games, Hay!"

Haley squawked, "Don't scream at me, you son of a ——"

"Haley, let the man in!" Kev's stern voice growled from behind Haley. "He does live here, doesn't he?"

Pulling the door open, Haley rolled her eyes. "He only paid for half. It's *my* place!"

Inside was a tragedy. I thought Mum's house was dirty and rotten. The room was still standing, even though mould grew between the skirtings, and cockroaches sprinted from one side of the lounge room to the other. Empty sachets and broken plastic bags covered the floor. The kitchen bench had a chunk of laminate chipped from one of its corners, the couch looked as though a dog had gone mad with bite marks stretching its beige fabric, and lots of sock fluff was sprinkled throughout the carpet.

Kev stood, shaking my hand. "Good to see you, Tyler. What can I do for you, boys?"

I ordered, "I want a ——"

"Let me!" Cameron muttered. "He um … Kev … Tye needs, uh ——"

"Spit it out already!" ordered Kev.

"Tye needs a job," said Cameron. "*Can he work with me?* is what I'm askin'. I'll show him the ropes, deliveries, how to sell, what to do with the boys in blue. The works. He's a good listener, an' he'll work hard. But it's not a permanent thing, okay?"

Kev nodded, "Who said it would be? No, I can't trust him. Not after the morphine went south."

"But Kev!"

"Don't nag, Cameron!" Kev rubbed his chin, examining my face. "Do you want this, Tyler? Do you really want it?"

I clenched my fist, standing tall. "I do! I'm sorry about the morphine, Kev! I had it, the whole delivery. And if you let me work for you, it won't happen again, I promise! It was just Beau, and ——"

"Hush, hush, hush." Kev laughed, "No need to raise your voice. I like you, Tyler. And don't think I don't know about Beau—Cameron explained the situation. He's an old customer of mine. I'll pay him my respects later. For now, you'll have to prove yourself. Deal?"

"Deal."

Kev looked at Cameron. "You're his boss, Cameron. If he stuffs up, it's not just on him. It's on you! Understand?"

Cameron gulped, "Of course."

Smiling, Kev shook my hand again as if we had just signed a contract. "Well then, you're going to come with us tomorrow morning. We have some business, a little dilemma of sorts. I suppose it will provide some insight into what we plan to do to Beau."

I grinned with him, and Haley howled, "Yay, new boy. Tye-Tye's my very own new boy. Can I take him for a spin, Kev?"

"No, Haley, he's mine!" Cameron pushed her aside. "I'm lookin' after him, got it. And he's sleeping here, I'll pay for his food."

I grabbed his shoulder. "Don't worry about food. I got enough money for that. You watch my back, I'll watch yours."

"Get some rest, all of you." Kev stretched his back, "Tomorrow is going to be interesting. Very interesting!"

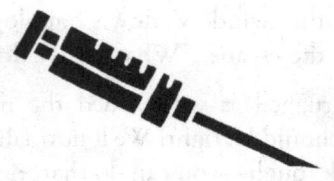

Day One

Like the heat of the sun, Cameron's palm burnt my cheek as if he thought I was dead. I was just sleeping, and the idiot started bossing me around before I could get the gunk from the side of my eyes.

Surprisingly, I was rather clean, covered in a worn-out blanket, an Adidas hoody and some track pants. From wall to wall, smoke blinded my eyes; the room reeked of marijuana and tobacco. As soon as I stood, I felt high and my vision clouded as I stumbled over a used syringe.

I rubbed my face and sniffed, "God, what have you been smoking? It freakin' reeks."

Cameron smacked the back of my head. "Don't worry about it, new guy. It always smells like that. We need to hurry. Kev needs us, so maybe the day after tomorrow I'll show you where we sell an' how to do it. We can go on a delivery in the city whenever ya need a break, all right?"

I followed him as we left through the fire escape. "Okay. Where's Haley, and why are we going this way?"

As Cameron leapt down the stairs, the scaffolding rocked. "It's quicker this way. Haley doesn't want the smoke to dissipate. Think that's the right word? Well, that's what she said. Did ya close the window behind you?"

The side window was open, breathing in the air. "Nuts, I'll go get it now."

"Come on, Tye! Think a little, yeah?"

I slammed the window down, apologised, and followed Cameron down the escape. "What are we doing exactly?"

Cameron shrugged as we reached the pavement. "Beats me, man. I think it should be right. We'll normally be back up, nothin' serious. Just look tough—you can do that, right …?"

I nodded.

"Good. We'll go get food after. Do you have anything in mind?"

"Yeah, actually. Pancakes?"

Cameron laughed, walking past the start of a bushwalking track.

We arrived at a car park, hearing Kev and Haley's voices behind a red minivan.

"Are you sure he didn't pay?" Kev demanded. "Haley, we gotta be sure. I don't need another bullshit ploy because someone said something you didn't like. What? Did he offend you?"

Haley spat, "He didn't offend me. Why would I lie? Not only did he not pay, but he ridiculed me and hurt my precious feelings. I want him, Kevali!"

"No! Don't take charge, let me. I'll teach him a lesson. One he won't forget." Kev took a step out from behind the van and welcomed us with open arms.

"Boys. Here we are! 'Bout time. Is he ready?" It was obvious Kev was talking about me.

Cameron shook his pale head.

Kev shoved his arm around me and opened the minivan. "Tyler, take a seat, we'll go a little slower today. Now, let me state this as clearly as I can. From now on, you do what I say. No thinking, no second-guessing, no maybes—what I say, goes! Do you understand?"

"Of course," I said, sitting inside the van. "Can I ask what we're doing?"

Kev smiled, and behind his back—I couldn't see—but Haley dropped something into his hand. "Tyler, we need you to stay quiet!

Now, Cameron's vouched for you. I, myself, can see what you're capable of, and we're going to get food after this. A feast for kings. Sorry for the sting; you'll get used to it."

A painful chill rushed down my arm. As I squirmed, Kev held a needle against my shoulder; its bubbling liquid froze my veins. I pulled back, but Kev held me against the van's seat. I was trapped.

For a moment, it felt as though my legs were broken. I thought my lungs were going to fall out, I was breathing so much, and Kev's voice went cloudy as if there was a wall between us. I could smell everything, from pollen to dust to the bits of leather next to my seat.

Finally, Kev let go, and I wanted to run away, but I couldn't! Everyone else got inside the van, and things got awfully dark.

"It's okay, man," Cameron grabbed my shoulder. "Just concentrate on one thing. I've been through it many times. Heck, I'm feeling it too."

My hands gripped at one another as the van began to move. The drive went on forever until Kev gave me a white papier-mâché mask. The mask resembled a rabbit with long stiff ears. On its mouth and nose, red smears shaped the words: Help Me.

I gulped as Cameron covered his face with a second mask shaped like a wolf. On its left ear was a purchasing tag, swinging back and forth. Reading the tag closely, I saw *Salvos* imprinted above a barcode.

The wolf spoke, "Put it on. Quick, Tye! We're almost there!"

I panicked. My hands were too buttery, but somehow, I managed to put the thing around my head. *Are we robbing a bank? What's going on?*

The breaks squeaked, stinging my ears as Kev's muffled voice ordered us to get out.

There was a couple walking across the road, laughing at our masks. But then something freaked them out. They both ran, holding each other as if a murderer was chasing them.

The wolf handed me gloves—cotton ones you'd typically use to avoid getting splinters when gardening. My heart was beating inside my head, my fingers were shaking, and before I knew it, Kev—who was now a bull—handed me a pistol.

Kev's face, it was gone. Holding the handgun, the bull demonstrated that the pistol wasn't loaded. Either way, it made my bones shiver. I could taste its metal through the gloves.

The bull loaded his own shotgun and threw Haley another larger gun. *Wait, that's not Haley, it's a sheep.* I didn't know what gun the sheep had. An AK, maybe? How would I know? I could barely hold my own.

It's like … is this a dream?

My sight was in theatre mode, blackening around the silhouettes of the bull, the wolf and the sheep.

Suddenly my head wobbled.

The wolf jabbed my temple with the end of his pistol. "Stay with me. No one's going to get hurt," he said, his voice heavenly. "Make sure no one moves or tries anything. Got it?" The more he spoke, the slower and deeper his voice became.

I nodded, I think, following the sheep towards a service station. *Wait a minute! I know this place. This is where I fill up Jess.*

The sliding doors parted for us as the bull yelled something. It was really bubbly, his voice. *No one move*, maybe. Something along those lines.

There were five people inside. A little boy and his mum, a tradesman in an orange jumper smeared with mud, an Asian lady who looked like she worked in an office building and Beverage at the counter.

The bull told me to take guard and deal with the little boy and his mum. *Crap! How the hell do I do that? I'm not going to shoot them.* My stomach ate itself. It was sour inside as I held the empty pistol at their heads. *What am I doing?*

The mother protected her boy, hiding his little body behind her own. She had tears in her eyes, begging me to shoot her, not him.

I pleaded for her to be quiet. "It'll be all right, kid. Your mum's got ya!"

Behind me, near the sliding doors, I heard the wolf's voice. "Shut it! If you speak again, lady, I swear, I'll shoot you square in the head. Don't tempt me, bitch, I'll do it!" He noticed my gaze and shrugged.

The tradesman was cradled on his knees, gasping for air. Next to him, the sheep leaned on the counter. "Beverage, Beverage, Beverage! You forgot to pay up. You know what we do to people when they forget to pay up, don't you?"

The bull pushed her aside. "Addermire, you know I don't intend to harm if there is no harm to give. Is there anything you'd like to say to my little sheep? Anything at all?" The bull pointed his shotgun at the mum. "I'm sure a bullet in that boy's head might trigger something, hmm? Tick-Tock!"

Beverage opened the register. "Take whatever you want. Whatever I owe you and more should be in here, I promise. Just don't kill anyone, man. They're just filling up their cars. Wait a …" Beverage squinted at the sheep. "Why the hell would I have something to say to her? I didn't do anything disrespectful—nothin' at all! She's actin' crazy!" Beverage folded the register's notes into his hand, pulling away from the bull.

The sheep screamed, "Are you joking! You piece of ——"

"Settle, women!" the bull urged. "I need you to bring me the man in orange. Quickly now, we don't have all day."

The sheep sighed, angrily lifting the tradesman up into the bull's arm.

The bull put the tradesman into a headlock. "Are you sure there is nothing you'd like to say to the woman beside me?" The end of the shotgun was placed beside the tradesman's head. "Quickly now! My trigger finger's getting lazy."

Beverage fiddled with his purple hands. "Well ... I think I may need to apologise about ——"

The bull raised his voice. "Uh, uh! Do you think or do you know? Make it clear to her, Beverage! CLEAR!"

Beverage gulped, "Fine. I know I want to deeply apologise to this crazy loon of a woman about ..."

My vision faded as everyone's voices went hazy. I couldn't see straight as the bull uttered threats. The sheep mentioned something, and Beverage continued. However, after all their debating, I heard the sheep's croaking boredom between the lines of Beverage's apology, and then it stopped!

The sheep screamed something, and an aggressive explosion of colours hit my eyes.

Then, the bull screamed Haley's name. He was pissed! He dropped the tradesman and pushed the sheep away from the counter.

Blood dripped down the register and was splattered on the wall behind Beverage's shoulders. The stench of gunpowder tickled my nose as many frightful screams echoed around the room.

The mother held her crying boy, covering his eyes from the vulgar image. Beverage was faceless with only half a mouth left. Blood poured from his nostrils, which were now caved into his eyes. All that was left of him was a blank stare that gave me goosebumps.

The bull shot another round into the roof. Beverage's body fell, and the sheep skipped out of the building.

The wolf screamed something to me. Either *we gotta run* or *let's get out of here*—I don't know. I kept looking at the survivors, back and forth, back and forth. All I heard, felt and smelt was my own breath and the distinct aftertaste of Beverage's face.

Finally, I staggered off behind the wolf.

It felt like hours before we made it to the van, but once we were inside and the bull sped away, my body gave in, and the world went black.

Voices murmured quietly beneath the veil of my unconsciousness, getting louder and louder as though they were angry. Bits and pieces managed to form, like Kev arguing with Haley, Cameron's worried face as he checked my temperature, and the white rabbit mask in my hands.

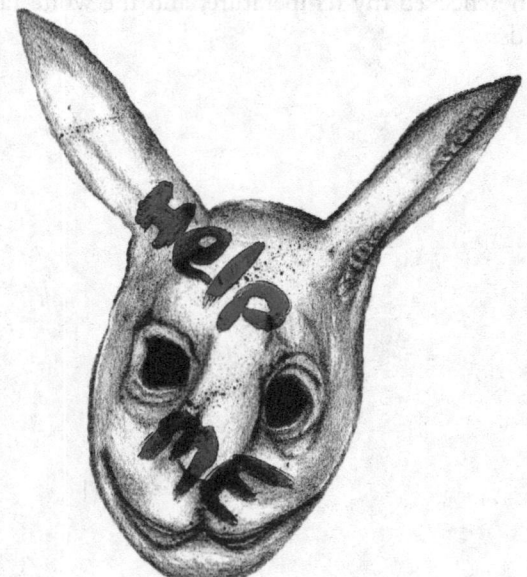

The People I Fear

Kev yanked on the handbrake, his voice loud with rage. It sounded as though he wanted to break something. Or someone. He pulled the side door open and snatched me up like I were a doll, tossing me over his shoulder. All I saw was an alleyway covered in red graffiti, a dirt track that led to a dark forested abyss and a staggering staircase.

Inside Haley's apartment, I was tossed aside, too weak to run away. My head was heavy as I leaned against a wall.

Cameron crawled to my side and clicked his fingers in front of my eyes. As he clicked, several white lights flickered like fireworks.

"Jesus, Haley! I think you've fried his brain." No one responded to Cameron's concern.

Haley roared, "Don't blame me, Kevali! That a-hole deserved everything he got—he abused your system. My goddamn kindness!"

Kev swore his head off. "That does not give you the right to kill the man! And in front of that boy—what the hell were you thinking? I told you not to do anything, to let me deal with it, and you shoot the idiot in the head!"

Haley raised her voice. "It was my problem, Kev. I dealt with it my way! And if you don't like that, well, I might as well get rid of you too."

Kev howled, sprinting at Haley and holding her up against the front wall. I could see the sweat on Haley's forehead as her face turned purple

"*You take that back, you frickin' brat!*" Kev screamed. "That's all you are without me, you know that? You're nothing! *Nothing!*"

Cameron leapt onto Kev's back. "Get off of her, ya freak!"

Flying into the air, Cameron crashed his head into the concrete next to me. He was out of breath with tears in his eyes, rubbing a new bruise on his forehead.

Kev pushed against Haley's throat as her eyes began to swell. "You want to get rid of me! After everything I've done for you! Given you the apartment, money, drugs, support for your family, bail! After all that, you want to kill me?"

"Enough!" I was surprised I could stand. "No more bloodshed. No more killing. Hasn't there already been enough of that? Just let her go, Kev. No one else needs to die." My voice was like a whisper.

Kev tightened his fist. "Why ...?" His tone changed as he smiled. "You're right! Tyler's right, everyone." He dropped Haley, who began gasping for air when her feet touched the ground. Kev turned to me, "Did you hear me, Tyler? You're right! *No more bloodshed, no more killing.*" He towered over me. "Did I say you could speak?"

I gulped, "Uh—um, no. You didn't."

Argh! My head. That prick, why'd he punch me?

Damn it. Again! My forehead was burning! I held my temples, hoping the blur would fade away. But it never did.

"Then why did you speak?" Kev screamed. "Mind your fucking business and keep it to yourself. God, it's bad enough with Cameron jumping on my back, but now you're arguing with me."

He stormed off into the bathroom; his hands were red. I couldn't smell it, but as my fingers soon revealed, there was blood dripping from my nose. Kev threw me a towel, and it fell to my feet, landing atop the carpet.

The sound of the sink stopped, and Kev sauntered to the exit. "Clean yourselves. I'm going to get rid of the van. No one leaves or does anything until I get back." He slammed the door as Haley began to wheeze and cough. No one spoke, no one argued, no one did anything.

From then on, we did what Kev said. Nothing more, nothing less.

¶

It was May—a reunion of sorts. I had extra cuts and new bruises swelling across my back. There was a nice deep gash against the side of my right cheek, and many holes curdled with dried blood trailed up my arms like a connect-a-dot. Let's just say I was sick and needed a cure. But being sick, it was addictive.

I laid awake under a pile of decaying cardboard. My nose was runny and red, and the bags beneath my eyes were like a skin infection. My pasty lips crumbled and peeled, and my fingertips were weak; the layers of skin around my nails had begun to scab.

I lifted myself, admiring the ground's imperfections. The grass was too high, the sidewalk was too clumpy, and the road was too low. Chewing on the raw gums that had been shredded behind my teeth, I counted the shoes that walked past.

One, two, three, four, five, six, seven.

Now!

Merging into the crowd, I followed the footsteps of some lady CEO blasting orders into her phone. The Salvos store's dark-blue hue burned my eyes as the smell of the elderly lingered not too far from its entrance. I strutted into the carpark and searched for my keys.

I swear they were in my pocket, weren't they? I couldn't have … Aha, found 'em.

I owned three keys. One for dad's garage, a second for Jess and a third for the Salvos' donation bin, *zx2h5ow*. I kneeled, fighting the rusty door as I shoved the key into the lock. I threw the door open and finally felt the five hundred thousand in my hands.

"Where the *hell* have you been?" Cameron demanded. "Where'd you go last night? Haley almost killed me!"

I spun around and threw him the cash. "Our savings for the last two months. And Haley's. We'll have to split it with her."

Cameron looked inside the paper bag. "Why did …? Kev gave you the key? When?"

"'Bout a week ago. He said I could be in charge of our finances."

"Don't listen to his bullshit, Tye. It's just …" Cameron sighed, "He gave the key to you! Damn, Haley's really pissed him off. Come on, let's get some lunch."

We went to Noodle Paradise, scoffing down their big bowls of ramen. I laughed at Cameron as a single noodle dropped from his teeth and landed on his neck. He argued that it wasn't as bad as ordering honey chicken.

I mixed my bowl as if I were drawing a spiral. "With you and Haley screaming at each other, I can't think straight. It hurts!" I said. "And that croaking cough she keeps doing. It freaks me out. I had had enough, so I found somewhere else to sleep."

Cameron slurped his final noddle. "On the street? Look, I get it, but if you do it again, be careful. The cops are still out there, looking ——"

"They've already interviewed me about Beverage. I've got no connection to any of you." I rolled my eyes. "You're the one who should be careful. Especially being out in the middle of the day. The investigation ——"

"I know it's not over, Tye!" Cameron crossed his arms. "It's not even my fault. I'm just keeping an eye on you, all right?" Relaxing, Cameron lost his anger. "Why didn't you sleep in the garage?"

"'Cause of Kev!" I played with my noodles. "I was with him most of the night. We were talking about poetry."

"Poetry? Like rhymes and hymns and crap like that? Sounds like you and Kev. What'd he say?"

I shrugged, "Something about hands. You wouldn't care."

"Tell me." Cameron leaned forward.

"He just quoted some Alan Watts guy, and … It got me thinking. I didn't sleep at all last night. Almost did. Got cold and ended up lying under some cardboard." I avoided Cameron's eyes. "I don't want to talk about it. How'd you guess I was going to be at the bin?"

"I didn't. I was heading there to break it open. Lucky you were there. An extra five minutes, and I would have found something to smash it with!" He paused for a moment. I could feel him notice that half my bowl was still full. "So a weird night, huh?"

I nodded, "Yeah. I was just lost in my head. I ended up writing Mum a letter. When I went to put it through at the post office, I bumped into Kev."

"That's good. I'm sure she'll read it, man." He smiled, "You know, I don't have a good memory. But today's a sort of anniversary. It's about the time last year when I met this really amazing girl. I think it's good to remember things like that, don't you?"

Tears burned my eyes but never fell. "It is." I stood, "Let's head off. Is the teddy bear inside Jess?"

"We won't talk about her then." Cameron nodded, "Yeah, the bear's ready. We'll go to the skateparks first. Usual. Do you want to drive?"

I left the table. "Sure. I've been counting the stash. With the next payment, I think we can leave. Cam, we can get out of here!"

He joined me. "I like it. It's settled then, we'll leave in August!"

When we found Jess at the Salvos' carpark, I noticed an oily handprint against the building's main window. Like a stain, it etched itself deeply into the glass, and as my eyes adjusted, it revealed the one person I feared

I feared this person far more than Kev, and much more than Haley—it was the person I feared the most … Myself.

"The only thing I know is that I know nothing."

SOCRATES

Reminders

I was sitting on a reminder. It was a hard-cushioned wooden chair, and next to it was a sizeable spiky shrub and a concrete urn. The chair was outside a Centrelink office, where many poor souls came and went. I didn't know how long I'd been waiting. Deliveries in the big city seemed to take longer and longer the more I did them.

Although the bench reeked of burnt cigarettes, its rough slats were almost comfortable in comparison to my old spot at school. Nowadays, the ants seemed distant. There weren't too many being plundered under the crowds of herding feet. The clomping sound of leather shoes and bony heels was only a blur in the city. At home, it was vivid, echoing endlessly; here, it was diluted with honks, subtle murmurs of pointless chitchat and the obnoxious wind.

Amid the abundance of shoes, one pair came to a halt.

"Tyler! I haven't seen you in ages. How are you?"

Glancing up, I saw a familiar face. "Xander! Holy crap. I'm good, how are you? What are you doing here?"

Xander sat next to me. He looked skinnier with stubble under his chin. "Just got out of my university class."

"Right. How is it?" I asked.

"Great! Better than school. Are you still going to the one near Central?"

I shook my head. "No, I never started. I'm here with Cameron. Some business ..." I watched the ground for a moment. "Have you eaten?"

"I was just going to get a kebab and eat on the train."

"Nonsense." Waving away his plans, I smiled. "Catch the next train; it's been too long. I'll shout ya, whatever you want!"

"Tye, you don't ——"

"I insist!" I stood. "Do it for an old friend."

We went to a bar called *Homeless Happiness*.

"A little insensitive, don't you think?" Xander asked as our food came to the table.

I shrugged, "So the name's a little out there. Just ignore the sign. What are you doing at university?"

"Law." He took out his knife and fork. "Well, kind of. At the moment, I'm doing a course on human rights. Have you ever done charity work?"

I nodded, "I have for Vinnies and this tree company. Plant a hundred trees in a day, pick up litter, that sort of stuff. Why?"

"I've been volunteering at campus for the homeless. It's pretty fun, hey? I never knew you had done things like that before." Xander looked back and forth. "What are you up to with Cameron?"

"This and that. The usual. Nah, it's good you're doing what you're doing."

Xander smiled, chopping up his steak. "Thanks. You know, to be quite frank, I was worried about you, but you seem pretty happy. It's just … last time I saw you, it was … Amberley's funeral."

My stomach churned, and my heart jumped. "So it was. You don't need to worry about me. I've always been like this."

Xander shook his head. "I mean, how's your mental health? How are you feeling on the inside?"

I grinned, laughing away his comment. "What kind of …? I'm great! Normal, Xander. It's an odd question." Although I had answered him, Xander continued to pursue a mindless tangent.

He stared above my head, admiring a historical picture pinned on the back wall. "I'm really glad I introduced you to her. Like from that day on, man, you changed for the better. Like, I'll always— and I mean always—consider you as a friend. But when you and her were together. *Wow!* You started talking more, you made the funniest jokes, and I knew you liked her from day one." He took a moment to eat his steak. "It's good to be away from everyone. Like, getting clarity with new people and just really knowing yourself. I've made some top new friends at university; but don't worry, Tye. I'll never forget you. If you need someone to talk to, whenever, just text me ..." Lowering his knife, Xander frowned, "Did I say too much? I'm sorry."

"A bit." Examining the bar staff, I gulped and confronted Xander's innocent gaze. "Don't worry. Now that you mention it, I never did say thank you. So, thanks."

"What for?"

I bit my lip. "What not for? Like you said ... *her!* And you always had my back, even before. When I was rude. I mean it, thank you for everything!"

We reminisced on the good times, about how Xander was single, and at that moment, I realised something. But before I could explain myself, Cameron had called my flip phone. "Hold on, Xander. One sec." I put the phone to my ear. "Hello. Gotcha, on my way now."

As I put the phone away, Xander finished his beer. "What was that about?" he asked.

I stood, "I have to go. Thanks for having lunch with me." I shook his hand and placed a hundred on the table. "Should be more than enough. Don't forget to tip the waitress. She's cute." I gestured to a sistering table, and Xander peeked at the waitress.

She was our age, there was no doubt about it. Her knotty hair was neatly done in a bun, and she wore a black wench outfit. Her brown eyes were frantic as she talked to an older couple.

Xander's body drooped. "Maybe I will talk to her after you leave." He went to grab the hundred dollars. "No, I'll pay for my half——"

I grabbed his arm. "Don't worry about it, Xander. See you around, all right?"

Holding himself back, Xander nodded, "You can text me whenever. I'm always keen for a chat, Tye!"

As I reached the next table, I waved to him. "Hey, Xander. Thanks for the reminders. I almost forgot what her name sounded like."

He put his thumb up, and the waitress went to his table. She gasped at how much he was tipping her. Shielding himself, Xander apologised, and soon after, asked for her name.

Like music to my ears. I walked out with a smile on my face. It felt so foreign.

The Centrelink office was a cold building. When I entered its sliding doors, my smile got sucked away and my feet found it hard to walk. It smelt like an absence of money, leaving a steel tinge that made my tastebuds curdle. From newly born to nearing death, people of all ages sat in crummy couches that had this awful green sheen.

Behind a round table, Cameron called my name and waved me over.

I joined him, rubbing the goosebumps off my arms. "The hell are you still doing here? What about the delivery?"

Cameron focused on his papers. "I got it! What else would be in the bag?" He nudged a duffel bag that was on a chair next to him. "If we're leaving the mountains soon, I'll be needing a medical card so I can visit the doctors." He leaned in close and whispered, "I say, once we leave Kev, we get off what we're on. Like slow down, heal a little. Stop pumping the crap through our bloodstreams and start being high on life. So, we might need to get check-ups. I'm thinking positive."

"Fair enough. At least you're being honest."

Cameron bobbed his head, writing with a wobble. "I'm looking forward, like you told me. The right direction." He laughed, "Honesty! We're finally freakin' leaving. I can't wait."

"Honesty's the best philosophy," I said.

"Philosophy? Call it whatever you want. What's the date?"

I told him it was the ninth of June, and he swung his pen on top of his ear. Gosh, I hadn't seen the idiot this happy in ages. He was like a little kid with a familiar joy in his eyes the whole way home.

Jess was anxious; like a scared stallion, she continued to mutter from one road to the next. It was giving me a migraine, so half an hour in, I asked Cameron to turn down towards the beach to give the ute a break. But, if I was honest with myself, as soon as we passed the highway's sign, I knew the beach wasn't just for Jess.

When Cameron pulled up at the carpark, I leapt out, marching onto the sand with my shoes and socks. The dark clouds had emptied the beach, leaving only the haunting sound of the waves.

Cameron stuck his head out of Jess' side window, asking what I was doing.

"I'm going for a stroll," I mumbled. *I needed to look!*

And Cameron followed my every step. Trudging through, we reached a ghostly inlet, and in its cove, I found a small rotten journal resting in the sand. I couldn't believe that it was still there!

It was warm to touch, smelt like salt and seemed almost story-like. No one had picked it up, taken it or stolen it. The bucket list had been here for months, and as soon as I opened its worn pages, Cameron gasped.

"This is ... where she died, isn't it? I'm sorry I stopped here!"

I sniffed, tears burning my eyes. "It's not your fault. I just left something here, that's all." I glared at the spot where Amberley had died. "You got a pen?"

Cameron checked his pockets and tugged at his ear. "Ah, crud. I forgot to give this back. Oh well. Here."

When he passed the black pen, I clicked it, turning to the first page in the bucket list and crossing out number eleven. *We had finally done it, Amberley! We watched the sun rise!*

I met Cameron's gaze. "I'm ready to leave now. Leave everything!"

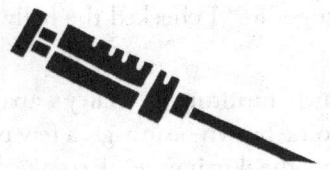

Cold Hands

"Jesus, Haley! I thought you could hold your shit together!" My pants were covered in a layer of chunky vomit.

Instead of helping, Cameron laughed, scavenging through the delivery bag we had received in the city. Every time we sold half a bag, Haley and Cameron loved to have a little celebration, injecting, snorting and smoking the other half. To keep the money straight, they'd pour their own cash into the bag, and get super high in Haley's apartment, telling Kev they had sold it all.

I stood with saliva dripping from my track pants, ordering Cameron to see me outside.

Haley swore at me, laying on her belly with her legs curled in the air, sniffing another white line.

When I closed the door, I was moments away from screaming, but I held myself back.

"Really, Cameron!" I pointed at Haley's apartment, "We gotta do this today. How are you going to drive tomorrow?"

"Don't worry, Tye." Cameron laughed, "It's a tradition between Haley and me. You've joined us before; it's fun. I get it, tomorrow's the big day, and I'm excited to get out of here. But a little fun never hurt. Get the vomit off your pants, have a few lines, and I'll roll ya a joint. If you really want, have some alone time in the bathroom. There's crap everywhere in there. I'll be sober enough to drive in the morning." He wiggled past my side. "If you'll excuse me, there's a little lady in there named Coco and Haley's in the mood for a threesome."

"What? Oh, just get in." I checked the hallway and opened the door.

There wasn't much furniture in Haley's apartment. Beside the couch, there were some brown beanbags, a few posters of musicians and termites infesting the skirtings. Pink smoke drifted from Haley's joint. It bounced off the unplugged fire alarm, which hung off its bracket like a chandelier, and into my nostrils. Blocking the stench with one hand, I grabbed Beau's tool bag and headed towards the bathroom.

Haley offered me a second joint. "Have a puff, Tye-Tye!" She burned its tip and smiled. "It's the new stuff. Makes your stomach turn inside out."

I plucked it from her fingers and took a drag.

Yuck! It tasted worse than it smelt. Like I had just swallowed a piece of charcoal, it burnt the sides of my throat and made my nose tense.

"The hell's in this?" Pink smoke rippled out of my mouth every time I wheezed.

"We ran out with the last rollie, so I improvised. " Haley giggled, "I found whatever was in the kitchen and crushed it up. I think it's cat food!"

Cameron began to laugh, and I threw the joint away, sprinting into the bathroom. I had to get whatever was in my lungs out. For a minute straight, I vomited until the sink was yellow.

Kicking the door shut, I felt the dryness of my throat and the wetness of my pants. Behind the wall, Haley and Cameron complained about my crappy sense of humour.

I can't wait to get out of here. I think Cameron was right, I did need some time alone.

My chest heaved as I smeared the vomit away from my cheeks, tasting the numbness of a stale addiction. My teeth felt grimy and my hands were freezing as I unbuttoned my pants and changed into the spare pair in the bag. My legs looked unstable, wobbling as the bone of my knees pushed against my skin. Different sized cuts staggered across my calf and thigh. My shoes were rough around the edges, split with dirt in between the cracks. Getting the new pair over my right leg, I felt comfy again—warm even. However, my left leg was not the best support.

Hopping into the pants, I misplaced my foot. My forehead burned, and a smacking sound made my brain shake. When I glanced up, I realised there was blood on the towel rack. A rushing pain made my eyes shut, leaving my head throbbing. I could taste the crisp metal as a cold stream of blood dripped down my temple from an open gash.

Stuff it!

As I held back the bleeding, I sat next to the toilet, sliding my back against the wall. I wanted to cry, but could only manage a sigh, slamming the back of my head against the grubby tiles. It was silent as a passing train howled like a whirlwind.

Next to my leg was a syringe. It began to blur as I eyed off the empty teddy bear that sat next to the door stopper. It had a missing eye, limp from its opened sack. Next to it was the bathtub, its surface moist even though no one had used it since Beverage died.

I reached for the syringe, but my arm didn't quite make it. *Damn!*

After a few more failed attempts, I realised I had nothing to use it with. Feeling around in my clothes, both in my jumper and in my spare pants, I found a half-full bottle of morphine.

Wait a tic. There was something else in my pants. Something that was caught against the pocket's edge.

I dug at the cotton until I freed the object. It was a piece of paper, and as I unravelled it, it hit me; it hit me so hard that tears began to build under my eyes.

In my hands, I held my old survey, the one Amberley had filled in. I swear it smelt like her!

My body gave in, and I couldn't move a muscle. It felt like I was almost high. Amberley's writing made my fingers loose, my bones weak and my hair sticky. But damn, did it make me smile.

Every word I read brought back her blue eyes, her perfect skin, her smile and that innocence she had. And after all the questions I read, I was surprised to discover that she wasn't happy. *She was just like me.*

Past question twelve and thirteen, on the second page, Amberley had filled in the empty space below, after I had typed, Thank you for filling in my questionnaire.

As though I could hear her voice, the subtle breeze of the beach echoed within each word she wrote.

I don't know if you like me all that much, Tyler. You seem to be going along with all of my demands as if curious about something that isn't my sickness, but I still can't figure you out. I'm sorry if something bad has happened to you. I really do like you and so does everyone else. And I guess you'll be surprised by my answers to some of your questions, but to be honest, I haven't been happy in a long time, and it sucks. I don't like showing it, and I probably will never tell you, so if you read this, give me a hug and don't tell me why. I'll know!

She scratched out the next line. She would do that; probably thought it sounded cliché.

And if you do read this, I hope you're not only hanging out with me because I'm sick and you feel bad. You don't seem like a person who'd do that. I don't know why I'm writing this; I keep laughing. I guess I wanted to tell you that you're a good person, Tyler.

A really good person! And no matter who tells you 'you speak too much' or 'you're not worth it,' you're an amazing person to me. After only knowing you for what feels like three days, I like talking to you. You're one of the only people I've ever met who actually listens. Not half-listens or just gets the basics to reply; you take every word I say and hold it in. You understand! And I've never met anyone who takes the time to do that. I'm running out of paper, so I'll continue on the back.

On the back page, things got harder to read.

By the way, I love this bucket list idea. I'll never say it to your face. It's cute. You're a lot different to what I was expecting, but take that as a good thing. I'd like to spend lunch with you every day if that's okay. And recess! You're a fun person. Perfect for someone who's dying …

I took a break, crying away all of our memories. The tears were so heavy that I had to close my eyes and rub at their rawness.

When I reopened them, I found myself at the beach; the one where she died. The clouds glowed like symphonies, the ocean crashed as if it was a thousand kilometres away, and the wind messed up my buttoned-up white shirt.

Amberley stood next to me, barefoot in the sand. Her voice sounded brand new as her hair waved about in the breeze. She smiled.

"Thank you, Tyler. For keeping my secret, for listening to me, for always being yourself. And for being my antidote. My one and only cure!" She turned away and looked at the water. I swear those few metres between us felt like mountains and canyons. I wanted to reach her, but she continued, looking up.

"Oh, look. The sun's out."

I glanced at the sky and we both admired the sunrise. Up and up it went until I closed my eyes again and smelt the piece of paper in the darkly lit bathroom.

As though a spotlight was on me, the toilet, the bear and the bathtub were gone.

Amberley held my hands, sitting across from me. I shook, staring at her, and the room faded with just her and me, staring at one another. She giggled, "I get you. You have cold hands. Like me!"

Gosh, she makes me smile. "I do? Yeah, I do. I get you."

"Is that a smile? You should do that more …" Sighing, Amberley tightened her grip. "I wanted to say one last thing."

"No, Am," I pulled her closer. "I want to listen to you. Don't go."

"I know you'll listen. And I'll always love you. Look up, Tye. It's okay to be alone!" With her final words, she let go and faded into the whiteness.

I blinked and was back in the bathroom with vomit on my chin, blood drying above my eyebrow and morphine next to my leg. Tears fell like my head were a waterfall, I couldn't hold them in. Cameron's voice re-emerged, but all I was concerned about was the syringe next to the toilet seat. I kicked at my legs, punched the tiles and whacked my head against the wall, but all the pain led to the same thing.

The more I reached and pulled, the more tears came out. My face had gotten sticky, and my nose twitched. I could taste the salt, feel the redness to my face and hear all the will in my body.

Don't take the morphine!

But I couldn't stop myself. I wanted to so badly, but I kept moving forward until the syringe was in my hand and the survey was on the floor. I wanted to remember her, I wanted to!

My grip tightened and I swore at the needle. It stung my eyes as my resting hand had trouble grabbing the morphine. I was shaking so much! I couldn't read any of the words on the bottle—no title, no prescription. Nothing.

What was I doing?

The bottle was a pain to open one-handed, so I put the syringe in the creases of my dirty hoody and went at it. Each bend of my wrist made me madder. It was like I wasn't in control.

I swore again, hearing the thud of the lid bounce from tile to tile. Leaning forward, I crossed my legs and filled the syringe.

Why did I have to read that stupid survey? No, I didn't mean that—did I?

I could hear my nose exhausting itself as my legs trembled. When I heaved, pulling up my sleeve, the whole world stood still.

It wasn't me. Don't blame me, please.

Things began to cloud over; the walls became fuzzy, the teddy grinned and the stinging in my veins vanished. There was no need to kick anymore, no reason to hurt my head; I just needed to chill. Relax!

Why was I angry? That was so silly, wasn't it? I should probably put that questionnaire in my bag, I'd be littering if I just left it here.

Huh? I'm still crying.

I smiled back at the teddy. *This is pretty funny. I saw her!* I saw Amberley. *But she's dead!*

Huddling into a ball, I laughed with the bear. I laughed so hard that snot dribbled down my chin. I couldn't smell a thing! My arms were like a T-rex's, my back was like a rocking chair and my smile was like a clown. I murmured to the insanity.

I hear you. I hear you.

Finally, my whispers croaked. "She's gone." I giggled hysterically. "She's gone … I'm at the beach. I've got cold hands! I've got …" The laughing stopped, becoming a cry. "Cold hands. I've got cold, cold hands … I'm *alone!*"

There was nothing but emptiness.

A thud from outside made the sidewall jump. Cameron and Haley were going crazy, screaming about lunch. Pizza this, pasta that. *Hey, why does every good food start with a P?*

I took out my phone. Yikes, I had been in here for almost two hours.

Struggling to stand, I opened the bathroom door, and Cameron fell into my arms. On the other side, Haley was roaring about how she wanted Indian for lunch.

Cameron staggered to his feet, rubbing his crown. "Then we'll go get Indian. Jeez, Haley. Don't do that again, you piece of ——"

"You finish that, and I'll cut your dick off," Haley screamed. "I swear, Cameron, I will."

Cameron raised his arms, turning to me. "Okay, okay! Didn't say a word …" He grinned at me. "You were in there for a long time, huh? Told ya there's crap in there."

Pink smoke covered the room, wall to wall, as Haley chopped her herbs with a knife.

I laid on a beanbag. "Haley, can you pass some papers please?"

She ignored me, throwing the Tally-Hos at my chest. As she muttered to herself about how much she wanted Indian, Cameron sat down between us.

I rolled myself a joint and plugged in my headphones, smoking and listening to the Alan Watts lecture, *Acceptance of Death*. As soon as the paper was burnt, reaching the filter, Cameron and Haley got louder.

I closed my eyes, but they kept at it for an hour. *Why worry? They always argue.*

Rubbing my hands together, I tried to warm them, seeing colours sparkle inside my head. Like a playful drama, my daydreams enticed me as though I was asleep.

Haley's voice shrieked louder and louder until a thumping sound vibrated the carpet. She howled, and Cameron swore at her.

I inhaled, closing my eyes, listening to Mr Watts. "So, therefore, in the course of nature, once we have ceased to see magic in the world anymore, we are no longer fulfilling nature's game of being aware of itself. There's no point in it anymore. And so we die. And so something else comes to birth, which gets an entirely new view ..."

Something struck me, teasing the hair on my arms. It was freezing!

When I opened my eyes, the colours had vanished. I turned to Cameron as he gasped for air. Blood erupted from the front of his neck; his face was white, and he was trying to eat the smoky oxygen. Atop his frantic body, Haley continued stabbing her red-covered knife into his chest.

I leapt up, pulling out my earphones and thrusting Haley off Cameron's belly.

"Get off him, you freak. What the ...?" Climbing on Cameron, I covered his neck wound with both my hands. "Look at me! It's going to be okay. Haley, call the goddamn doctor. Where the hell is Kev?" My fingers got painted in red as my shaken body pressed as hard as it could. "Cameron, don't worry. It's just a little cut. I got you. Kev's here, he'll make things right. We'll get you some help! Breathe slowly."

But it was too late.

I watched his eyes drain themselves as a splatter of blood shot through the sides of my fingers and into my face. I yelled for Kev, but we were alone.

Haley stood. Her eyes widened as if she had just taken control of her body, and she began to spaz out. Squawking, she crawled into a ball.

"Haley, find Kev!" I demanded, but she was too awestruck. "Haley? Gah, it's all right, Cam! I got you. We're leaving tomorrow, remember? We're leaving! We'll be free."

Cameron choked as his eyes met mine. Panting, he rubbed his hand across my face, smearing a bloody handprint across my cheek. And with one frightened cough, those hard-pressed eyes drifted to a halt, and his head went limp.

I bawled my eyes out. "Don't do this. Please. I can't do this anymore. We were going to leave. We were going to leave!" His neck bubbled as my hands pushed down and nothing changed.

He was dead.

Haley pleaded for help. She apologised over and over again, and I couldn't bear to stare at Cameron's lifeless face anymore. I grabbed my tool bag, covering its strap in blood and pulled the door open.

Kev ventured from behind the main staircase. His eyes grew round. "Tyler! *What on Earth?* What happened? Are you okay?"

I cursed, rubbing my hands on my forehead. "It's Cam … Cameron. He's gone."

"Gone?" Kev frowned, "What do you mean *gone?* Where's Haley?"

I dodged past him.

"Where the hell are you going?"

I pointed at the apartment. "Haley's inside crying. She killed him, Kev! With a freakin' knife! She killed …" I kept crying. "I'm sorry, I can't anymore! I can't do this."

Kev grabbed my shoulder, swearing at the top of his lungs. "Bloody Haley. Look, things are going to work out, Tyler. Don't worry. I …" He sighed, "Haley! She just had to do it, didn't she? I ain't letting her get out of this one! Not this time." I tried pushing him off, but his grip was too strong. "I'm sorry, Tyler. I truly am. Go! I'll deal with everything. Find a doctor, get some help."

I nodded, stumbled down the main staircase, hearing the stars whisper during the daylight. Each step felt like a hike, each pant was like a heart attack, and when I reached the door to freedom, I lost my whereabouts.

Scouting past the red graffiti as if it were a map, I wandered onto a dirt track that was soon engulfed by a changing forest.

The dirt was heavy, and the strong scent of pollen illuminated the stench of blood. As I drifted further, heaving the duffel bag along, I heard a loud ringing noise.

A bike bell!

Turning around, a familiar voice called my name. "Tyler? God damn, son! What the hell …?"

Amberley's father leapt off his bike and caught me as I collapsed. His stupid biking gear felt funny against my sticky arms.

I laughed, "Hunter! I've been meaning to visit. I'm sorry for everything. I'm … I'm …"

The world turned black.

"Cold hands—something you get when you're too busy worrying about the past or admiring the future."

TYLER MCBAKER

The Moment

A white glare and the stench of sanitiser filled the room. The stainless-steel bench I laid on was cold. It shocked my back, making me sit up. To my left, Doctor McNeill was checking a monitor. He rushed to my side.

"Tyler, you're up. Hey, lay back down, you've got a lot of drugs in your system."

I nudged his hand off my shoulder. "I've already vomited. Thanks. How'd I get here?"

"You don't remember?" McNeill rubbed his chin. "Hunter rushed you into the emergency room about an hour ago. I've checked as much as I could, but there are still a few things I'd like to test. For beginners, whose blood is on your hands?"

I shook my head. "The blood, it's …" I looked at the dried blood that covered my fingers. "It's mine."

"Tyler, listen," McNeill leaned against the bench. "I'd suggest that you tell me. The authorities aren't going to be so gentle about it. Do you understand?"

I shoved him away. "Why should I tell you anything? You'd just lie!"

"Tyler, I want to help ——"

"Don't give me that. You lied to her!" I yelled. "You know you did! Have you even told Hunter and Tegan?"

McNeill's face sagged and his head dropped.

"Of course you haven't! They're here, aren't they?"

McNeill nodded, "Outside, in the waiting room. They're worried sick about you. I promised I wouldn't call the police until I was certain you hadn't done anything ... bad. Tell me I'm not going to have to put you in rehab? Or jail?"

I eased off the bench. "You won't do anything! Because I haven't done anything *bad*. I'm not you!" I stood face to face with the doctor. "Why didn't you help her?"

McNeill put down his notepad and sighed, "Amberley was always going to die. I didn't lie. She really was getting better. Her vital signs were recovering, she was breathing at a normal rate, yet she was losing time. And I wanted her to be happy—not to suffer. You saw her those last few weeks. She smiled every time she saw my face, laughed about how amazing you were, about how grateful she was for her parents. She wanted to excel in school; she planned on buying plane tickets to New Zealand and Canada. She dreamed of an absolutely adventurous future. She got to live, not suffer! That's why I lied, so she could have every moment."

"That didn't give you right to *lie* to her!" I scowled. "She was the same before ..." Lowering my voice, I kept my chin up. "She kissed me the day after she found out. It's when we started going out. I loved her. And I know it sounds dumb because I'm young, and I've got my whole life ahead of me, but I'm never going to have someone like her again. Never! You didn't just lie to her, you lied to me. To her parents. You pretty much killed her." I reached for the doorknob. "Thanks for checking on me. I just want to be alone right now!"

"You'll get cold hands thinking like that!" McNeill laughed. "You ever find out what that poem means?"

"Yeah," I looked him in the eyes. "Cold hands—something you get when you're too busy worrying about the past or admiring the future. It's a metaphor. I hope I never see you again." I left, and the doctor sat against the bench, smiling as I closed the door.

Down the corridor, Tegan yelped my name. "Is everything okay? Gosh, you scared the living daylights out of us."

She had a coffee in her hand; it made me grin. "I'm okay. A little heatstroke and shock. Should be fine with a good night's rest. Good coffee?"

"I've had worse," she sighed. "Are you going home now? Because you're more than welcome to sleep at ours."

Hunter jumped in. "We'd be happy to give you a bed, some dinner, a shower. Gee, lucky thing I went riding today."

I nodded and hugged them. "Don't worry about me. I'm a people person, I'll get around somehow. Thank you. Really! I haven't visited either of you, and I'm sorry. I'm sorry for a lot of things."

Tegan's warm grip grasped my shoulder. "There's no reason to apologise. None of us knew. You're welcome in our home whenever you need a place to stay or just want someone to talk to. You're family, Tyler."

Hunter handed me my tool bag. "Might need this. I'm always in need of a biking partner. You know, we tried that Turkish place you recommended in Blaxland. It's not bad, Mr People Person." He paused and frowned. "You're not sleeping the night, are you?"

I shook my head. "I'd love to, really, I would. But there are a few things I'd like to do. I'll visit soon, I promise, and we can talk about everything that's going on." I hugged them again, smelling Tegan's coffee and Hunter's cologne. "Thank you. For everything."

Seeing Cass on my way out of the hospital almost broke me in two. She wished me luck and didn't ask any questions. I guess she was just happy to see me.

It was late when I reached the train station. The stars were beginning to shine as the sun set outside the carriage's window. The moon was almost full when I reached an old street, searching my pockets and tool bag. People stared at me oddly, gasping and sniggering behind my back. And not a single one of them helped.

I heaved the garage door open and emptied everything that was in Beau's bag. Climbing onto the main table, I stood where it all began.

Hmm?

A pipe was broken. It was the one I had tied the rope around, but now it was bent, and a crack pierced its neck.

I dropped down and pushed one of the office chairs towards the back left corner. Using the chair like a ladder, I pulled out a grey brick in the wall. Behind it the brick, there was hundreds of thousands in cash. From five-dollar notes to a hundred, money piled on top of itself like a rapid ocean during a thunderstorm.

Holding the duffel bag to my waist, I shovelled the money on top of my spare clothes until Cameron's stash was empty. It took so long, my fingers got used to the feeling of wealth.

Afterwards, I placed the key to the Salvos' donation bin into the empty space, put the brick back and closed the stash forever.

When I dropped down to the ground, I heard Kev's dismissive groan. "What do you think you're doin'?"

I faced him, too frozen to run. "I'm taking Cameron's money and leaving, Kev! There's no reason for me to be here anymore."

"Cameron's money?" He sniffled, adjusting his jacket and putting his hand on his waist. Holstered under his belt was a handgun. He played with its handle and eyed me down. "You're not going anywhere! Get in the car. Now!"

My hands were shaking. "Okay, okay! I didn't do anything. Please ——"

"Just get in!" I crept forward as he opened the passenger door to a black Mercedes-Benz.

Driving up a hill, we ventured past a dozen lights until we turned right, then left, reaching a mansion in the middle of nowhere. The house was amazing; every brick looked like a million dollars, every window was as pleasant as a motionless lake, and every light was as vibrant as a firefly.

After he parked, Kev guided me to the mansion's front door. He wasn't angry, but his voice was raspy. "Haley's been dealt with."

I raised a brow.

"Don't look at me like that," spat Kev. "My husband's not a fan of such fragile peculiarities. I told the authorities that she was the one who killed Cameron and that if they found any other evidence, to call me. I am the landlord for their apartment after all." He looked me dead in the eye. "None of it is going to blow over onto you. You have my word. Now, come in. Sebastian's excited to have a guest over for dinner."

"Sebastian? Dinner? This is your house?" I asked.

Kev smirked, opening the door to another world. It was like a medieval castle with a modern chandelier that glowed above a dark lacquered wooden staircase, which spiralled two, three, maybe four storeys high. The dining room was to my left with an exquisite table and several mighty chairs to match.

Doctor McNeill sauntered down the staircase in a purple dressing-gown, calling my name as if my arrival was unexpected.

I dropped my tool bag. "You two are married! This whole time, you two knew each other. Holy crap, you're his morphine source. You … you deleted the security footage of ——"

"Of you stealing it?" McNeill said. He opened his arms. "Tyler, Tyler, Tyler! Don't look so shocked. Kevali and I don't mean to harm you; we simply wanted to discuss things. Over dinner perhaps? Should be finished …?"

Kev nodded, "Soon. I'll check the oven. It's a lamb roast. You must stay for some food at least."

"And a shower wouldn't do you any harm either," McNeill added. "You're free to have one. Looks like you've been through god-knows-what."

As Kev marched around the dining table, I gasped again. "But you're married! To *him*! What the hell's going on?"

McNeill handed me a towel and explained that money was hard to come by when he was in med school and that he and Kev had met during a hard time in his life. Yet the more he talked, the more my head burned. Admittedly, it did clear during my shower, but my fingers never stopped shaking. The water felt so amazing, absorbing the heaviness of Cameron's blood as it dripped off my arms and face.

When I was out of the shower, there was a pile of folded clothes on the toilet lid. They smelt new, felt warm and were way too comfortable. A band-aid had fallen on the tiles.

Where did that come from?

I rubbed my forehead, feeling a cut that had blistered down my temple.

As I snuck out of the bathroom, I saw Kev fiddling in a cupboard in what seemed to be the master bedroom. He turned to me and smiled. "How was your shower?"

"Nice. Thanks," I said. "I really should get going now."

"Nonsense!" he marched to my side. "You won't make it far without food. I insist, for Cameron's sake. You know, I should be the one apologising. You must think I'm a monster, leaving him and Haley where they were, knowing how they lived and ate when I went home to a place like this. I did it to you too."

"Don't! It's just how it is sometimes," I admitted. "It's who you are. You're not New Kev, Big Kev, or anything. You're a businessman. I thought I should tell you that Cameron and I were going to leave in the morning. *Forever.* I guess it's not worth waiting for things, is it?"

"Wise words," Kev smiled. "I knew. Knew about the stash, his plan, you! And I would have let him leave. Because at the end of the day, for me, he's replaceable. Doesn't mean I'm not going to grieve. He was a good person. And you were his safety line."

Downstairs, in the backyard, there was a balcony where Doctor McNeill was sitting behind an empty round, timber table. There was no roast on it, just a gun.

After ordering me to take a seat, Kev hugged McNeill from behind. I leaned, watching Kev kiss McNeill's temple. It was perplexing, making my gut heave and feel mushy.

Laughing, Kev left to prepare dinner, while McNeill's eyes met mine.

The doctor asked, "Where do you plan to go?"

"Away," I said coldly. "I've got some ideas. New Zealand, Canada, Sweden. I'm going somewhere else ——"

"For a fresh start?" guessed McNeill.

"No!" I stared at the table. "You can stay somewhere as long as you want, but if you feel like you don't fit in, there's no point in trying to push through. Especially after eighteen years. It's a big world."

McNeill crossed his arms. "You're going to look for a place that makes you happier?"

I shook my head. "Happiness isn't the key to life. I just want to listen to people, talk about their lives and understand."

"Then why don't you stay?"

I looked at him. "Because this part of my life is over."

He nodded, shoving the gun closer to me. "It has one bullet. Now, I may be a doctor, but seeing someone like yourself go through what you have, I'm worried about your ——"

"Mental health?" I scoffed. "It's always been messed up, Doc."

"Just take it as another way out. If all seems lost." It was like McNeill was pleading.

Rolling my eyes, I snatched the gun from the table. "You want me to kill myself? You're worse than Kev!" I pointed the barrel at his head. "Tell me why I shouldn't shoot you?"

W.I.P.

"Because that's not you." McNeill kept his eyes focused on me. "You don't have to do anything. It's just a precaution. Do whatever you want—throw it in a river, melt it in a furnace, give it to someone else. I just wanted to help!"

"You disgust me, thinking I'd kill myself!" Resting my arms, I placed the gun in my pants. "I know my life may seem terrible, but at least I don't think like you." I stormed off, running into Kev as he held the roast with two oven mitts. Grabbing my bag, I turned to the two of them. "At least I'm not like either of you! I actually know who I am. I'm not four different things! Give Cameron a nice funeral, okay?" Slamming the front door, I leapt down the driveway and found Jess parked at the kerb.

Yes! She was open. Searching under the passenger seat, I found the keys. She had half a tank. *That'll get me somewhere.*

Speeding off, I bought paper and pens at a two-dollar shop. I sat in Jess' tray, writing a letter for Mum. She may have only left me an address, but I could still picture her reading it—like all the others—and smiling to find that I was okay.

I sent it through at the post office, and on my way to the motorway, I made a small detour. One final stop.

Sneaking under the fence was hard on my back. Things were a lot neater now. I tiptoed past newly made walls, smelling the scent of paint as several rolls of carpet laid above different sized boxes of furniture.

Unlike all of the other boring walls, there was one that made me stop. It was covered in different-coloured handprints, and in its centre were mine and Amberley's, as bright as the moon.

Climbing dozens of timber steps with a steady railing, I reached the rooftop, noticing the apartment block was almost ready to sell. At the top, the stars seemed almost like the droplets from a waterfall—*white ants in the sky.* So many filled the darkness, and I was so encapsulated that I stood on top of the roof's concrete bannister.

The gun was in my hand, loaded and ready. My feet were shaking, yet they were not afraid to fall. For the first time in what felt like forever, I didn't feel cold.

I saw all the faces of the people I loved. My mum. My best friend. My cure. Amberley would always make me smile. I inhaled as much as I could and watched my hands.

A gunshot echoed, and the world was set alight. I reminisced on the handprint-covered wall as many questions sped alongside the echoing sound.

Am I happy? *Yes and no.*

Do I want to die? *No.*

Am I hungry? *Always.*

Are the stars beautiful tonight? *Definitely.*

Is this place where I live amazing? *Of course; I wouldn't want to be raised anywhere else.*

Will I miss anyone? *Probably.*

Will they miss me? *I don't know.*

What's around? *I see the stars, the buildings below, the canopies above and the night lights ahead.*

Am I depressed? *Only when I feel empty.*

Will I leave? *I think so.*

Will I survive? *I hope so.*

Do I have cold hands? …

Please Read

Cold Hands showcases several mental illnesses, including the impacts of clinical depression, social anxiety, schizophrenia and post-traumatic stress disorder (PTSD). Each of the conditions expressed within the story currently impact one in four people worldwide. Moreover, according to the *World Health Organisation (WHO)*, it was estimated that in 2017-18, around 4.8 million Australians suffered from a mental health disorder. Although this data is outdated, there is evidence from companies like *Mindframe*, that deaths from suicide have increased from 2018 to 2019.

Below are websites, companies and resources that can help people with mental illnesses and teach readers about the importance of mental health.

If you are feeling low, empty or socially anxious, please call **Lifeline Australia.**

Call today: 13 11 14

Link: <https://www.lifeline.org.au>.

If you'd like to learn more about the factors that impact mental health, **Health Direct** has a three minute read that goes in depth on depression, anxiety and eating disorders.

Link: <https://www.healthdirect.gov.au/mental-health-resources-for-me>.

Beyond Blue offers wellbeing support after the mental health effects of the 2021 Australian Lockdown.

Call today: 1800 512 348

Link: <https://coronavirus.beyondblue.org.au>.

Kids Helpline wants to help young people with their mental health. They have videos, stories and quizzes about mental health and their resources are perfect for kids.

Call today: 1800 55 1800

Link: <https://kidshelpline.com.au>.

If you do not want to call Lifeline Australia, there are other companies like **Suicide Call Back Service** who can help break negative thought loops and suicidal risks.

Call today: 1300 659 467

Link: <https://www.suicidecallbackservice.org.au>.

MensLine Australia offers support for males with anxiety, stress, addiction, separation and counselling.

Call today: 1300 78 99 78

Link: <https://mensline.org.au>.

If you want to find a local service that helps with mental health, **Health Direct** also offers a 'Find a health service' search engine based on location, preference and the type of service.

Link: <https://www.healthdirect.gov.au/australian-health-services>.

Don't forget, **YOU** are the most important person who can help the impacts of mental health. I know the world can be scary sometimes, but try and talk to someone new, start a new hobby or class, find something you enjoy, and never compare your life to others.

The Videos and Lectures in Cold Hands

Throughout Cold Hands, Tyler listens to several audio recordings from writer, Alan Watts. Mr Watts, who popularised Buddhism and Taoism in western communities, was a crucial influence in the writing of Cold Hands. Below are the links for the videos/lectures used in the story.

I would highly recommend that you take the time to watch at least one of these recordings as they do offer an interesting insight on life, death, depression and meaning.

Videos:

It is Impossible to Tell if Anything is Good or Bad — Alan Watts.

Created by AfterSkool. (1 August 2018).

YouTube Link: <https://www.youtube.com/watch?v=j4TZMxkxySc>.

Life is NOT a journey – Alan Watts.

Created by AfterSkool. (7 September 2017).

YouTube Link: <https://www.youtube.com/watch?v=rBpaUICxEhk>.

Lectures:

What Have You Forgotten? – Alan Watts.

Created by DoYouFeelLucky. (8 June 2014).

YouTube Link: <https://www.youtube.com/watch?v=voIovM07_JI>.

Alan Watts - Let it Happen By Itself.

Created by Wiara. (25 November 2017).

YouTube Link: <https://www.youtube.com/watch?v=rC-IsCryRlE>.

Alan Watts - Acceptance of Death.

Created by Life Eternal. (1 February 2015).

YouTube Link: <https://www.youtube.com/watch?v=qK1BJkBJdtY#t>.

Sharron's Letter

Dear Tyler,

I have decided to take Beau's offer and move with him down south to a town near Wollongong. Although I know this news will break your heart, I really did want to stay and celebrate your birthday. Unfortunately, sometimes things don't work out, and we have to make sacrifices to save the ones we love.

I will leave the address Beau gave me at the bottom of this letter so you can visit me sometime in the future when things are a little easier to explain. However, I will understand if you never want to see me again.

I wish we could have had more time to talk like we did yesterday. It was really nice to meet Amberley, and I can she makes you very happy. Happier than what I've seen you in a long time!

You're eighteen now, a good age to figure out what you want to do with yourself. And you're a good boy. I know you have an amazing life ahead of you! Good luck with school and study hard. You and your father will always be in my thoughts.

Happy birthday. I hope one day we can reunite!

I love you, Tyler.

Mum.

P.S. I left the photo upstairs of you, me and your father. Please take care of it for me.

82a Merrick Circuit,
Kiama, NSW, 2533.

Tyler's Final Letter

Hey Mum,

I don't know if you've received my previous letters, but because you haven't replied, this will be my final one.

I had a really bad day today! Everything's falling down around me, and I'm scared. I think the world hates me. But that's okay. Because I don't mind being alone and I do have some good news. I'm going to be leaving the Blue Mountains to go travelling. I don't know where I'm going to go, but I think it's time.

I'm going to be visiting you. Maybe not tomorrow, maybe not even this year, but I will see you soon. I promise! Just give me some time and don't move away again. Okay?

Anyways, I hope you're doing well. I wanted to let you know that I'm taking the photo of you, me and Dad around the country. I try not to look at it but thank you for leaving it behind.

Take care of yourself,

Tyler

P.S. Cameron's funeral will be soon, maybe in the next few weeks. It would mean a lot if you went and gave him some flowers.

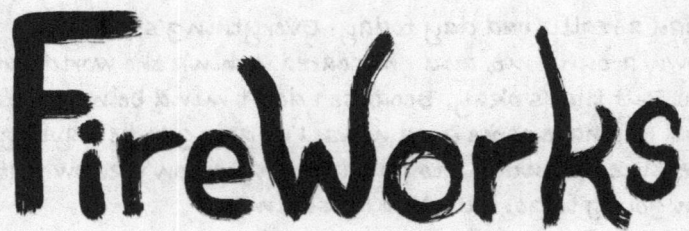

FireWorks

What happens after the events of Cold Hands?

Inspired by true events.

Come gather, come gather, for Illuka, the koala, is ready to explain how he and his friends survived the Australian bushfires.

Yes, yes, he is, he is! All of the animals in the bush have come together to uncover the truth behind Alinta, the flame, and her dancing orange lights.

Please, join us, join us! Come follow Illuka and Bouddi, the sugar glider, as they explore the Blue Mountains and face the black sky.

Quickly now. The family herd is waiting!

 /oliver.smuhar/

The Quotes in Cold Hands

Oliver Smuhar has used inspiring *quotes* from 8 figures. These *quotes* have been chosen as they best represent the philosophical ideas within the story. These *quotes* allow readers to reflect on their own personal life stories. The *quotes* used were recorded on several websites by different companies, articles and published books. Cold Hands would like to acknowledge the following sources: BrainyQuote, Business Insider Australia, Epic Quotes, Goodreads, Inspirational Stories, Katrina Chambers (Blog), Minimalist Quotes, and Teach Different.

Cold Hands would like to further reference:

Cummings, D. 1 September 2014, *Questions For The Dalai Llama*, Penguin Random House, New York.

The Art in Cold Hands

Cold Hands uses certain artworks to add depth to the overall narrative. These artworks include the 21 sketches by Amberley and Tyler and the 6 chapter symbols. Some of the artworks have been inspired by other artists' creations, photographs and royalty-free images. Oliver Smuhar has reimagined, recreated and adapted each of the artworks within this book through acrylic paints and pencils. The artists and companies Cold Hands would like to acknowledge, include alexblacksea (123RF), Artontax (PNG Item), booblgum (Deposit Photos), Bring a Trailer (Pinterest), deepblue4you (iStock), EatenRibs (Clip Studio Tips), FrankRamspott (Getty Images), How2DrawAnimals (YouTube), istry (AgeFotoStock), John Smith APS (Dreamstime), LEOcrafts (iStock), liftarn (Open Clipart), Marielle de Groot (Pinterest), maudis60 (123RF), Nazneen Kane (Pinterest), nikiteev_konstantin (Shutterstock), Open Clipart, PngFind, Seamartini (Vector Stock), The Custom Bag Company, thewet (iStock), Void Nottingham Limited and Wild Dots (YouTube).